When I Set
Myself on Fire

W. W. Singer

ISBN: 0692342435
ISBN 13: 9780692342435
Library of Congress Control Number: 2014921552
Cactus Jack Press, Dallas, TX

For information:
7324 Gaston Avenue, Suite 124-349, Dallas, TX 75214

Be Thou my vision, O Lord of my heart.
Naught be all else to me, save that Thou art.
Thou my best thought by day or by night,
Waking or sleeping, Thy presence my light.

Irish poem and traditional hymn

Chapter 1

The monkey wept.

Chapter 2

Things aren't always what they seem at the time or the way you try to remember them later. Even vivid memories of things fall away like crumbling edges of old, brittle newspapers, but I've begun to suspect that the essence of lost memories can remain as lingering proof of what is more real than not. I have no other words to explain it.

I'd been monitoring things at the university's medical research lab since the day the Houston Chronicle blindsided us with an article about the genetic experiments with monkeys that were being conducted by our medical science department. [1] The general

---

1   HOUSTON, TEXAS – Researchers at Texas University at Houston have brought gene-splicing experiments closer to the realm of science fiction by inserting human genes into the embryos of rhesus monkeys. After fertilization, the embryos were injected with human genes linked with Parkinson's disease. Scientists said the technique will enable medical researchers there to confirm their understandings about genetic links to certain diseases and to better study the possibility of using experimental drugs in the early treatment of those diseases.

In a telephone interview, Jim Drewry, associate general counsel of the university, acknowledged that some people could be disturbed by the ethical implications of the experiment. Drewry said, "I am monitoring the experiment protocols personally and am satisfied that the highest standards for humane treatment of these animals is being followed."

A source disclosed to this newspaper that eleven pregnancies resulted. Three ended in stillbirths. Eight monkeys were born, but only five incorporated the human gene into their own monkey DNA.

counsel of the university, who was my boss, decided that, going forward legal oversight of the human gene-splicing experiments was of critical importance in protecting the university's reputation—and that avoiding the slightest whiff of public scandal was of critical importance in protecting *his* reputation. He wasn't eager to be quoted or to have his name associated with any of it, and so he called me into his office and said, "How'd you like to try something a little different, Jim?"

I was associate general counsel at the university, one of the most senior lawyers in the legal department. But much of my work for the university in recent years had been writing policy manuals that were gathering dust on shelves and in desk drawers throughout the university system, so this was, indeed, different. He told me what he thought that I needed to know about talking with the press, and on the way out of his office, he put his arm around me like I was family and said, "This has become one son of a bitch of a political hot potato, my friend. Don't let this turn into some kind of religious brouhaha or there'll be hell to pay by somebody." Mindful of those prophetic words, I agreed to take on oversight of the monkey experiments, thinking that there might be a related university policy that needed to be updated or written.

So I became a regular visitor to the Medical Science Building. I read—and mostly understood—the experimental protocols for the animal drug testing. Science isn't foreign to me. I was a physics major for almost three years when I was working on my undergraduate degree. I was a straight A student in all the classical physics classes, but once the professors started dealing with quantum physics and subatomic particle behavior, I could no longer master the concepts. I reluctantly changed majors—to pre-law.

I'm as good as anyone when there are concrete rules, but when there aren't any rules, I don't deal with things like everyone else does. I intuit other alternatives. I create my own logic. What else can you do? At the time, someone in the physics department—the assistant dean, I think—pulled me aside and told me that there were medicines that could have helped me contain my thought process better. I didn't tell him, but I'd already tried medicines of various kinds and found them…lacking. I had my own strategy for containment, and it worked well for me for a long time. Containment. What a great word. It was as if something combustible were fluid inside of me, maintained inert for years by force of will—my will. And then….

But I'm getting ahead of myself.

Once a week, I observed the monkeys in their cages, confirming that the cages were always relatively clean and that the lab in the basement of the building was comfortably air-conditioned. Since it was now public knowledge that five of the university's lab monkeys had been genetically altered to carry human genes, the university had a heightened official interest in their well-being. I made several appointments to question Dr. Hermann, the mercurial faculty member heading the experiments, but each time, he postponed our meeting, with excuses of varying levels of credibility. He could get away with it—he was a money machine for the university, bringing in one big grant after another for medical research projects and clinical drug trials. No one at the university was going to force him do something he didn't want to do.

Initially, I had been enthusiastic about taking on this assignment. It seemed to have more substance—and more genuine relevance—than my other responsibilities in the legal department. There was something disturbing and wrong to me about the idea of science conducting experiments that could create some kind of near-human animal species—like the unhappy half-human creatures portrayed in the old horror novel, <u>The Island of Dr. Moreau</u>. But that wasn't the reality of what I was finding. Not at all. The animals that I saw when I visited the lab were just monkeys. The genetically altered ones didn't seem to be any more intelligent than any other monkey in the lab. Their appearance was no different. They moved with the same crouched gait as the others. And in the weeks since I had taken on oversight responsibility, nothing I saw gave me any cause for alarm—until the night that a grad student named Bonnie Norton, one of the most annoying and frustrating people I've ever known, called me from the lab.

Bonnie was primarily responsible for the lab animals. She had a gift for getting the monkeys to relax and cooperate, but she wasn't as adept at getting along with people. She had a reputation for being a loner. She wasn't always nice to the faculty and other students, but she was particularly rude to me. She rarely returned my phone calls. On a few occasions when I ran into her in the lab and tried to talk to her, she acted as if my questions were unintelligible and sighed dramatically as if I were wasting her time. When I asked her to help me organize a complete set of the team's research files, she just laughed and walked away, repeating the words "a complete set of files." I pointed out to her once that she was smoking in a non-smoking area, and after that, almost every time she saw me, she pulled out a cigarette and asked me for a light.

And so I was surprised to hear her voice on the phone that night and even more surprised when she said: "We need to talk. When can you get over here?"

It was after eight o'clock in the evening and I was still in my office. I looked at scattered, marked-up pieces of paper on my desk, an early draft of a controversial new policy that would change all the rules on faculty tenure—something the legislature was requiring us to implement in the coming year. Another political hot potato that had become mine alone to handle. The policy had to be finished and delivered to the university president before the week was over. I said, "How about tomorrow, some time after lunch?"

"No, now."

"I'm sorry—"

"We can't do this anymore."

I was exasperated. "Do what?" I assumed it had something to do with me, but I couldn't remember having asked her—or any of the grad students—to do anything.

"I need you to see you."

"Maybe tomorrow morning."

"Tonight. Jesus, what don't you get about that?"

I thought about hanging up on her to teach her a lesson about the consequences of being rude to people. But she'd made me curious. "Fine, I'll be there in a little bit," I said.

I drove my car, so that I could go straight home afterwards. The university has a sprawling campus, and the Medical Science Building was on the opposite side from where I worked. I was hungry. Earlier in the day, I'd promised my wife Grace that I'd meet her and our son Buck for dinner at 6:30. That time had come and gone. I assumed that they'd gotten tired of waiting and had gone without me—I hadn't called her and she hadn't called me. It wasn't that big a deal. Grace was beyond being mad at me, given all that had gone wrong for us.

I parked in a spot reserved for faculty and staff and went in through the side door. There were a few students leaving, as I was coming in, with backpacks slung across their shoulders. It was quiet inside the building. The only sound I could hear was that of my own footsteps, the clicking of my hard-soled shoes on the tile floor. I walked down the stairs to the basement. I didn't see anyone there either. Assorted empty chairs were scattered along the walls. The basement smelled like a veterinarian's office, with the odors of disinfectant and animal waste. I walked down the hall to the room that served as an office for grad students. I didn't want to startle anyone, so I knocked and called out "Hello?" as I opened the door.

The room was full of bookshelves and filing cabinets and had desks in all four corners. Bonnie was standing behind one of them, with her hands resting on a tall stack of multi-colored files. She was probably in her late twenties, had an angular Germanic face and straight hair chopped off above her shoulders. Maybe she would have been more attractive if she'd tried, but she didn't try.

After a few moments of silence, she reached into the side pouch of her backpack, pulled out a cigarette and said, without emotion, "Got a match?"

I couldn't believe it. What I wanted to tell her was, "Kiss my royal ass," but as associate general counsel for the university, I couldn't say anything like that to a student, particularly a female student, one whom I was seeing after normal hours in an otherwise empty building. Instead, the words that came out of my mouth were, "No, I don't have a match. I never carry any damn matches. My mother told me I'd *end up setting myself on fire* if I carried matches around with me."

A smile slowly appeared on Bonnie's face. She said, "You know, you ought to let people around here know that you've got a sense of humor. It would help."

Sometimes people think I'm funnier than I really am. Bonnie thought I was making a joke, but my mother really did say that.

She had her reasons.

Bonnie put the unlit cigarette in her mouth and pointed at the stack of files, nine or ten folders, each half an inch thick. They were the only thing on her normally cluttered desk, except for her backpack. Everything else was gone. She said, "These are for you—what you've been asking for. As they say in the cop shows, 'We've protected the change of custody.'"

"Chain of custody. They say '*Chain* of custody.'"

"No, they don't."

I saw no point in arguing the fact. We stared at each other for a few moments. I broke the silence. "That's it?"

She frowned. "So what happens next? Do you, like, take these files and try to read them yourself? Or do you go hire somebody who actually knows what they're looking at. Or what?"

The cigarette hung from her lip, nearly vertical. It distracted me, but I tried to ignore it. I also ignored the insulting way in which she'd framed her question. I shrugged and said, "When I get around to it, I'll look at the files, and then if I have any questions, I'll call somebody."

"It won't be me."

"Fine." That didn't upset me. "It won't be you."

"I won't be here." The cigarette fell from her lip, but she caught it, expertly.

"Over the Thanksgiving break?"

"Anymore."

"You're graduating?

"No."

She could tell that I wasn't grasping the significance of what she was telling me, and so she abandoned all subtlety. "I'm quitting. Getting away from this place—away from Herr Doktor Hermann and his cadre of prissy sycophants—and you, of course—to somewhere far, far away. Now do you get it?"

Bonnie had once said that doing research here was her life, working under Dr. Hermann alongside the other grad students—and with the monkeys. She largely avoided the people, but had a special bond with the monkeys, treating them as if they were her children, even as they were subjected daily to experiments and dying prematurely. I never understood how she rationalized all that. Maybe that was part of being a scientist. But whatever moral compromises and personal sacrifices she was making would have been worth it for her. When the experiments with these monkeys were complete, she'd get international recognition for her role in the research and co-authorship credit for whatever papers were published. She'd been involved with the experiments since the very start, even before the monkeys were born. It was inconceivable that she would quit now. But as a lawyer for the university, I was more than just curious. I wanted to be sure she wasn't intending to sue the university for some real or imagined transgression. "Because...?"

"She cries all the time now, and I can't make her stop," she said quietly. "I can't stand it anymore. I can't let a monkey like Evie just—" She stopped in mid-sentence, turned and walked toward the lab.

I followed her. As we entered the lab, I squinted for a moment, until my eyes adjusted to the harsh glare of the fluorescent lights overhead. The floor was spotless, but the room had a pungent, ammonia-like smell. There were muffled, shuffling sounds that came from all sides of the room.

There were more than a dozen cages in the lab, sitting on metal tables that lined the walls. A few were empty; the rest held monkeys, most of whom were curled up in the corners of their cages and visible only as dark humps. We walked past one cage in which a monkey sat holding a metal bar in the cage door with one hand and a ragged, yellow teddy bear in the other. The grad students had named him Smokey. Smokey stared at me, unblinking. I say that, because that's the best way to describe how he looked, but of course, monkeys blink. I had learned quite a bit about monkeys over the past few weeks. Physiologically, a rhesus monkey's eyes are almost identical to a human's, with eyelids and tear ducts. Their tears wash dust and other foreign particles from their eyes, like ours do. Their bodies are almost identical to ours—except for their tails and the proportions of their limbs—and that's why we use them for research.

But their minds are not like ours. They don't have ideas any more complex than the thoughts needed to implement their basic instinctual drives. They have no awareness of things beyond their senses. For monkeys, if they can't see, smell, taste, touch, or hear something, it doesn't exist. Whatever it is that elevates humans above the rest of the primates, whether it is a soul or some other kind of divine gift or lucky accident, monkeys don't have it. And that's why we use them for research.

Bonnie stopped in front of a cage that had a pink, fringed tablecloth draped over the top. It covered the back and sides, but was pulled up in front. That was Eve's cage. I'd heard grad students talking about Eve more than a few times. Bonnie pointed at the cage door and said, "Look at her. Just look."

I leaned down and looked in.

Eve sat on her haunches, inches from the cage door. Her head drooped and her long, furry arms hung limp at her sides. I couldn't see her face at first. Her shoulders shook in time with quiet sobs. The sound was unfamiliar, but unmistakable. Her sobs had a high-pitched, bleating quality about them.

And when she looked up at me, tears were streaming down her pink cheeks to the tufts of amber fur that framed her tiny face. Our eye contact lasted for several seconds—she didn't look away at first and I didn't either. And in those moments, I felt an uncomfortable connection to Eve that I didn't expect. I felt something else too, a mild panic that stemmed from something I couldn't quite articulate. There was no sense of expectation in her glance in my direction. I didn't sense any extraordinary intelligence. But there seemed to be awareness there—awareness of me, yes, but also a tangible *self*-awareness.

I was at a loss for words. I said, "Is that...normal?"

Bonnie stared at me with her mouth open and then bumped me aside with her boney shoulder. "Normal? Jesus."

As I was moving out of her way, I stumbled when the cuff of my pants got caught on something small but stiff that was protruding from the steel mesh door of what appeared to be a another cage under the table. When I bent down to disentangle my cuff I saw that it was actually the bare leg of a Barbie doll that had snagged my cuff. I said, "What's this...leg?"

Bonnie lifted the latch that secured Eve's cage door. Without looking at the doll, she said, "Nothing. It's just a bin where we put...stuff. Toys and stuff."

Bonnie reached out her hands and Eve climbed into her grasp and cuddled up against Bonnie's chest, like a small child, with one arm behind Bonnie's back and the other resting on her breast. Bonnie cooed, "It's okay, Evie. It's okay."

Eve lay her head on Bonnie's shoulder. I noticed that Eve's hand was trembling. I pointed and said, "Is that the Parkinson's, or is she—?"

"Yeah. But just early stage. She's three years old—she'd be a blossoming young women in if she were in the wilds now. Or even in a zoo with other eligible males."

All five of the test monkeys carried a human gene that researchers had isolated which appeared to be connected in some way to Parkinson's disease. They were injecting the test group of monkeys with high doses of an experimental drug that was believed to have a beneficial effect on the disease. The idea was to treat the disease early, before symptoms had developed. If the drug was ever approved by the FDA, it would be given to people who carried the Parkinson's gene when they were young, to slow the progression of the disease. With the high dosages being used on the monkeys, the drug had very unpleasant side effects, but testing the drug had been the reason for creating genetically altered monkeys in the first place.

Eve continued to cry softly. Her back quivered with each breath she took.

I glanced up at Bonnie. "I didn't know monkeys could cry."

Bonnie looked at me as though she'd come to the final, inescapable conclusion that I was truly stupid, and, in retrospect, it wasn't a particularly smart thing to say. I knew better. Monkeys *couldn't* cry. Weeping was an exclusively human reaction to despair. Watching Eve cry gave me the same sense of disorientation that I would have had if our cat laughed out loud or if one of my son's gerbils winked at me. I was nervous as it dawned on me what we, the university, had done. We had made this monkey into something somewhat human—how human, I was afraid to learn. "Are the other four test monkeys…the same way?"

"No. Just Eve."

"Why is she crying?"

Bonnie began to pace around the perimeter of the small, cluttered lab, gesturing with her free hand. "Why do you think? Look at this. This is her daily existence—this ugly room, that tiny little cage…she's all alone here. Alone."

I followed behind her and pointed toward the cage where Smokey, the monkey with the stuffed animal sat passively. "This one seems okay." I gestured toward a row of cages, identical, like little tract houses, that held quiet, docile monkeys. "And them too."

"I know."

"Why's this one different?"

Bonnie shrugged and looked away. It was a non-answer. She had an opinion, but she wasn't interested in talking about it. Abruptly, she turned back to me and said, "So, do you need a sack or something for all of my files. I'm giving them to you. Complete files. Did you catch that part?"

"A box would be better. Is there an empty box around here?" I wasn't stalling exactly, but I wasn't in a hurry now to leave. I've always liked animals. As a kid I watched Tarzan movies on TV on Saturdays. I remember fantasizing sometimes about having a pet monkey like Tarzan's monkey Cheetah, wondering how that would work in a neighborhood without trees. Eve had stopped crying. I reached out to pet her, then stopped. "Does she bite?"

Bonnie shrugged. "She might. She's a monkey."

I leaned closer. "Eve?"

The monkey turned her head in my direction.

"Eve, are you...sad?" I wasn't expecting a response of any kind. It was like talking to my dog—like when I'd walk out the back door and say, "Hey, Daisy, how are you doing?" and the dog would jump around and bark because she recognized her name.

The monkey—Eve—nodded one time, a clipped, quick nod.

I looked at Bonnie. "Did she really understand what I said?"

"No. It just means—I don't know...that she thinks you're not a predator."

Eve's face registered indecision. She reached out and pulled the pen out of my pocket and looked at it from multiple perspectives. Then her hand started to shake and she dropped it.

I asked, "What does Dr. Hermann think?"

"He said for me not to tell anybody about her crying—and specifically, not you."

"Okay." That didn't surprise me. Dr. Hermann told me the first time we talked that anything I did to interfere with his research would delay the availability of a more effective treatment for Parkinson's. He'd said, "Just remember that every time you give me and my team more busywork to do."

Bonnie continued, "He spent time with Evie at first, observing her and running some behavioral tests, but he's lost interest now. It's the results from these drug tests that are going to make him a rich research rock star, not another study on monkey behavior."

I felt the monkey's fingers exploring the front of my shirt with a light touch. I looked down at her. "Eve?" She raised her head. "Shake?" I held out my hand for her to grasp.

Eve turned her face away. I could see tears, still clinging to the tufts of hair below her cheeks.

Bonnie said, "She doesn't do that. Shake. Save Timmy. Roll over. None of that shit."

"But she's...smart, right?"

"They're all smart. I assume what you're really asking is whether the genetically altered ones are smarter than the others."

I nodded.

Bonnie shrugged. "Not that we can tell."

As I pieced all the bits of information together, it was clear to me that the gene-splicing experiment had resulted in an unintended consequence—a monkey that cried, that showed a uniquely human reaction to its own suffering. I knew that much, but I didn't know much else—didn't have any idea yet why Bonnie had called and demanded that I come to the lab that night.

I didn't have to wait long to find out. Bonnie took a deep breath and then blurted out a few words at a time. "Okay. You need. To do. *Something.*"

I waited for her to say more, and my hesitation made her lose all remaining patience with me.

She said in a louder voice, "Don't you get it? It isn't right, to create a monkey like Evie and then do this to her." She gestured at the rows of cages and the research apparatus around the room. "She can't stand it. I can't stand it."

"I understand." I didn't know what I could do about it, but I did understand.

"Those files on my desk? You need to get them out of here—tonight. If you don't, Dr. Hermann will shred them."

"Haven't they already given me copies of everything?"

"No," she said, pointedly. "They haven't."

"Okay."

"I think there're some empty boxes in the supply room. Let's go check—and get out of here. Okay?"

My pen was still on the floor, where the monkey had dropped it. It was jade colored with gold trim. My dad had given it to me. I squatted down to get it. From that position I could see Barbie's legs again. I looked closer. They were sticking out of a small animal crate under the table, a lightweight blue plastic cage with a handle on top, made for transporting animals. We had one just like it at home that we used to take our dog to the vet. The Barbie doll was inside, with her legs sticking through the mesh door. I also saw a rolled up pink blanket inside. With my free hand, I pulled the crate out from under the table. "What's this?"

Bonnie scowled at me. "I don't know," she said sarcastically. "Why don't you tell me?"

I didn't answer her, and she looked away.

When I pulled the crate out from under the table, I saw that there was a bulging white plastic grocery sack behind it. I got down on my knees and pulled it out too, accidentally spilling its contents on the floor, brown pellets that looked like dog food. There was also a small plastic bowl in the sack and some pill bottles.

It all made sense now. Bonnie was planning to take Eve with her… somewhere. When Bonnie had said that she was leaving, she hadn't meant that she was leaving alone. I started to say something like, "What the hell are you thinking?" but she held up her hand and said, "Don't. Don't even start."

I couldn't help myself. I began lecturing her about how Eve was university property—*valuable* property, given all the money that the university had sunk over the past five years into the experiment. That was the lawyer in me, always considering what should be said on behalf of my client, the university.

The monkey began to cry. The tone of my voice had upset her again.

And without warning, Bonnie thrust the monkey up against my chest. "Fine, then. You can deal with her. It'll be on you."

Eve reached out to accept me, and, without thinking, I took her and held her like a toddler, nestled in the crook of my arm. She looked back and forth between Bonnie and me, uncertain about what was happening, but she stopped crying and wiggled her body down into the crook of my arm.

Bonnie said, "He's your lawyer now."

Eve nodded, one somber nod.

"Look at that. She thinks she can trust you." Bonnie allowed herself to smile, a bitter smile that lasted only an instant. "Go figure." She reached out and stroked the top of Eve's head. "Dr. Hermann has decided to add a large daily dose of morphine to her drug regimen. That's his idea of a solution to the crying. I was supposed to give it to her tonight. That'll pretty much be it for Evie. She'll become a junkie monkey—we've got a few of them around here. They're zombies, but it's the humane thing to do when the experiments make their lives too much of a hell."

I nodded, but I found the idea abhorrent. I looked down at Eve in my arms. Her eyes were closed. I suddenly wished that I hadn't guessed Bonnie's intentions—her plan to save the monkey from all this. I had the irrational desire to turn back the clock and handle things differently.

"Dr. Hermann wants to get just a little more data from her. Then they'll put her down—that's what he said. And that'll be it." Bonnie turned and began to walk toward the door to the lab.

I wished that Bonnie hadn't even called me, that she had simply taken Eve away from this place and gone somewhere—as she had said—far, far away. I looked down at Eve, who was now peacefully asleep, nestled against my chest. "What am I supposed to do with her?"

Without slowing down or turning to look back at us, Bonnie said, "Whatever you think, Jim. Whatever you think is right."

Chapter 3

I took the monkey. Let me explain.

When Bonnie Norton walked out of the lab and left me standing there alone holding Eve, I looked down at the monkey, asleep in my arms like a baby. Her eyes were closed, but I'd seen something in them earlier, something that had connected the two of us, something I didn't quite understand yet.

I wasn't thinking. I was acting on emotion. If I'd been engaged in rational thought, I would have followed university procedures—and ordinary common sense, right? I would have called my boss first, before doing anything, and given him a heads up, asked him what the hell to do. Something unintended, but unthinkable had occurred in our university's medical research lab. And people were in the process of covering it up. That seemed pretty clear.

I had to protect this genetically altered lab monkey. There was no one else who could—who *would*. No one. I didn't want her to die—and she would die, if I didn't do something.

Bonnie had told me that I had to "do something," and I had realized within moments after she walked away that she was right. But what I did would have surprised her—it wasn't at all what she had had in mind. I was a lawyer. What she had wanted was for me to do something lawyerly, like lawyers do in movies, like taking on the system to force researchers everywhere to abide by strict guidelines on experiments involving human DNA and primates…or like spearheading an investigation and then holding press conferences to herald the results.

That could all have been part of a grand strategy—if I'd let Bonnie take Eve away from the lab to somewhere safe. But I hadn't. I'd stopped it.

There are university procedures to follow when any serious allegation of misconduct is made. I knew that very well—I'd written the policies that laid out those procedures. If I initiated an inquiry, Dr. Hermann would have the right to defend his actions, the right to request a hearing. There would be no disruption allowed of these important, high profile medical experiments without adequate proof.

Proof? I had no proof, no proof that Eve was anything other than a specially bred, but otherwise quite ordinary lab monkey. But I knew what my gut told me. This monkey had *something*…something resembling human awareness—maybe like an awakening soul—but I didn't know. How could anyone know? She was only a monkey and couldn't talk.

But I did know that if I put her back in her cage and left her there in the lab, this intriguing creature would be dead before any official decision-maker following official university procedures came to any official conclusion.

I couldn't let that happen. It was wrong.

Eve woke up when she felt me trying to put her into the plastic animal carrier that Bonnie had left behind. She squealed and lunged toward me, grabbing a lapel on my suit coat. When I tried to pry her strong little fingers open, she bared her teeth as if she was getting ready to bite me. So I got the Barbie doll out of the crate, wiggled it in her face and had Barbie say, in a girly voice, "Hey, monkey, want to go for a ride? Come on!" I'm glad no one was there to witness it.

When Eve relaxed her grip on my lapel to reach for the doll, I shoved her into the crate and shut its door. I was sweating. I wiped perspiration from my upper lip with the back of my hand and realized that my hand stank—smelled a bit like feces. It made me realize…I didn't know much about monkeys, about their interest in personal hygiene or their bathroom habits. I didn't know if Eve was housebro-ken—or could be.

I carried the animal carrier and Bonnie's tall stack of multi-colored research files to my car. I walked briskly, afraid at first that a security guard—or maybe someone who knew me—would stop me and ask what I was doing, carrying off one of the lab animals. But as it turned out, I didn't need to be worried about that. The halls were empty and the parking lot outside was deserted. No one saw me, but as I began to drive away, the thudding sound in my ears that came from my pound-ing heart grew, drowning out all other sound.

I quickly had huge misgivings about what I was doing. I thought about parking my car and taking the monkey back to the lab. I even thought about driving over to the general counsel's house—he lived near the university—and forcing him to make whatever decision had to be made. But I knew it would turn out badly—not only for the monkey, but for me and my boss—if we brought the problems to light. The university's primary concern—hell, its only genuine concern—was protecting its ongoing ability to raise research funds. Anyone or anything that stood in the way was expendable.

As I was considering my options, I had sudden intense feelings of déjà vu. I had the vivid sensation of having taken this monkey before—a ridiculous possibility, of course. But I had what seemed like recent, clear memories of taking Eve away from the university, but circling the large parking lot outside the Medical Science Building, undecided about what to do—just as I was then doing. I've had experiences of déjà vu before—we all have, right? I suppose sensations of *having been there before* always seem real at the instant they occur. But what seemed strange to me then was that in my déjà vu memories, the monkey was crying—weeping inconsolably. In the reality of the present moment she was quiet, probably sleeping.

I made my decision. I said, to no one in particular, "It's going to be okay," and I turned from the parking lot onto the street that led to the freeway that I drove every day. It was going to be okay. We had an old dog at home that my wife Grace had found on the highway, a three-legged cat, and two gerbils. Helping strays had become fairly routine for our family and even something of a passion of Grace's—a diversion, I suppose, from her own troubles. She was on the board of an animal rescue place that took in dogs and cats that needed homes and medical attention. I didn't think she would object to another rescue. And my son Buck would help. It would be okay.

Grace was lying on the couch, reading, when I got home. Without looking up at me, she said, "What's her name?"

"Eve."

"Is she pretty?"

I looked down at the monkey through the plastic slits in the top of the crate. I wasn't sure how to respond.

When I didn't answer, Grace turned on the couch and looked at us. "So what have you got there?"

"A monkey."

There was a long pause. "Okay. What are you going to do with him...her...is it a him or her?"

"It's a her."

"Does she have a name?"

"You already asked me that. Her name's Eve."

Grace smiled, or at least her mouth was turned up in a smile, but her eyes were uncommitted. "Oh, I thought we were talking about your girlfriend." Grace was joking, of course. Sometimes when it seemed as if I were spending an unusually large amount of time at the office, Grace would ask me random questions about me having a girlfriend, but she didn't actually suspect anything like that. She often said that if I were having an affair, she'd just know. And I think that's probably true.

Grace's flat response to the highly unusual fact of me bringing a monkey home from work was her way of expressing quiet anger, anger that had nothing to do with Eve or even the fact that I was five hours late getting home.

Grace wasn't asking questions, but that didn't mean she didn't have any, and so I gave her the essential facts. I explained that Eve was a genetically altered monkey and I said what I thought was true at the time—that we were only going to keep her in our home for a couple of weeks—no more than a month, enough time for me to figure out a solution to the problem of Eve's existence, and probably find a zoo somewhere, where Eve could live out the remainder of her life in relative anonymity.

By the time I had finished my abbreviated explanation, Grace was standing beside me, bent over and peering at the monkey through the door of the crate. "I hope you know what you're doing." She stood up straight, looked at me and said with some alarm, "So…do we have to buy diapers for her?"

"I don't know. What do you think?"

"I don't want to take any chances."

"I agree."

Grace sighed. Then she took my arm and leaned against me, worn out from another day of living. "Why do you hate me?"

I turned to face her. "I don't hate you. I love you."

"So why do you love me?"

I shrugged. I was worn out too, too tired to articulate a reason that sounded credible.

She didn't care.

Eve began to whimper. Grace bent down again to look at the monkey. "Why in the world would somebody name a monkey Eve?"

I wasn't there when the grad students named her, but it obviously wasn't a random pick. One of the other monkeys that died prematurely was named Adam. The grad students were aware of what they were doing—creating living creatures with a combination of human and monkey DNA, creatures that hadn't previously existed—and, as it turned out, with unintended consequences a little bit like the Bible story. In the book of Genesis, Adam and Eve ate fruit from a forbidden tree and became like God in some respects. But the price for a more godlike awareness was high—an existence filled with suffering. We as humans are different from other living creatures in that way. We're *aware*—aware of all kinds of things, ranging from commonplace feelings of anger and fear, to elevating feelings of love, to puzzling feelings

20

of intuition, déjà vu and the like. Having all those complicated feelings isn't something that we necessarily like, but when we suppress them, we don't like that much either.

Psychologists are kept in business by people who want to learn how to feel anger…sadness…even joy, emotions that have been buried or locked down so tightly that they might as well not exist. That had described me pretty well until four years earlier.

My first son was named Thomas Byron. He was named after his two grandfathers. I was working for one of the big Houston law firms when he was born. Grace and I were living a charmed life at the time. It was easy to be Baptist. God was good and we were blessed—truly blessed—there's no sarcasm in that statement. I had just made partner at my law firm. Some small real estate investments we'd made had paid off handsomely. Our parents were all alive and healthy. We had good friends—not a huge number, but more than enough, more friends than we had time to see.

When Thomas was born, I called almost all of them from the lobby of the hospital, and I told each of them essentially the same thing: that Thomas was healthy and that Grace and I were "ecstatic." Everybody I called responded with nice words, as one would expect, except for my friend Neal, who just laughed at me and mimicked what I'd said, repeating in a deadpan voice, "Grace and I are just ecstatic." Neal was giving me a hard time about something that was true about me. I rarely displayed genuine emotion. My words weren't matching my tone of voice. I wasn't ecstatic. I should have been. I should have been giddy with happiness, but I couldn't feel anything more powerful than a general sense of well-being.

As it turned out, Thomas wasn't healthy for long. Several years later, shortly after our second son Buck was born, we discovered that Thomas had leukemia. That was a bleak, dark period in our lives. I spent long hours at the hospital with Thomas. Grace stayed home, focusing most of her energy on the needs of our newborn and retreating deep into her own private world, finding hope in our Baptist beliefs. We held much the same beliefs going into the crisis, but we each reacted quite differently. I kept my fears to myself, but she told all who cared to listen that it was going to be okay, because God was in control of everything and all things work together for good for those who love God.

I wasn't sure anymore.

Throughout those months, despite everything, Grace found the energy to go to church almost every Sunday. I didn't go as often, but I made time every day to read the Bible and pray. I read the Book of Psalms over and over again, from first to last. There is a jarring juxtaposition of suffering and thanksgiving in Psalms. If you only hear the commonly quoted snippets, you don't realize that. "Yea, though I walk through the valley of death, I shall fear no evil." We all know that one. But there are many passages that vividly detail the psalmist's despair and suffering, like this one: "My soul is in anguish. How long, oh Lord, how long?" It gave me a new perception of prayer...and a first inkling of some unnoticed symmetries. One day I asked Grace if she'd like to join me in my reading and prayer, and she said okay, but before we were done, she stood up to leave and said, "I can't do this." That was okay. I understood. Grace could not square the reality of undeserved suffering with her belief in a god in control.

You need to know this: Thomas survived the leukemia, but he died from pneumonia within six months after we were told that his cancer appeared to be in remission.

The day that the doctor told us his honest opinion—that Thomas' organs were failing and that he wouldn't live through the weekend—I had been at the hospital for more than forty-eight hours straight. Grace came to the hospital to stay with Thomas, and I went home to take a shower and try to sleep for a little bit. I sent the babysitter home and sat in a rocking chair in Buck's room watching him sleep peacefully in his crib. And without knowing what I was about to do, I began to weep—the first time since I was a child. I actually can't remember crying as a child, but I'm sure I did. All children cry. Indulge me for a moment as I explain this. Most of you probably know how it feels to cry, but maybe some of you don't remember. Sobbing out loud is a wrenching emotional experience. You feel the pain. You don't hide it or rationalize it away. But buried in the intense grief is a sense of connection to things outside of you. For me, a burden of self-imposed isolation had been lifted and a barrier had been removed. After that I cried frequently—and got angry sometimes and yelled when I felt like it. And I admitted to myself how afraid I was about so very many things in my life.

But the barrier that had isolated me from my emotions had also helped me curb my…let's call it my style of unique thinking—throughout my life. It had been a coping mechanism I had learned as a child—to impose cold rationality on my feelings and thoughts. And to always follow rules that I set for myself. Cold logic had helped me come this far. I never allowed myself free rein. My mother had drilled it into me—for good reason—that I should not carry matches.

But that's what happened. My friends soon noticed a change in me. Grace did too and wasn't altogether happy about differences in how I viewed things and how I behaved.

No one but me knew how hard it had become to control my thoughts and impulses.

I had set myself on fire.

Grace still goes to church and Sunday school at the Baptist church in our neighborhood almost every Sunday, but I haven't been back once since Thomas' funeral service.

Grace and I are good parents to Buck. We sleep in the same bed and we've never talked of divorce, but when Thomas died, something in our marriage also died. I mourn for that too.

Chapter 4

Circa 85 C.E.

Many have undertaken to write accurate accounts of the miraculous things that have taken place among us, things that we have observed or that have been recounted by reliable eyewitnesses. Therefore, since I, myself, have been investigating diligently, it seemed fitting that I should write an objective account for you, most excellent Theophilus, so that you may better understand the mysteries that you have been taught.

Now, most of the Eleven were already in the courtyard waiting and arguing among themselves. Mary Magdalene and Joanna had come down from the room where they had been staying, and seeing that anger had already driven John and his followers to stand apart from the others, Mary Magdalene asked that everyone wait in silence for Cephas to arrive. It was the day of Pentecost.

A large room had been obtained that opened onto the courtyard. The air in the courtyard was still and stifling. Birds were nesting in a crevice in a corner of the courtyard where bricks had fallen away. The stone floor under the nest and in various places around the courtyard was stained by bird droppings.

Clouds overhead gathered and then broke apart, causing harsh sunlight to intermittently fill the center of the courtyard.

Several strangers appeared and stood in the shade on one side. They looked at John with curiosity and suspicion.

A boy carrying a large, tattered basket tripped on one of the uneven stones of the courtyard floor, spilling loaves of bread onto the floor that was layered in gray dust and stained by the birds' droppings. As he was kneeling to scoop the loaves back into the basket, he also gripped one of his toes tightly with the hem of his garment. A red blood stain appeared and spread along the hem.

Cephas, who had appeared in one of the doorways, came and knelt beside the boy. He prayed, as the Master had taught him to pray, and then quickly stood, unable to hide his frustration. He lacked the power to heal even such a minor injury. Cephas looked in the direction of John and those around him. They were engrossed in their own concerns and were paying no heed to the boy's mishap. Cephas glanced at Mary Magdalene, who mouthed words that he understood to mean, "Be patient."

But Cephas couldn't be patient. He had seen enough, experienced enough, that he had become despondent in his inability to wield the powers that he had seen. At the Master's death, he was there—at least once—and had the revelation of having been there multiple times, each time in circumstances that were slightly different. In one memory, faint as an old dream, the Master had been there himself, outside the tomb. In another memory, there had been one angel, and in yet another there had been two. Cephas distinctly remembered a violent earthquake that had dislodged the stone from the Master's tomb and scared away the guards, but everyone else, except for Mary Magdalene, denied that such a thing had happened and admonished him not embellish the facts of the Master's resurrection any further. But others had. Differing accounts had already begun to circulate. Mary Magdalene refused to discuss it, but he could see in her eyes that she shared his confusion and awe at the manner in which things had been revealed to them. It was as if the same pivotal moments had occurred again and again and again, but each time with subtle differences, until—and this was Cephas' uncertain speculation about the matter—*matters were somehow settled, no longer in flux.*

Cephas lowered his eyes again, praying once more for healing, of the boy's injury and of the growing dissension among the believers who were there with him in the courtyard.

The clouds had thickened again, blocking out the sun. Large drops of rain began to fall, sporadically, at first. The whispering breeze grew into a stiff wind that caused unseen doors to slam against their frames. John and those around him moved into the room that had been prepared for them to observe Pentecost together, and he shouted over his shoulder, "Come. There's no reason to wait any longer for the stragglers."

As the men began to sit down, the noise from the wind outside grew into a moan as it forced its way through gaps around those of the windows that were held closed by their worn latches. A single, sharp thunderclap sounded, interrupting individual conversations. As the conversations resumed, rain began to fall outside, filling the room with the sound of the muffled drumming of raindrops against the flat roof overhead.

Cephas was the last to sit. A place of honor had been reserved for him beside John. Ignoring the questions that were being shouted from various sectors in the room, Cephas lowered his head once again and prayed silently, with an expression of desperation clear upon his face.

The room was lit suddenly by a flash of white light that came through the windows that faced the courtyard and then, as suddenly, was returned to the dim light put out by a few lanterns that had been found. Again and again, lightning flashed, creating the illusion of frozen images shifting magically. And then the lightning became jagged, branched like the bare limbs of a tree in winter, touching or appearing to touch the ground outside the doors and windows. The sound of wind and thunder was deafening. The web of lightening around them was blinding and disorienting. Several men struggled to close one of the windows, and at the same time, another man opened a window that faced into the storm, to gaze at the awe-inspiring display outside. And light entered the room, in the shape of tongues of fire that blazed white-hot in arcs across the room and then disappeared. Those who had been touched by the fire found that they had new understandings and powers.

Chapter 5

The monkey and I shared a fascination with thunderstorms. When I was a kid I liked to stand outside in the summer and watch thunderstorms. There was a pregnant smell in the wind—I didn't know the word for it then, but I do now. It was a fertile, earthy smell, almost at odds with the deluge of water that was soon to come. And I remember the colors, the way the storm tinted the outside world a luminous, greenish gray. I waited and watched for the lightning, with its jagged white lines, and the heaven above seemed less infinite, as if there was a ceiling to the world, as if all the real and imagined powers of the universe were hovering there, close enough to see, if you looked hard enough. And I looked hard.

I should say, early on, that I became attached to Eve very quickly after I brought her home. There were things that connected us—similarities in our temperaments—despite the fact that she was just a monkey. She seemed genuinely happy accompanying me in whatever I was doing. She was very quiet and docile and adapted so well to life in our household that I lost most of the sense of urgency that I'd had to find her another home—other than ours.

I had expected for there to be an uproar at work when it was discovered that a grad student had resigned without notice and a lab monkey was missing—but that wasn't the case. When I made my next regular Friday afternoon visit to the science lab none of the grad students said anything about either one of them. I nonchalantly pointed at Eve's empty cage and asked one of them, "Where's that one?" He said, "You'll have to ask Dr. Hermann about that." I said, "Hey, where's Bonnie? I haven't seen her around today," and he said in the same stiff tone of voice, "Ask Dr. Hermann." When I recounted the conversation to Grace that night, she said, "Are you sure you know what you're doing?"

At the time, I thought so.

It was on a Saturday in January—almost seven weeks after I brought Evie home—that I first discovered her interest in thunderstorms. Buck and I had just come back from one of his soccer games—Grace was at the game too, but she had driven her own car so that she could run an errand afterwards: shopping for a baby clothes—a gift for some new parents at church. Buck was five, which was a little too young to be able to focus on genuine soccer technique, but in Houston, kids start sports early. And it was an outlet for some of his abundant energy.

There's a covered walkway from the garage to the back door of our house, and so Buck and I could see Eve at the den window as we came up, wrinkling her nose and looking around.

I said, "I thought I told you to put her in her crate."

His face assumed a look of innocence. "I did...I think."

It wasn't the first time that Eve had accidentally been left alone un-caged, and, honestly, I wasn't particularly concerned. When we were home, we usually let her roam the house freely, and we'd only had one significant mishap—and that was mostly Buck's fault. We have a wall clock that makes bird sounds on the hour, instead of chimes—each hour of the day has the sound of a different bird. The clock was cheap, but the sound quality is very realistic. Buck noticed that whenever the clock would chirp or coo or caw, Eve would run over to it, looking for the bird. Buck began egging her on, yelling, "Get the bird." It was funny at first, watching her get excited—until once when she jumped from a nearby chair, grabbed the clock and pulled it off the wall. The clock still works, but the minute hand is bent now, and sometimes when the hands on the clock get jammed together, time just stops.

Buck knocked on the window and yelled, "Hey, Eve, did you miss us?"

She ignored Buck and moved over so that he didn't block her view and stared in the direction of the dark clouds overhead. A few fat, slushy raindrops had begun to fall and thunder was rumbling in the distance.

I gave him a nudge and said, "Come on. Let's get inside before the storm hits." I looked around the backyard for our dog Daisy. I didn't see her. I assumed that she was keeping dry under the gazebo. Grace made me build her a doghouse, but she never used it.

Buck said, "Do they ever let kids play soccer in the mud? Like if it rained really hard, would you and the other dads let us keep playing anyway? That would be so cool."

"I don't know." That had become one of my all-purpose answers for Buck. I wasn't ready to dampen his enthusiasm for life that came out of his wild, childish ideas. That would come in due time without my intervention.

We walked in the back door into a small room that has a closet and our washer and dryer. Our three-legged orange cat, Porky, was curled up on a rug that was in front of the dryer. His food bowl was in the corner of that room. It was full. Eve liked to feed Porky, and, unless we stopped her, filled up Porky's food bowl every time she saw that it was empty. Not surprisingly, Porky treated Eve like his new best friend. Eve had even begun using Porky's cat box. We were weaning Eve from diapers, and she was adapting—pretty well—no more accidents than some other animals Grace had rescued in the past.

Buck ran past me, through the kitchen and into the den. I stopped in the kitchen and shook the coffee thermos to see if there was any coffee left in it. There was, and so I poured myself a cup—it was at least two and a half hours old and there was still a wisp of steam coming off of it. We don't properly appreciate the miracles of science.

Buck came back into the kitchen, with Eve beside him, holding his hand. He said, "She wants to go outside." He let go of her hand and she climbed up my pants leg and into my arms. Her touch was light, as she grabbed a wrinkle in my jeans and then my belt on her way up. She didn't stop at my arm. She climbed onto my shoulder, where she balanced with one hand resting on my head. With her other arm she reached toward the kitchen window. I didn't really like having her that close to my face. In between baths, she sometimes smelled like an unwashed armpit. I reached up and took her in my hands. She began to twist and started to squeal, still reaching toward the window.

Buck said, "She wants to go now."

I said, "I get it." I began walking toward the back door. She calmed down immediately, grabbed the collar of my shirt and clung to my chest. I turned to Buck. "You coming?"

"That's okay. I'm going to go upstairs and do some stuff."

"Okay."

"Hey, Dad, can I have a Dr. Pepper?"

"No."

As I shut the back door, I could hear him saying, "Please?"

We don't have a covered patio behind the house, and so a couple of years ago we paid someone to build a gazebo in the middle of the backyard. It was a prefabricated structure that has some Victorian inspired trim. I like sitting out there in the morning. We bought a table and chairs so that we could have dinner outside, but we don't do that very often.

I trotted to the gazebo. The branches from the huge pine trees by the house sheltered us somewhat from the falling rain. Just as I climbed the steps, there was a loud crack of thunder and within moments, the rain began to come down hard. I stood, with the monkey still in my arms, at the very edge of the gazebo, leaning against the iron railing. There was little wind, and the rain was falling straight down. The air was moist, but the roof of the gazebo kept us dry.

Lightning filled one corner of the sky and another clap of thunder followed. I turned my face to Eve and said, "So, what do you think, Evie?"

Holding onto my shoulder, she leaned out into the falling rain so that she could look up at the sky, where the lightning had been. Raindrops fell on her face. She jerked back close to me, then touched the water on her face and examined it on her fingers. She lifted her hand to my face, and with her tiny finger, pointed toward the corner of my eye. If I hadn't blinked, she might have poked me in the eye.

31

She began to wiggle and I let her jump down. She climbed up on the iron railing and reached out her hand, palm up and let rain fall on it. She looked at me again. And the connection hit me: the rain struck her as being like tears—or maybe in her mind, the raindrops *were* tears. I was speculating, of course, but weeks earlier she'd been crying all the time. Even for a monkey, that kind of memory would linger. It made sense.

She stood on the railing and, holding on to one of the columns, leaned out as far as she could and looked up at the black clouds. She stared at the sky for a long time. I sat down in one of the chairs that was in the gazebo and watched her—and the storm. After a while, she turned and looked back at me. Eye contact was becoming an important means of communication between us, a very imprecise means of communication to be sure, but it told me when something was on her mind. I could tell from the gleam in her eyes that what she saw above her—in the churning storm clouds and in the falling rain—meant something.

Two of our closest friends are Elaine and Barry. My wife and Elaine were roommates in college. Barry and I have always gotten along well too. Elaine is a psychologist and Barry is a Presbyterian preacher. His church is twenty miles away, on the other side of Houston, so we never seriously considered joining it. There are reasons in addition to the convenience factor. Grace still wants to be part of a Baptist worship culture. Also Grace and I talked about it and decided that it would change the comfortable relationship we have with Barry—and probably with Elaine too—if they had to fill the roles of preacher and preacher's wife around us.

They came over for dinner on Saturday night for an evening without kids—for all of us. Buck was spending the night with Grace's parents, and Elaine and Barry had gotten a sitter for their two daughters. They were almost half an hour late arriving because of the wet roads. The early afternoon thunderstorm had ended, but a steady, light rain had taken its place. More thunderstorms were expected.

I can't tell you how much we enjoy the time we spend with Barry and Elaine. Elaine reads more than anyone I know and always has interesting—and frequently offbeat—insights on virtually everything. Grace talks more when she's around Elaine, and I'm sometimes surprised at what Grace knows and thinks. Barry has a sly sense of humor and charming demeanor, but underlying it all is a quiet, persistent passion for justice, which has sometimes aroused suspicion in the churches that he's pastored. Elaine says that in earlier times he would have been one of the prophets driven from village to village by threats of stoning.

We had a great dinner. Grace is a great cook. She's very serious about the details, the presentation and appearance of the food. She made a berry tart with a lattice crust top that was almost too beautiful to slice up and eat—but we did. And we enjoyed it, along with some special coffee that Grace had bought from a place nearby that roasts it daily.

I told them about my experience with Eve and the thunderstorm earlier that day and about my theory that Eve thought that the raindrops were tears.

As Grace was stacking up the dirty dessert plates, she said, "I think he's just projecting his own thoughts on her. She's just a monkey, for heaven's sake."

Sometimes Grace disagrees with me, even when she has no reason to. It makes me mad. "You weren't there," I said.

Grace smiled at our guests, ignoring my obvious irritation with her. "She's Jim's new best friend."

"Grace is starting to like her too," I said. "Although she won't admit it."

"I admit it."

"Can we see her?" Elaine asked. Elaine has a rather round face, framed by thick, unruly red hair. She's a pretty woman, with striking, pale green eyes.

"If you want." I looked at Grace to be sure she didn't object. She shrugged.

Elaine continued, "I wonder if she looks at other things that way."

"What do you mean?"

"Anthropomorphizing the things around her. Like what primitive people did in ancient times, making male and female gods out of the sun and moon. You know...." Elaine has a delightful urbanized Southern accent. Coming out of her mouth, even a mind-numbing word like anthropomorphizing sounds elegant.

Now it was my turn to say it. "She's just a monkey." I slid my chair back from the table. "I'll get her."

Grace signaled for me to keep seated. "No, I'll get her."

Barry held his coffee mug with both hands, savoring the warmth and aroma. "So you rescued her?"

"Grace told you?"

"Well, she told Elaine. And Elaine told our daughter Brandy, who told her granddad, who told me."

"That's strange."

"Strange, but true. I think the story was embellished some by the time I heard it. What I heard was that you disguised yourself as the president of the university."

"But that's a woman."

"Yep."

The wind was picking up outside. An overgrown shrub next to the dining room window scraped against the glass. I heard thunder in the distance.

Grace came back in the room carrying Eve, who was wearing a baby blue dress.

"You bought her a dress?"

"Today. When I was shopping for the baby gifts. Isn't she cute?" Grace grinned at Elaine. Grace has a beautiful smile. I didn't see it much when we were alone.

"Did she fight you when you were putting it on her?" I asked.

"No. I think she likes how she looks, don't you, Eve?" Grace smoothed the skirt over Eve's long, furry legs.

Eve nodded once, a quick, crisp nod. Then she looked around the table at the three of us sitting there. She held out her arms for me.

Grace passed her to me. "Jim is her favorite."

It thundered again, louder this time. Eve wriggled out of my arms, jumped to the floor and scampered over to the window. She burrowed underneath the drapes and disappeared from sight, although we could see a lump behind the drapes, climbing up to the windowsill and fidgeting around.

Elaine walked over and gently pulled back one side of the drapes. She said, "I want to see what she does when she sees rain."

"I don't think she'll do anything unless we're outside—in it."

"That's okay. Do you mind, Grace?"

Grace frowned. "Let me see how many umbrellas I can find."

"We can share."

Grace found three umbrellas. Barry poured himself some more coffee and the rest of us carried snifters filled with Bailey's—and I carried Eve.

As we walked down the path to the gazebo, Barry said, "Now is it a good idea or a bad idea to carry an umbrella in a thunderstorm?" Barry is quite a bit taller than the rest of us, but he has a bit of a hunch in his posture that makes him look older than he is. Even so, whoever shared an umbrella with him would have gotten their legs wet. So the monkey and I shared an umbrella with Elaine and let Barry have his own.

Grace trotted ahead of us. "You're a preacher. God wouldn't strike *you* with lightning. It would be me that he would decide to smite."

"Smite."

"What a great word."

As we climbed the steps onto the gazebo, Barry put his hand on Grace's shoulder. "Did you know...that the ancient Hebrew word for 'smite' was actually derived from the Sumerian expression, 'Oh, shit'."

"Barry." Elaine laughed. I think she enjoyed being around him more, when he didn't have to act like a preacher.

I let Eve down. She wrinkled her nose, made a snuffling noise, and looked around. Then she quietly moved over to the iron railing that went around the sides of the gazebo. She grabbed it with one hand and then swung up and stood on the railing. She looked out at the storm.

A storm at night has its own unique kind of beauty and mystery. In the blackness of night, the lightning appears between cloudbanks and illuminates dark, hulking shapes. The quick flashes reveal cascading avalanches of snow in the sky, or giant rows of misshapen cabbages, or maybe huddled gods—and then they're all gone.

There were several flashes of lightning and claps of thunder, followed by heavier rain.

Eve began to chatter and to scamper back and forth across the narrow iron railing, hopping and pointing at the sky and occasionally stopping to look at me, as if she was waiting for some word or reaction. The little blue dress she was wearing didn't slow her down a bit.

Elaine said, "Is she scared of the thunder?"

"I don't think she's scared." Barry walked to the railing where Eve was perched and looked down at her. "Just curious."

I said, "Maybe it's the lightning that's getting her attention. You like lightning? You want to see more lightning?"

She looked up and shook her body, then tapped her chest several times with her fist. She checked to be sure I was watching her and then she pointed at the sky.

Grace said, "I think she's pointing at that big, dark cloud over there. It looks like a monkey face."

Eve squealed and jumped into the air. When she came down, her toes curled over the railing, securing her landing.

"Eve, you want to get closer? To the monkey face?"

Barry said. "Charades. I love charades."

And it *was* like playing charades—but with someone who doesn't understand your language. It wasn't the first time we'd played charades with Elaine and Barry. We'd had more than a few spirited games over the years. I said, "There's nothing like a good game of monkey charades—outdoors, in the middle of a thunder storm. Right?"

Grace shot me an ugly look. This wasn't how she had intended to spend the evening with our friends.

Eve jumped off the railing, looked at Barry—who was closest to her—and then swung back up onto the railing and leaped into the air again.

I moved closer to Barry and said, "I'm on his team."

Gusts of wind began to blow rain into the gazebo. Drops of water were landing on Eve. She wiped water off of her forehead and then pointed at the sky.

"Raindrops Keep Falling on My Head."

"Eve, are we doing song titles?" Elaine asked.

Eve looked at us and nodded with conviction. Of course, she didn't understand anything we were saying, but her comic timing was perfect and fueled our enthusiasm for the game, despite the increasing velocity of the wind.

"The Sky is Crying."

"What's that?"

"A song title. We're doing song titles, right?"

"Was that by Eric Clapton?"

"Are you kidding me? Where were you in the 80's?"

"Perfecting her disco moves."

"Shut up."

The wind was blowing water onto us now. Grace picked up an umbrella and held it at an angle to block the rain. "We're all getting wet."

Eve hopped down to the floor, then climbed back up on the railing and jumped again, higher this time, bumping into Grace's umbrella when she landed.

Barry feigned sudden inspiration. "It's raining monkeys." He laughed. "You know, the old saying, 'It's raining cats and dogs?' Well… it's raining monkeys and…" He ran out of inspiration. "More monkeys."

Eve stared at us. Her nostrils flared and her face twitched.

Obviously, Eve didn't understand what Barry had said, but I did. And the words he'd blurted out as a joke came close to capturing her primitive thoughts—I was sure of it. I scooped her up off the floor and lifted her into the air. And like I used to do with Buck when he was a baby, spiraled her through the air as if she were flying. I stopped, tapped her chest—as she had done—and then pointed to the sky and then lifted her into the air and lowered her to the ground one more time. She climbed up my leg and into my arms, and then she lifted

37

her hand to my eye, as she'd done earlier that afternoon, and pointed. And then she looked at me and waited.

I said, "Monkeys come from tears...they come from the tears...of God."

Almost in unison, Grace and Barry said, "What?"

I repeated: "Monkeys came from the tears of God."

Eve hadn't looked away. She was still looking me in the eye, waiting to see if I understood.

I did. I understood.

She had come up with her own creation myth. Her memories of her own suffering, while caged in the university lab, had spawned a revelation of a higher monkey reality.

Chapter 6

Our old cat Porky died quietly, sometime during the day. Porky was the very first stray animal Grace and I had adopted, although it would be more accurate to say that he'd adopted us. Shortly after we bought our house, a few years before we had any children, he appeared on our back step meowing, with a note of criticism in his voice, as if we were shamefully late in feeding him that morning. He only had three legs—we have no idea how he was injured—and was a bit portly, even then, but he had a gentle, affectionate temperament and we let him move in with us.

Eve found him on the yellow shag rug in front of the clothes drier, where he liked to nap. Eve's crate is in the laundry room too. At night-time and when we're going to be gone from the house for more than an hour or so, we put usually Eve in her crate. She doesn't seem to mind. In fact, sometimes when things are hectic and noisy around the house—like when Buck has a friend over—Eve will go get in the crate and play with her Barbie doll or sleep.

I was in the kitchen. I had opened the refrigerator to check on a bottle of wine that I had put in there earlier, to be sure it was now cold enough to drink, and I heard whimpering coming from the laundry room. I recognized the sound—Eve whimpers about a variety of things—but I didn't know what was upsetting her at the moment. When I went into the laundry room, she was crouching beside Porky and lifting his head, letting it fall back onto his rug and then lifting it again. She stopped whimpering when I got down on my knees beside Porky, as though she thought I could fix things. I slid my hand under Porky's shoulder and lifted it a little. He was still warm, but he was dead. I pulled the other side of the yellow rug over him, to cover him completely. I'm not sure why we instinctively do that sort of thing. It seemed respectful. Eve tried to uncover him, and she began to whimper again, and when I pulled her hand away and covered Porky again with the corner of the rug, Eve began to cry.

I hadn't seen her cry since the night I brought her home from the university lab. I lifted her from the floor and took her in my arms into the kitchen. Grace was there, looking for scissors or something. She looked at us and said, "What's wrong?"

When I told Grace that our cat had died, she ran into the laundry room, and when she came back out, she was crying too. Porky had been part of our family for over ten years, Grace's constant companion at breakfast during good times and bad. Grace plucked Eve out of my arms and the two of them cried together, with their foreheads touching. Grace glanced over at me and said, "What am I going to do now?"

I didn't know what to say. My mind went blank.

———

Our old, three-legged cat Porky died quietly, sometime during the day. Eve found him on the old blue bath mat in front of the water heater, where he liked to nap. Eve's crate is in the laundry room too.

I was in the kitchen, taking one pill out of each of my three pill bottles, when I heard the sound of Eve whimpering in the laundry room. I accidentally dropped one of my pills in the sink and considered skipping that one altogether, but I'd promised Grace to stop skipping doses. She was right—taking the pills made me function better. My secretary had told me the same thing.

When I went into the laundry room, Eve was crouching beside Porky and lifting his head, letting it fall back onto his rug and then lifting it again. I knew when I saw his motionless body that he was dead. I got down on my knees beside Porky, slid my hand under his shoulder, and lifted it a little. I was right—he was dead, already beginning to get stiff. I took a red striped beach towel from a stack that was on the dryer, unfolded it and used it to cover him. Eve tried to uncover him, whimpering again, and when I pulled her hand away and covered Porky again with the towel, she began to cry.

I hadn't seen her cry since the night I brought her home from the university lab. I lifted her from the floor and carried her in my arms into the kitchen. Grace was there, with a glass of wine in her hand, curious as to what was going on. It was her first—and probably only—glass of wine for the evening, but I could smell alcohol on her breath. I was staying away from alcohol—since I'd started taking medicine again, it was better for me not to drink.

Grace looked at us and said, "What is it? Is something wrong?"

When I told her that Porky had died, she ran into the laundry room, and when she came out, she was crying too. I put my arm around her. The smell of the alcohol on Grace's breath, as faint as it was, bothered me.

I turned my face away and closed my eyes.

———

Our old cat Porky died. Eve found him, unconscious in the wicker laundry basket, where he liked to nap.

I was in the kitchen, pouring two glasses of wine from a bottle I'd just opened, and I heard the sound of whimpering coming from the laundry room. When I went into the laundry room, Eve was crouching beside Porky and lifting his head, letting it fall back onto the rags in the basket and then lifting it again. She stopped whimpering when I got down on my knees beside Porky, as though she thought I could fix things.

I had a sense of déjà vu about the moment, as if it had happened to me before—kneeling beside my motionless cat that way.

I slid my hand under Porky's shoulder and lifted it a little. He was still breathing, but they were quick, shallow breaths. I yelled for Grace, who was in the living room playing checkers with Buck.

41

But before she and Buck came in, Porky was dead. It happened that quickly. I took one of the large rags that was under Porky in the wicker basket and used it to cover him. Eve climbed into the wicker basket with him and tried to uncover him, and when I pulled her hand away, she began to cry. Buck came up from behind, lifted her from the floor and held her.

I put my arm around Grace, and as we stood in silence there, I was aware of her warmth and of the softness of her touch. Death reminds you of how precious life is and somehow intensifies the love you feel for those who are left. Grace and I exchanged glances. I think that the death of our cat Porky brought back memories for both of us of the time in our lives when he was with us—in particular, the early days when he first came to live with us, when we were new lovers, inexperienced and idealistic. I should try to relive those times more often in my mind. They're past—those exuberant days of new love—but they're really not gone. The fact that they once truly existed is part of who I am this very second, despite all the ways in which my capacity to love may have diminished with age and hard times.

I made a mental note that a romantic weekend away was long overdue—maybe even just an overnight trip to a secluded bed and breakfast in Galveston.

Grace said, "Well...Porky had a good life."

I was in the kitchen, pouring two glasses of wine from a bottle that I'd just opened, when I heard whimpering coming from the laundry room. At the doorway to the laundry room, I could see Eve crouching beside Porky and lifting his head, letting it fall back onto his rug and then lifting it again. It looked as if something was wrong with him. I stood for a moment in the doorway and stared at everything around me. I had an unusually strong sense of déjà vu about the moment, as if it had happened to me before.

Eve stopped whimpering when I got down on my knees beside Porky. I slid my hand under Porky's head and lifted it a little. Again,

I had a feeling, almost a certainty, that I had experienced the very same series of events before—getting on my knees like that, with Eve beside me. How does that work—déjà vu? I've read that it's a mild brain malfunction, sort of a mental stutter, but I wonder....I wonder sometimes if it's a hint of an aspect of reality more complicated than we can imagine. Grace rolls her eyes when I say things like that or cautions me not to say them in front of people who don't know me very well.

Porky turned his head slightly in my direction and opened his eyes, revealing slits of pale green, and then closed them again. I lowered his head and he rolled over and curled up with his back to us.

I said, "He's an old cat. Let him sleep."

Grace called from the other room. "Is everything okay?"

Eve poked the cat with her tiny finger. His tail rose in the air, twitched and then slowly came back down on the rug.

"Come on. I'll get you a snack." I held out my hand, and Eve gripped my thumb and went with me back into the kitchen. I gave her some Cheerios. Then I carried the glasses of wine that I'd poured into the den and gave one to Grace. She said, "Is something wrong with Porky?"

"No, he's fine." I sat down on the couch and tried to read a book I'd just bought. It was a non-fiction best seller, about quantum physics—about the intriguing and complex behavior of subatomic particles. Not everybody's idea of a fascinating read, certainly, but...it was for me. It was written by a scientist with multiple degrees from several prestigious universities and reflected accurate scientific theory, but it was written for people with only a limited knowledge of science. Grace doesn't understand why I would spend my time reading and struggling to understand a book like that.

I was having trouble focusing on the words that I was reading. My mind kept drifting back to what had happened a little earlier, when I was in the laundry room checking on Porky—I had a vivid recollection of Grace standing at my side and of experiencing intense love for her, a love far stronger than what I now felt—what *either* of us felt for the other.

I was staring at Grace, as that memory replayed itself in my head. She was sitting in a recliner near me, clipping recipes from a gourmet cooking magazine. The monkey had come into the den and was now at her feet, playing with colored scraps of paper that fell to the floor from her work. I could hear Buck bouncing around upstairs somewhere.

Grace looked up. She seemed uncomfortable at the unusual intensity of my gaze. "Are you sure nothing's wrong?"

I said no and looked back down at the pages of my book. The feeling I remembered having had for her moments earlier, a vital—and even passionate—love was tantalizing in its absence, like when a hungry person imagines a steak dinner. I wanted it. I wanted to feel that love for Grace, not just the rote expressions of affection that we settled for.

I also had some vague and confusing recollections of Porky having died. When I tried to focus on those memories, they began to slip away. Still, I had multiple images of him in my mind in which he was lying in his bed, stiff and dead. But I didn't care as much about that, not at the moment. He was alive, and any seeming memories to the contrary were irrelevant, something I could discuss with my psychiatrist another day…if I felt like it.

But the sensation of vibrant love with Grace that I'd experienced was something renewing, something I longed to experience again.

I made a mental note that a romantic weekend away was long overdue—maybe even just an overnight trip to a secluded bed and breakfast in Galveston.

Chapter 7

Circa 76 C.E.

In my earlier writings, Theophilus, I've described many of the things that I have observed or that I have learned in my investigations. Here is another. Take heed, so that you may better understand the mysteries that you have been taught.

Mary and Martha, who were friends of the Master, sent a messenger to bring him word of a grave illness that threatened the life of the women's brother Lazarus in a small village not far away. The Master loved Lazarus, and yet the Master seemed to be in no great hurry to depart from the peaceful stretch of land along the Jordan River where he and the Twelve were then staying. The messenger had been carefully instructed by the sisters to show deference to the Master, and so the messenger waited patiently. But on the fifth day after having delivered his urgent message, the messenger had become distressed about the Master's delay. He pushed his way through the small crowd that surrounded the Master that morning, interrupting their conversation, saying, "Didn't you understand what I told you when I first arrived? Lazarus, your friend, is dying."

The Master smiled and said quietly to the young messenger, "His sickness will not end in death," and then in a voice loud enough so that all of those who were gathered around him under the trees along the river bank could hear, "No, my friend Lazarus has only fallen asleep. I will wake him up when I arrive."

And the Master and the Twelve gathered their meager belongings and set out on the road for the village where his friends Mary, Martha and Lazarus lived.

When they arrived at the outskirts of the village, Martha came out to meet them. She was accompanied by her cousins and elders from the village. She said, "Master, my brother is dead. He died four days ago and is now laid in his tomb. If you had been here, my brother would not have died."

The Master was moved by the anguish in his friend's words. He said, "But he'll rise again."

Martha turned and saw her sister Mary running down the road toward them. Martha said bitterly, "Yes, on the resurrection day."

Mary slowed her pace as she came near to the Master. She began to wail as she drew closer and said, "Master, if you had only been here, if you had come immediately when we sent for you, our brother Lazarus would not have died."

The Master looked past them down the road and saw the tomb of his friend in the side of a hill. A stone had been laid across the opening to the tomb. The hillside and ground outside the tomb was dry and desolate. As Mary stared at the Master, waiting for him to explain, to say something in defense of his delay, many of the onlookers turned away, muttering contemptuous words. A hot, stiff breeze lifted fine dust into the air. It coated his cracked lips.

The Master wept.

Chapter 8

We're cleaning up the dinner dishes, and I'm listening to Grace talk-ing about the worship service that morning at Spring Road Baptist Church, talking about the preaching and the people who responded. I rearrange some of the dishes she's already loaded in the dishwasher and I ask her, "But what does it all mean?" And she tells me what she thinks: that they have found salvation. I say, "What does that *really* mean?" And she says, "That they've become children of God. They're saved now."

I say, "Hmm."

She says, "Hmm? What do you mean, 'Hmm'?"

I shut the door of the dishwasher and push the start button. "Sometimes I don't think we understand what we're doing. Do you? I mean…what was going on inside your head when *you* were saved? Can you still remember?"

She stares at me. The sound of rushing water comes from the dishwasher.

I say, "I just want to know. Can you remember?"

She looks away and says, "No, not really."

A half-truth, I think. My guess is that there are things that she still remembers but wants to protect from the diminishing effect that comes from saying them out loud.

Had she asked me the question, I would have said, "Yes, I remember." But like Grace, I would not have been eager to put my recollections into words. Words aren't adequate to explain an encounter with God—whoever or whatever God is—but words are all I have. I have no witnesses, no supporting logic.

Logic would distance itself from the idea that a teenage boy could experience a clumsy moment of transcendence like I did at Falls Creek Baptist Encampment almost thirty years ago.

I don't remember much of being thirteen, but I remember that week at Falls Creek. We arrive on the bus on Monday, forty or fifty of us, and by Thursday night we're all sunburned, tired and feeling good about the week so far, the hiking, swimming and volleyball—and about the coming evening's tame, but romantic possibilities. We've spent recent evenings paired up with someone we like, sitting shoulder to shoulder on one of the many hard, wooden pews in the huge tabernacle. There is a religious service every evening at seven o'clock, as the sun is setting. A few of my friends have been *born again*—as the Baptists say—at one of these services, called to action by the charismatic preaching, but not me. Others have walked down the aisle, alone or with groups of friends or strangers, to publicly declare their hunger to be better Christians, but not me. As the Thursday night worship service begins, it seems to me that almost every teenager at Falls Creek has already responded in some way to the presence of God that we feel in the tabernacle where we gather every night—but not me. Not me.

I'm too controlled, too careful. I'm an unlikely candidate for any impetuous religious experience.

My friends and I are all showered and splashed with cologne—an overpowering amalgam of sweet and pungent scents under normal circumstances, but Carla nuzzles my neck and says that *my* cologne drives her crazy. It is a time of awakening for me, my first experience being touched that way by a girl. Carla and I never kiss, but we hold hands every night, and let our bare legs and feet touch.

The outdoor tabernacle at Falls Creek is rustic and huge. It has a flat roof, but no walls. I think it holds a thousand people. The preaching each night is loud and emotional, filled with urgent warnings against wasting time. It calls each of us to make a decision now to follow Christ.

All of us have a sense that some of the mysteries of life are being revealed to us and that our decisions matter greatly.

A light breeze blows through the sanctuary. The sun sets outside and the amber lights overhead cast soft shadows on our faces. This evening's sermon outlines the steps to salvation in a methodical way, with each step backed up by one or two verses from the Bible. Like this: "For all have sinned and fallen short of the glory of God." And this one: "But whoever believes in me will not perish, but will have everlasting life." The sermon is simple and moves through the evangelical message of salvation point by point, with the last and most important point being that salvation depends upon each of us believing and asking Jesus to be saved. The preacher tells us how to ask. To receive salvation you pray words like these: "Jesus, I want you to come into my life."

I like the preacher. He'd been a street preacher for a few years in Hollywood and has exciting stories about Jesus saving gang members and their sexy girlfriends. He is in his thirties and has longer hair than anyone his age that I know. Each night his sermon has been more urgent than the night before, with an invitation that is longer and more forceful. Tonight, the invitation—the part of the service where we are asked to walk down to the front of the tabernacle and profess our faith in Jesus—lasts for half an hour, maybe longer. A few more of my friends walk down the aisle tonight, some of them in small groups. Carla whispers that she is going down to the front and asks me if I want to come too. She is crying. I say no. I don't want to.

The preacher paces across the platform at the front of the tabernacle, praying to God and pleading with us to open our hearts, to be receptive to the entreaties of the Holy Spirit. The choir sings verse after verse of hymns that speak of allowing the Holy Spirit to have its way with us. My friends are caught up in the emotion of the moment, but I feel nothing.

Sitting there on that hard pew, I know that we are God's children, brothers and sisters, each of us. But I don't feel the connection that others are feeling. I am shoulder to shoulder with my best friends, part of a mass of teenagers who are crying and hugging each other, and I am absolutely alone. They are drunk with something exhilarating and mystical, and I feel nothing.

When the service is finally over, my friends—those who are still in the pews around me—leave to walk back to our church's cabin. I stay behind and wait a little while for Carla to come back, but, as the tabernacle begins to empty, I can't see her anywhere. I watch the last of the kids who have gone down to the front during the invitation being herded off to talk to ministers about what they'd done. I realize that Carla is going to be tied up for a while talking with grownups.

So I decide to get a lime snow cone. There is a wooden shack near the swimming pool that sells snow cones and candy bars. It is a five-minute walk from the tabernacle. All the cabins are in the opposite direction, and so I don't see many people as I walk. It is after nine o'clock and dark, except for a few yellow lights on wooden poles. Falls Creek is in rural Oklahoma, so it has that empty sound that you hear when you're away from the big city—no freeway noise, no airplanes, no background hum of any kind.

When I get there, the snow cone shack is dark and no one else is around. There is a patch of grass nearby and I sit down to wait. I let my mind wander. I think about Carla and I think about the softball game scheduled for the next day and I think about the trip back home on Saturday morning, but my mind keeps coming back to the preacher's words about asking Jesus and the Holy Spirit to come inside me. I'd never done anything like that before. I'd been going to church all my life, but I'd never had salvation explained to me in exactly that way before—or if I had, I hadn't been paying attention.

A part of me wants to do it. The idea of it crowds out other thoughts in my head. I can picture God's Holy Spirit living inside me—like the preacher had described—and being with God that way forever.

And so I close my eyes, and in my head, I voice these incredibly naive, innocent words: "I want to be saved, Jesus. I want you to come live inside me."

And the memory of what comes next is as vivid to me now—almost thirty years later—as if it happened moments ago.

The first sensation I have is euphoria. It rushes over me and catches me unaware. I open my eyes and for an instant the world has lost its physicality. For a fraction of a second, there is no up and no down, no near and no far. And then my physical senses are jolted by intense perceptions of light and dark and of sound and smell. I perceive the stars more clearly than vision alone would allow. The darkness is infinite, but warm and inviting. Each blade of grass is alive and quivering, aware of my presence, full of light, but not light that can be seen. As I breathe in, I feel beauty, understand it through its smell and taste, but more than that, through a sense that the air that I am breathing is inside of me and mingling with the other elements of my being.

No one had prepared me for this. I feel like crying, but I fight back the urge and run as hard as I can back to our cabin.

Chapter 9

I want to tell you about the monkey's growing fixation with images of water—before I talk about some unfortunate things that happened. Some people might do this in reverse order, but it seems to me that context is important and often neglected. Grace says that people sometimes give me funny looks when I'm telling a story, because my digressions don't always seem to have a noticeable connection to the main thread of my story. Grace has better people skills than I do.

And she notices things that I don't. For example, she noticed soon after Eve came to live with us that Eve showed many of the same signs of depression that you see in people—Eve was listless and didn't seem interested in much. She slept a lot. We both agreed that it might have something to do with her Parkinson's disease, but probably had as much or more to do with her environment. She was bored. What is there for a monkey to do for fun inside the four walls of a house? We tried several things. We left the television on in the den and experimented with cartoons and nature shows, but she generally ignored it. I bought her a harmonica—that didn't prove to be one of my best ideas. We bought a Barbie dollhouse that we found in a garage sale and some furniture that went with it, but Eve didn't comprehend the idea of make-believe. She enjoyed sitting on top of it, until it broke.

It was Grace's idea to begin reading children's books to Eve. That turned out to be something that Eve loved. Grace usually invited Buck to participate if he was around, and sometimes he did and sometimes he didn't. Grace thought Eve would enjoy <u>Curious George</u>, which, as you may know, is a series of gentle stories about a mischievous monkey and a nice man who wears a yellow hat. But it bored her. Eve's initial favorite was <u>Goodnight Moon</u>. If I were a child psychologist or a monkey psychologist, I'd do a study on why that book is so appealing, why kids—and genetically modified monkeys—want to have it read to them over and over again. Part of it is the repetition of words and part of it is the warm colors in the simple illustrations. "Goodnight room, goodnight moon, good night light and the red balloon...."

We bought her a copy of her own of <u>Goodnight Moon</u>, one with thick cardboard pages. I don't know if a healthy monkey has the fine motor skills to turn pages in an ordinary book with paper pages without tearing them, but Eve didn't. Her Parkinson's disease made it too hard. She soon had her own small collection of books. Her favorites had simple pictures. I thought she'd like Dr. Seuss, but the complicated illustrations overwhelmed her.

She liked pictures of water—any book that had images of pools of water became favorites. One was an old book about bath time. Another one had pictures she liked in which silly looking animals were diving into a swimming pool—two of the animals were wearing swimsuits and the third one was wearing a hat. Another favorite was about Jesus being baptized in the River Jordan.

Grace pointed to images in the books and she read the words on the page or just said the word for what she was pointing to. We could tell that Eve was learning to understand a few words of spoken language, but not many. She developed a sign language for a few basic wants, such as snack time, diaper problem, come here, and "Where's Barbie?" But she didn't try very hard to learn to communicate with us. She always seemed to think that I, in particular, knew what she wanted, without any effort on her part to communicate—and many times that was true.

The book about Jesus' baptism was one out of a series of books that Grace's brother gave to Buck. That was the book which Grace was reading to Evie the afternoon when I arrived home after my last day of work at the university.

It was the middle of the afternoon. Unlike my normal practice, I hadn't called out, "I'm home," as I came through the back door. I was in no hurry to begin any discussion of why I was home so early or how my day had gone. Buck was still at school. I walked quietly through the back of the house and stood at the doorway into the den, watching Grace and Eve sitting together—Grace didn't know I was watching. Her brown hair was pulled back in a ponytail. When her hair was pulled back, she had the face of a model—the high forehead and prominent cheekbones. I always told her that, but she didn't believe it and preferred to wear her hair loose in a way that covered up more of her thin face.

Eve was in her lap, like a small child. When you read to a child— or in this case a monkey—you read the words on the page, but you also talk about the pictures. You point and you explain in simple words what's happening. Parents do that instinctively. If we don't, most books are far too dry for little kids to understand and enjoy.

Grace said, "And here's John the Baptist, and he's frowning, isn't he? He says, 'Repent.' And here he says, 'You brood of vipers!' Because he's mad at the people. He baptizes people, see? He says, "I baptize you with water but someone is coming after me who will baptize you with the Holy Spirit *and with fire.*" And look. Here comes Jesus. And Jesus walks into the river. And then what happens? John tells *everybody* about who Jesus is. See? So John takes Jesus and lowers him into the water. See? And then John lifts Jesus out of the water. And look…the sun comes out and a dove flies down from the sky. And God says, 'This is my son in whom I am well pleased.'"

When she was finished, Grace noticed me standing in the doorway. I smiled at Grace—not a particularly contagious smile, apparently—and said hi.

She shut the book which they'd been reading and said, "Are you laughing at me?"

"No." On a better day I might have been laughing—at the absurdity of reading New Testament stories to a monkey—but not that day.

"You're home early."

I began stumbling over words, not knowing what to say first, what to leave out until later. I'd been fired—well, technically, forced to resign. I'd been escorted out of the building by the security guard as if I were some kind of criminal. I had taken the fall for an ugly public scandal, because at a university like ours, somebody always has to—but I'd received an unnecessarily generous severance package—because at a university like ours that's what they do…to make people like me shut up and go away.

Grace looked at me with growing concern. "What's wrong, Jim?"

"They fired me."

"No!" She stood up and Eve slid off of her lap onto the floor. "Those bastards." It was a word her father used from time to time. I'd never heard her use it before. "They found out…?"

"That I took Eve? No. Nothing to do with that."

"Then why? Why would they do that? You're the only one there who does anything."

"Politics…it was just politics."

I'd known when I went into work that morning that it would be a day filled with questions, finger pointing and butt-covering. A front page article had been published in the Houston Chronicle the day before, claiming that the lab monkeys—or some of them—had far more human DNA than was needed to create lab animals with Parkinson's disease. [2] The university had been asked to comment, but had responded by

---

2 HOUSTON, TEXAS – An unnamed source has made allegations that unauthorized gene-splicing experiments are being conducted at the University of Texas at Houston. Researchers there have been producing genetically altered primates by inserting human genes into the embryos of monkeys. New reports indicate that in at least one of the tests, strands of so-called "junk DNA" from human chromosomes had been injected into the monkeys' embryos.

Dr. John Luther, a cell biologist from UCLA, in a telephone interview, said that he is generally familiar with the experiments being conducted in Houston. "Experimenting with human genes that are clearly linked to disease will accelerate the availability of a new generation of treatments. That is medical science at its best," said Luther. "Playing God with gene experimentation is another thing entirely. Junk DNA? There is no such thing as junk DNA. Simply because we don't understand the function of certain segments of our DNA doesn't mean that no purpose exists. Every single strand of our DNA makes us, as humans, what we are."

The phrase "junk DNA" was coined by researchers to describe repetitious sequences of DNA that don't appear to have any function.

The university did not respond to requests for an interview.

saying only that it was conducting its own investigation and was confident that the accusations were false. Reporters from major newspapers around the country had been calling, asking if, indeed, godless scientists at the university were creating a new subhuman species—serious accusations for any university, particularly one that depends on the generosity of religious foundations and conservative alumni to fund its medical research. After an emergency meeting with the president of the university, my boss had called me in and said, "I thought you were on top of this. Why am I hearing about this for the first time from goddamn reporters? Why didn't I know this shit-storm was going to be coming before now?" He'd often told me that in the general counsel's office we were political handlers first and lawyers second.

I assumed that Bonnie Norton, the disgruntled, former grad student, was the unnamed source for the newspaper—that she'd gotten tired of waiting for me to do something. But the claim that one or more of the monkeys had extra human DNA was news to me. Bonnie hadn't told me that—or if she did, I didn't catch it. And if Eve's chromosomes included extra human DNA—even a substantial amount of junk human DNA, as the article said—what would it mean? Obviously, that she could cry, but what else? Was that the sole consequence? I tried to get in touch with Bonnie to ask her these questions, but couldn't find a working telephone number for her.

Right after chewing me out, my boss—his name is Bob Townsend—took me into a meeting with Dr. Hermann, who was accompanied by the dean of his department. Bob said that he wanted me to come, but he didn't want me to talk. He said that Dr. Hermann would lie less if I was there.

But Dr. Hermann denied everything. He said, "What proof do they have? They have no proof...of anything." He showed us a tall stack of files in which the sequences of human DNA that had been injected in the monkey embryos were listed with code numbers that meant nothing to me. He explained, as if talking to children, that the DNA specified on each chart was empirically connected to Parkinson's disease and was not found in the so-called strands of junk DNA. Each file was the same—the same scientific procedures that had been used to alter the monkey embryos were described succinctly—but a few of the files reflected that the monkeys had been stillborn.

Bob said, "So how many of *them* are there now...five?"

Dr. Hermann spoke without emotion. "Four. One died...later."

Even though Bob had told me not to ask any questions, I couldn't stop myself from asking, "Which one?"

Dr. Hermann looked at me as if my question was irrelevant. He flipped open a couple of files and then slid one across the table to me. "This one."

"The file just assigns the monkey a number. What was her name?"

He turned and whispered something to the dean, who nodded. Then Dr. Hermann turned to face us again and said, "I think the students called her Eve. Are we done?"

Obviously, I didn't stand up and shout, "Eve is not dead! She's... living with me!"

I wasn't sure what to think. It was possible that the grad students had hidden the truth about the monkey's sudden disappearance from him, afraid that it would jeopardize their roles in the experiments somehow—and their futures. But that didn't seem likely. I suspected that he knew about it—and had decided to cover it up. Dr. Hermann would have nothing to gain and potentially much to lose by acknowledging an unexplained disappearance of one of his lab monkeys—if nothing else, there might be questions about whether it was arranged to eliminate a monkey that wasn't showing benefits from the drug being tested. My guess was that he believed that Bonnie had taken Eve, since Bonnie had walked out on the same day. The bigger question was whether he knew that Eve's embryo had been injected with extra human DNA—if that was, indeed, true, as the newspaper claimed. Why would Dr. Hermann do that or let somebody else do that? Unbridled scientific curiosity? Or just because he wanted to and could? My guess was the latter. Nothing more compelling—or more sinister—than that. He wanted to and he could.

Regardless of his motives for whatever he had done, he appeared to be confident that his future was in no jeopardy. He believed that Eve was gone forever, probably in the care of Bonnie—who was also gone forever. He had felt entitled to do the things that he had done. He perceived no problem whatsoever going forward. That's how men like Dr. Hermann think.

I made notes of the DNA code numbers listed in Dr. Hermann's file, intending to go home and compare them with those that were in the files that Bonnie had given to me—to see if official university files had been altered. But shortly after the meeting with Dr. Hermann, I was told that it *would be better for everyone* if I resigned immediately.

Bob said, "Jim, I like you and I respect your work ethic, but you're just not cut out for this type of work. I mean, look at what happened with that new faculty tenure policy you sent to everyone in the whole goddamn world to read. I mean, Jesus, it couldn't have gone worse if you'd…well, we don't need to rehash that miserable debacle, do we? Trust me, a year from now you'll thank me for doing this. Trust me on this."

On my way into work that morning I had called Barry and told him that I was nervous about what lay ahead. I was afraid that somehow it would be discovered that I knew of problems with Dr. Hermann's experiment months earlier and had dealt with it by, in essence, hiding one of the monkeys—that's how it would look. Barry knows how to say things that are comforting. He said that my intentions had been good from the start, and he expressed confidence that I'd have the wisdom to know how to deal with whatever happened.

He asked me if I'd like for him to pray with me. His voice was a little stiff when he asked, as though it was a phrase he said a lot that had lost some of its emotional punch. I said yes, and while I drove and held the cell phone to my ear, Barry said a short prayer. I thanked him, and we were done. I ended the call and put the phone down. Then I prayed, asking God to help me keep my job, or at least to cause everything to work for the best, or at the very least, to give me strength to face getting fired with dignity.

When I finished, I felt nothing. It was as if my words and thoughts ended inches above my head, completely within the confines of my car. I sensed no presence other than my own. I was alone and felt nothing.

If religious experience were commonplace there would be no unbeliev-ers. We like to touch things. We want to inspect the evidence for our-selves. What if miracles abounded? What if swirling winds and tongues of fire were a routine part of every Sunday morning church service? Or even, as the hymn says, the joy, joy, joy, joy down in our hearts? Good preachers don't lie to us. They warn us that tangible personal experi-ence of God's existence is fleeting and rare. But we want it anyway.

I still remember the experience I had at Falls Creek Baptist Encampment—vividly. The details of certain moments are etched into your brain forever. I assume you've experienced that. People often say that about their first sexual experience, that they can remember every scent and sound. That's true for me. I can also remember, as if it happened moments ago, when my first son, Thomas, first kissed me. It was a long time ago, when he was a little older than one, and of course, he'd been kissed a lot, but this was the first time that my own son, of his own free will leaned over to kiss me on the lips, and I remember where I was, the color of light coming through the window.

And I remember in complete detail that short walk out of the build-ing the afternoon the university fired me, escorted by a security guard, the expressions on the faces of each of the people who watched me leave, the parting words they said. I would rather erase that moment from my memory, and maybe I will over time.

My Southern Baptist friends assure me that what happened to me at Falls Creek was my *personal* experience with Jesus Christ, me becom-ing born again. I believed that once, but I'm not so sure now. I'm not a Southern Baptist anymore, but I haven't strayed too far. I'm more of a Presbyterian now than anything else, which is really just an agnostic Southern Baptist.

But whatever it was that happened to me as a teenager at Falls Creek hasn't happened again. The overwhelming, spiritual connec-tion I felt to something outside of me was brief and has never been reestablished. So what was it? The hell if I know. But I know this: it wasn't just my imagination.

Something real happened and I can't explain it anymore. I'm flex-ible and would consider almost any explanation, even if it didn't fit neatly into the framework of things I already believe. Was it a Zen-like moment of enlightenment? How could that have happened without years of prior meditation? Was it like the Pentecostal experience that Jesus' disciples had when they were touched by tongues of fire and became filled by the Holy Spirit? Why would that have happened to a teenager who mostly wanted a lime snow cone?

Whatever it was, I desperately want for it to be something real.

All I know to do is to try to shoehorn my experience into the framework of one of the many fine religions that are out there in the world, unless I decide to create my own myth to explain it, one that feels right in my own gut.

I may have to do that.

Chapter 10

When I found small pieces of broken pretzels and an empty Dr. Pepper can in the downstairs hall closet, I immediately blamed Buck. We have a rule that he can't eat junk food without our permission. My suspicion had been that Buck sat in the dark closet, defiantly eating pretzels and sipping on his favorite soft drink on an occasion when he'd asked and we'd said no. He sheepishly admitted tossing the empty Dr. Pepper can into the closet, saying, "There's nothing but junk in there anyway, Dad." But he earnestly and convincingly denied having anything to do with the pretzel crumbs that were in the closet, and so my next theory was that we had rats—which wouldn't be startling in Houston. So on Saturday morning I got my flashlight and began the process of pulling clutter out of the closet, to check for other evidence of rodent activity and to see if there were any gaps along the baseboard or other holes big enough for rats to get through—things that I would need to fix.

Every homeowner in Houston has a problem with rats sooner or later. Before we had kids, we let our cat Porky sleep wherever he wanted at night, until one day when we found evidence that a rat had been eating from his bag of dry cat food which we kept in the laundry room. So we started making Porky sleep in the laundry room at night, and that eliminated the problem.

When the hall closet door is opened, an overhead light automatically comes on. The switch is in the doorframe. I probably didn't need the flashlight, but Buck had used his own money to buy it for me for Father's Day and I wanted him to see me using it for something important.

The closet used to be a useful walk-in closet that held coats, umbrellas and our hardwood floor polisher—and had a few shallow shelves, on which we kept jigsaw puzzles and baby toys, all arranged neatly enough for visitors to see. It's under the stairs, so the ceiling slopes off to the left behind the hanging coats. Now the closet was filled with stacked boxes of various sizes, along with clutter crammed in there over recent years on occasions when we were making the house presentable for unexpected company. This past year, it was also where I put the Christmas decorations, rather than taking them all the way to the attic.

I'd pulled half of the Christmas boxes out of the closet, when Grace came by to check on things and to caution me not to move anything that belonged to her. She sipped on her cup of coffee in between sentences. She said, "Every time you organize *my* things, I can't find them later when I need them."

I said okay.

She pointed at the boxes of Christmas ornaments that I had stacked outside the closet. "But you can move *those* somewhere else. How'd they wind up in there anyway?" She smiled and poked me with her elbow. "Hey. Maybe you can make enough room in there for that great big wine storage vault of yours."

I had to study her face for a minute to decide whether it was a good natured joke or a taunt. I'd bought a big, brushed stainless steel wine refrigerator almost a year earlier because it was on sale for a really good price—and I really wanted it. It was the kind of appliance that wine lovers buy to store a hundred bottles or so at just the right temperature. When I bought it, I had imagined myself buying wines I like by the case, but I hadn't given much advance thought to where I'd put the refrigerator once I got it home. As it turned out, there wasn't any room for it in the kitchen or the laundry room, and so it was still sitting in the garage unused, still in the original unopened box that it came in.

I thought about it for a minute. She hadn't been serious, but she was right. It would fit perfectly.

She knew me well enough to know what I was thinking, without me saying a word. She shook her head from side to side. "Oh no. You're not putting that thing in there."

"It was your idea."

"I was kidding."

I glanced inside the closet again. There was even a plug in exactly the right spot. It would be perfect. I said, "We could keep all your coats upstairs somewhere."

She gave me a stern look and said, "I'll divorce you, mister. And I meant what I said. Don't touch my stuff. I'll do it myself. Later." She smiled, but it was a weak smile. "Someday."

She stood there for a moment, looking at me, as if she wanted something—or wanted me to say something.

I knew that she was upset and worried about my jobless situation. We both were. Periodically, she'd hug me and tell me that things were going to be okay. This morning, it was my turn. I said, "Things are going to be okay, sweetie."

She said, "I know, but it's just... I can't sleep. And last night that neurotic dog of ours started barking."

I'd forgotten—because I'd gone back to sleep without any trouble—but I'd woken up too and looked out the back window to see what Daisy was barking at. It was probably a snake. She was keeping her distance, but was barking ferociously at something under an azalea bush. And then she just stopped and turned and walked calmly back to her dog house—mission accomplished. When it rains a lot, we get snakes in our backyard under the bushes or the gazebo. They don't stay around very long.

I blurted out something I had been thinking about all morning. "Some weekend soon we ought to go somewhere fun—just the two of us."

She looked away. "Yeah. We should.'

"Soon. We wouldn't have to spend a lot of money."

"Well...let's see how things go." She turned toward the stairs and yelled, "Buck, come help your dad." Then she walked away, toward the kitchen.

I wanted for us to try to find some good things in our relationship that we seemed to have lost, but I couldn't do it alone. I couldn't do it alone.

Buck came bounding down the stairs, skipping stairs at random. The monkey was riding on his back. Buck was still in his pajamas, and his blond hair was sticking straight out on one side. He obviously hadn't combed his hair since getting out of bed.

I said, "How did you teach her to ride on your back?"

"One day she was messing with my hair, and I just took off running. It was so funny."

That was his explanation. It obviously left a lot out, probably details that were better for me not to know. "Well, don't do anything that hurts her."

"Yeah, right."

"I'm serious."

"Dad, she's stronger than I am. Sometime you need to tell *her* not to hurt *me*."

Sometimes Buck was too rough with Eve, but she never seemed to hold it against him or to retaliate. She hadn't shown any aggression as long as we'd had her, none at all. She didn't have many bad habits. For the most part, she was a calm, quiet guest in our house, better mannered than some of Buck's friends. But it wasn't an arrangement that could go on indefinitely. Grace kept mentioning how much the house had begun to smell—in her words—like a zoo. It was true. She asked me almost every day now what I was doing to find a new home for Eve. It wasn't particularly logical, but Grace had begun to show occasional animosity toward Eve after I got fired, as if, somehow, it was Eve's fault. I think Grace just wanted this episode in our life to be over. I did too.

So I began corresponding with zoos in other states. There was a zoo in Mississippi that had a large, shaded outdoor space in which rhesus monkeys and other compatible primates lived. Driving Eve to Mississippi would have made a lot of sense for her and for us, but in a lot of ways, I'd become dependent on her—on the novelty of having her around. She distracted me from my worries. I hadn't made much progress in my search for a new job, and having her around gave me something else to think about.

I had a lot of time on my hands. More than once I'd gotten out the research files that Bonnie had left with me and flipped through them. The lab notes were barely legible and didn't mean a hell of a lot to me. Eve's file and the files of two dead monkeys listed DNA code numbers that didn't appear in other files—at least that's how it appeared to me. I got access to several on-line university databases and tried to do some research to figure out what the code numbers meant, but it was all pretty foreign to me and I found it difficult to stay on task—other random thoughts and ideas cavorted in my head like unruly children, chanting, "Can't catch me...can't catch *me*."

While Buck and I were talking, Eve slid down Buck's back and scampered over to the hall closet. She shut the door and stood with her back against it, staring at us. Her brow was furrowed and her bottom lip protruded as though she was frowning.

Buck turned to me and said, "So what are we doing? I mean, how long's this going to take?" He smiled mischievously at Eve as he yanked the closet door back open, giggling as the door pushed her across the terrazzo tile floor, with her feet scrambling helplessly on its slick surface, unable to get traction.

"Hey, come on. Be nice to her," I said.

His eyes sparkled. "It's okay. She thinks it's fun."

Then Eve darted between Buck's legs, around the open door and into the closet. I hadn't ever seen her move before with that kind of urgency.

Buck followed her in, squeezing between the remaining stacks of boxes and pushing aside coats that were hanging from the coat rods. I stood just inside the closet door, waiting. Seconds later, I heard a low-pitched, growling sound coming from behind the coats—and Buck yelled, "Dad," and started backing up on all fours, knocking over the hardwood floor polisher with his feet in his effort to get back out quickly.

"What's wrong?" I grabbed his ankles and pulled him the rest of the way out.

His eyes were wide. "She acted like she was going to bite me or something. And she's got a couple of my guys back there."

Buck has a big collection of three inch tall action figures, everything from super heroes to military men to grotesque monsters. Buck always seems to have a few in his hands or pockets. His "guys" have melodramatic conversations and arguments with each other and they fight—mostly with each other, frequently bashing chests and flying into the air. We find them—and broken pieces of them—scattered all over the house and in the car. I wasn't surprised if Eve had taken a few of his unused action figures to start her own collection.

"Did you do something to…mess with her…you know." I stopped myself from explicitly accusing him of doing something that hurt her, but that was my suspicion.

"No. I was just trying to—I was going to get my guys back, and I was checking out the—all the weird stuff she has piled up back there." Buck's words came in spurts. "Mom's little gold mirror is in there, and other stuff, and an apple—I think. It's really wrinkled and gross."

That probably explained the pretzel crumbs that I'd found. It hadn't been rats snacking in the closet—it had been Evie.

"Let me see." I leaned in, to smell the air in the closet. There was the smell of moth balls, but also the cloying, sweet odor of over-ripe fruit.

Buck tugged on the back of my shirt. "Maybe we should just leave her alone. What do you think?"

"We can't have food rotting in the closet."

"You know, Dad, you and I saw something like this on television. What's it called?"

I was thinking that we might need Grace to distract Eve while I went into the back of the closet to clean everything out. Grace was in the kitchen now, maybe puttering around with some new recipe, or maybe just morosely staring into space. I turned and yelled, "Grace, can you come in here?"

She didn't answer.

Buck continued talking to me. "Remember that TV show we watched about Day of the Dead, where people put those cool skeletons and candles and food and stuff like that on little tables. What's that called when they do that?"

"I don't know." I wasn't paying complete attention to Buck. I took coats off the metal rod with both hands, leaving them on their coat hangers, and stacked them on the floor. There were jean jackets, overcoats, rain coats, ski jackets, and some coats I didn't recognize as even belonging to us. Some were in bags from the dry cleaners and slid sideways as I stacked them. To maximize the storage possibilities, we had put in two closet rods, so the coats were two layers deep.

He tugged on my shirt again, with greater force. "Yeah, you do. What's it called?"

I stopped to think about his question. "A shrine?"

He nodded enthusiastically. "That's it. She's made a shrine back there."

"Maybe." I wasn't convinced, but I hadn't seen it yet.

"That's what I think." He lowered his voice, as if what he was saying next was private, just between the two of us. "Didn't you and Mom take Thomas once to some kind of shrine where they had holy dirt?"

"Who told you that?"

He looked away. "I don't know. Never mind."

There's an adobe church in Chimayo, New Mexico. It's famous. Thousands of people come every year longing to be healed—or out of curiosity. There's a shrine there where people leave photographs of their loved ones and hand written prayers thanking God and the saints, and they leave behind crutches and objects that are precious to them. And from a hole in the floor people take a pinch or a small handful of dust and sprinkle it on someone who is ill. Miraculous stories of healings have long been connected with the place.

And so Grace and I take Thomas there, maybe a year before he dies. We don't tell anyone that we are going—it seems too irrational. We go there at the point in his treatment where he is going through his weekly regimen of chemotherapy. He looks terrible, pale, gaunt. When he's asleep he looks like a corpse. I am terrified that the chemotherapy will kill him before the leukemia does. I really am. Grace and I are both afraid—actually, all of us are, Thomas included. But for him, it is the only life he knows.

I remember what it was like. We pull into a parking place outside the church. That part of New Mexico has its own kind of beauty, desolate and lonely. The wind blows dust across the churchyard. There is a priest nearby as we walk in with Thomas. He looks me in the eye and nods, but doesn't say anything. In that context, sometimes the greatest act of kindness strangers can take is to remain distant, not to ask questions or offer false platitudes of hope.

Grace and I both pray before scooping up the dry dust and sprinkling it on Thomas. I remember her kneeling as she prays, but my recollection may be wrong. Maybe she kneels down so that she can reach through the old wooden floorboards. I honestly can't remember now. The room is small and there is a steady stream of polite, somber visitors who avert their eyes from us and whisper. All around us, there are painted carvings and photographs and plastic flowers and things I don't understand. What exactly do they mean to God?

I have this memory of the church at Chimayo being a place of distracting mystery. It feels to me as if God had been there, but had left a long time ago—a hundred years before we could get there with our precious, dying son.

What the hell is a shrine, precisely speaking? Is it just a historical marker, to inform all who come after that they just missed a genuine experience of God's presence? Or maybe it's like a searchlight directed at the heavens, surrounded by people crying out, "Here we are. Here we are."

As I pulled clothes from the second rod the view was completely unobstructed for the first time. Buck said, "See? See?"

In one corner, against the back wall of the closet, where the ceiling sloped down almost to the floor, everything was in the shadows, but I could see that Eve had piled up a variety of things. It had to have been Eve—a rat couldn't have done it. There were dead leaves pulled from one of our indoor ferns and scraps of colored paper and a random assortment of little things—a brightly colored dishtowel, a key chain, and two of Buck's action figures. I could see an apple and some popcorn—and pretzels—and what looked like shriveled-up grapes on the floor at the foot of the pile. There was also a small plastic bowl that appeared to have liquid standing in it.

Eve crouched between us and the clutter. She glanced at me a couple of times, but her attention kept returning to the mirror. I ducked down so that I could get under the closet rods and move closer. She twirled around and began to chatter and run at me, before backing up and charging at me again.

She had my attention. I'd heard stories about monkeys getting wild and biting off fingers, but we'd never seen any indication of aggressiveness from her before. Obviously, she was determined to protect her stash of things.

Buck said, from behind me, "Can you grab my guys? That's all I need."

I moved back a little bit and shone the flashlight on the things Eve had stacked in the corner, so that I could see exactly what it was that she had. There was order to what she had done—and purpose. It wasn't just a pile of things she was hoarding.

Buck had squeezed in beside me. "Hey. Do you think this is like a little monkey church?"

I didn't think so, but I didn't know. I shrugged. My guess was that Buck had gotten it right the first time. It was a shrine of sorts. But why would a monkey make a shrine? I didn't know.

He said, "That's what I think. It's a monkey church."

"How could she even know about something like that?"

Buck said, "Maybe she saw something like that on TV or maybe in one of the books Mom reads to her. Or maybe she had a dream about it. I heard Mom and her friend talking about that a couple of days ago."

"Elaine?"

"Yeah. Mom had a dream about Jesus, but in the dream Jesus was a woman."

"Really?" I was curious what happened in the dream, but decided to offer parental guidance instead. "You know that you shouldn't be eavesdropping."

"I wasn't. I was in the back seat of the car. What was I supposed to do? Cover my ears?"

"I guess not."

"Elaine said that everybody *everywhere* has dreams about the same religious stuff, even though the dreams aren't exactly the same—and are sometimes really weird."

I'd heard Elaine talking about that kind of thing too, especially right after she got back from a month at the Jungian Institute in Switzerland. Some of it makes sense.

Eve dipped her fingers into the bowl and then lifted her hand in the air. Drops of water fell from her fingers onto the floor of the closet. We looked at each other. There seemed to be something she wanted me to understand about what she had done.

I decided not to try to clean up her accumulation of trash and treasures—at least not right then. I said, "It's okay, Evie," and I went and got some of the coats to hang back up on the closet rods.

Buck said, "Don't forget to get my guys back for me."

"No. We can get them later."

"But they're two of the best: Robo-Cop and Iron Man.

"Later."

70

Buck looked up at me with frustration, but I didn't see any reason to take anything away from the shrine—or whatever it was—unless we were ready to completely clean up the whole thing. Eve wasn't going to make it easy for us. I was thinking that it might be best to wait until we'd found a new home for her, in Mississippi—or wherever.

Buck frowned at me and watched me, with his arms crossed over his chest, as I hung all the coats back up. And when I was bringing in the first load of boxes, he said, "Be right back," and lowered his head and squeezed through the coats.

Within seconds I heard him scream. It was a shrill, warbling scream—the kind that comes out of pain, not fear—and I felt my heart stop. And the monkey was shrieking too. I started ripping handfuls of coats back off the rods, but before I could do anything else, Buck came stumbling out backwards, swinging his small fists at the monkey who was hanging onto his face. And in a high-pitched voice that I'd never heard before, Buck was crying, "Get off me. Get *off* me."

I turned him around by the shoulders. Blood was streaming down his face. I began to yell, calling for Grace. A chunk of his cheek the size of a golf ball was missing—torn away, the wound a sickening pale white that oozed blood. And Eve was tearing at one of his eyes with her hand, scratching and pulling. I pulled her away and dropped her. I yelled again for Grace. One of Buck's eyes was rolling upwards in its socket—he was passing out—or worse. The other eye was hanging—hanging from the thick optic nerve, loose against his cheek. Blood was gushing now, down his face from wounds around his eye socket. Buck bent forward and retched on my legs. Then his knees gave way and he stumbled forward. I grabbed him in my arms and whirled around to carry him away from the closet.

I looked down, and the monkey was there in the doorway of the closet, looking up at me. Her hands and mouth were bloody. She began to shriek at me, hopping around and charging toward us.

I felt dizzy and my vision blurred. My only son—the only thing I had left—was disfigured and bleeding. I pulled back my leg and kicked that goddamn monkey as hard as I could. I felt bones in her body crunching with the blow from my foot. She bounced hard off

71

the toe of my shoe into the closet. I slammed the closet door as hard as I could.

I stood with my back against the door, holding my bleeding, motionless son in my arms and screamed, "Grace, where are you," and I began to cry.

Buck said, "So how long is this going to take? Evie and I have stuff to do." He smiled mischievously at Eve and then lifted her in the air and tossed her, like a basketball player shooting free throws, to the banister at the top of the stairs.

She caught the banister effortlessly with one hand, pulled herself up on top of it, squealed loudly, and then jumped down—eight feet or so—into Buck's arms.

"Hey, come on. Be careful," I said. "Both of you."

Buck said, "So what do I have to do?"

"Whatever belongs to you, grab it and carry it up to your room."

I'd already moved a stack of boxes into the hallway and a red plastic crate that held random sports gear and Nerf guns. His skates and a couple of toy hockey sticks were in a pile of things that either needed to go to his room or to the garage.

As I was talking to Buck, Grace came into the hallway to ask if I knew where our dog was. She hadn't come to the back door for breakfast and Grace didn't see her anywhere. She wondered if I'd let Daisy in the house. I told her no. She said, "She sure was barking last night. What do you think that was about?" Then standing there, Grace began inspecting my work. She said, "I'm glad you've got the energy and focus to do that." She hesitated. "Do you think...it's the medicine?"

I ignored the question about my pills. I wasn't convinced that the benefits were worth the side effects, but I didn't want to talk about it where Buck could hear. I stuck to business. "If we just clean out all the junk that we've accumulated in there, we can start using it again."

While we were talking, Eve slid out of Buck's arms, skirted the piles of boxes, toys and old coats that were on the floor and darted into the closet. I couldn't imagine what would have made her move with that much speed and urgency.

I said, "Buck, would you go get your monkey?"

He looked at me with an exaggerated look of surprise. "My monkey? She's not *my* monkey, she's your monkey." But he went into the closet after her, squeezing between the stacks of boxes that remained in the closet, pushing aside coats that were hanging from the rod.

Grace gave me a playful jab with her elbow and said, "Whose monkey?" She was trying very hard to make things pleasant and normal between us.

I appreciated the effort and tried to respond in kind. "I'm sorry. *Your* monkey."

She shook her head from side to side. "No, no, no."

She put her arm around me. I was thinking about mentioning the idea I'd had of a romantic weekend away—just the two of us—when a sudden loud commotion came from inside the closet. The monkey started chattering and barking, and Buck yelled, "Dad." I stepped into the closet, and could see Buck backing up toward me on all fours. I stepped out of the closet to give him room to maneuver through the clutter.

Grace yelled, "What's going on?"

At the doorway to the closet, Buck lifted up on his knees and screamed, and my heart stopped. His back was still to me, and I couldn't tell what was going on. I grabbed the shoulders of his shirt and yanked him up and out of the closet. He was still screaming, and he was swinging his fists at the monkey who was wrapped around Buck's face, holding on to Buck's hair, ears, nose—I couldn't tell exactly—and clawing at his cheeks and eyes. They were twisting around so fast, their movements were a blur. I saw blood and I saw Eve biting Buck's face, and in a shrill voice that I'd never heard before, Buck was crying at the top of his lungs, "Get off me. Get *off* of me."

Buck said, "So what are we doing? I mean, how long's this going to take?"

I said, "It won't take very long if you and your brother both help. Where is he?"

"He's coming. I think he's still in the bathroom. Watch this." Buck tossed Eve into the air, almost up to the ceiling, flipping her in a backwards summersault. Then he closed his eyes and waited with his arms outstretched.

Eve landed in his arms without a wobble, grabbing his hair with one of her little hands and wrapping the toes of her feet around his arm. Her tail moved gracefully from side to side, like a snake through water.

"Hey, come on. Be careful," I said.

His eyes sparkled. "She thinks it's fun." Buck noticed that my treasured, but never used wine connoisseur storage vault was sitting just inside the front door. I'd already slit the thick corrugated cardboard crate at each corner and pulled away the pieces of Styrofoam that protected its glistening stainless steel surface. It was beautiful. Through the smoky glass door you could see scallop-shaped empty racks that were waiting to be filled with my favorite rare bottles of cabernet and pinot noir. Buck said, "How'd you get it in here by yourself?"

"I got William's dad to help me."

I felt Grace's hand on my back. I hadn't heard her come up. "And me. I helped too," she said.

"Yes, your mom helped too."

Her voice had an upbeat lilt. "I was the one who said, 'Hmm... why don't you put it on a blanket and drag it, rather than ruining your backs by trying to carry it.'"

I turned around to face her. "What a clever woman." I saw that she had one arm behind her back, as though she was hiding something from me. "What have you got there?"

With a dramatic flourish, she presented me with one of the two long, thin sacks that were dangling from her hand. "Enjoy," she said. The sack she gave me was gold, with faint curlicues on it. The other was bright, glistening red.

I looked inside and saw the embossed foil label on the top of a wine bottle. Before I could pull it out of the sack, she said, "It's your favorite, but you can't drink it—at least not...soon. It's for your wine vault—the first bottle for your collection. From me." She was shifting from foot to foot, like an excited little schoolgirl.

I kissed her, aware again of how lucky I am. With her arms around me, I could feel the thump against my back of something hard in the other sack—it was obviously another wine or champagne bottle. I said, "So what's in the other one? Another present for me?"

She whispered, "For us...if we can get the scamps to bed a little early tonight."

Buck elbowed his way between us. Eve was still in his arms. They both peered into the sack that Grace was still holding. I could hear the sound of Eve sniffing, trying to smell what was inside. Buck said, "Anything for me in there?"

I said, "Sorry, big guy."

There was a shuffling noise on the stairs. It was Thomas. I'd woken him up an hour earlier, and he'd said he would get out of bed if I'd just leave him alone for a few minutes. He'd probably gone back to sleep. He stood on the bottom stair and yawned. "So what was it you needed me to do?"

I looked at him and started to laugh, "What do you have on your ears?" There were red and white socks hanging down from each of his ears, the long socks that he used for soccer. He had pulled the tight, stretchy part of each sock over an ear. "You look like dog."

He shrugged and said, "My ears were cold."

Buck dropped the monkey to the floor, hurried to Thomas' side and jumped up and down next to him, trying to pull the socks off his older brother's ears. "Can you do me? Can you make them go on my ears?"

Thomas grimaced. "Leave me alone. I just woke up." He meandered toward the downstairs bathroom and shut the door behind him.

A lock of hair had fallen straight down over Grace's face. She put her red sack on the floor, unfastened the clasp that held her ponytail and held it between her teeth, as she collected all the loose strands of her hair and pulled them together behind her head.

Thomas came out of the bathroom and stood facing us, with a sheepish grin. The socks were still hanging from his ears.

With the clasp still between her teeth, Grace said, "Thomas, are you going to leave them there all day?"

"Maybe."

Buck said, "If I get some socks, can you do me?"

"Nope."

"Please?"

"Nope." Thomas sighed. "It's too early for me to be awake. What is it you want me to do, Dad?"

"I'm going to put my wine refrigerator in here." I set my present on the floor next to the sack that held the bottle that Grace and I would share that evening, and I opened the door to the closet. "If everybody will grab a few loads, we can empty all the junk out of here in no time."

Eve vaulted over the sacks and darted past me, into the closet.

I said, "Just be careful not to step on Eve."

Buck said, "I'll get her." And before I could stop him, he ran into the closet behind Eve, squeezing past stacks of boxes that were inside the closet doorway.

As Buck went into the closet, I felt intense panic, even before anything else happened. I don't know how to explain it, other than that I had an immediate premonition of disaster. It made no sense, and I froze for a few moments. And then it was too late.

I heard Buck say, "Hey, Eve, what're you doing with my guys back in here?" And then seconds later, I heard him scream, "Dad," at the top of his lungs.

I felt my heart stop.

———

Buck said, "So what is it you need me to do?" He looked down at Eve and gave her head a gentle scrub with his knuckles. She slid down from his arms, scampered over to the closet door and shut it. She stood with her back against the door, shifting from foot to foot. She looked nervous about something.

I looked back at Buck and said, "I dropped the flashlight—the one you gave me for Father's Day. Sorry. Can you squeeze back there behind my wine vault to retrieve it for me?"

"What were you doing in there, Dad?" He wrinkled his nose and sniffed, and it reminded me of a face the monkey would make when she was thinking deep monkey thoughts.

I said, "Your mom told me that she smelled something in the closet, and I was looking for rats...or whatever." I didn't want to get into the details with Buck, but I had been trying to see behind the refrigerator, looking for signs of rodent activity—and also to see what smelled so bad. Before I dropped my flashlight, I thought I saw food back there—and other clutter.

It had been hard enough getting my wine refrigerator into the closet and plugged in. It was a tight fit. Because of the way the ceiling slopes, there was a lot of room behind it, but not a lot of space over it, or on either side. I didn't want to have to drag the damn thing out of there—for any reason. I'd gotten myself organized when I was on vacation a year before and cleaned out the closet so that the refrigerator would fit neatly where the coats used to hang. Through its smoky glass door you could see scallop-shaped stainless steel racks that were about half full. Grace and I had been talking about a trip to the Sonoma wine valley to find some bargains—and maybe a few collectible bottles—to help fill it up, but then our lives became too complicated to do something like that, with me getting fired and all. Adding to our wine collection was something that would have to wait.

I opened the closet door and pointed toward the narrow space between the refrigerator and the wall on one side. Buck followed me into the closet. I got on my knees in front of the refrigerator and showed him where I wanted him to go. There was easily enough room for Buck to get through there, but it would have been a bit tight for me to maneuver. My two hundred pound physique wasn't suited to stints as a contortionist.

He looked down at me and said, "Didn't you say there are rats back there?"

"Probably not. At least, not right now." With all the noise we were making, the rats—if there were any—would have already run for cover. Still, it made me think that Buck going back there might not be such a good idea. The more I thought about him crawling back there, the more nervous I got. I said, "You know what? Maybe we should just forget about it."

As we were talking, Eve darted past us, through the gap and into the darkness behind the refrigerator.

Buck said, "But you need to get back the flashlight I gave you. It cost me twenty five dollars." And he dropped down next to me on all fours and looked into the darkness where Eve had gone.

"Well, you wouldn't have to crawl very far. It should be right there," I said. Even as I was saying those words, I was having a stronger and stronger sense that my actions could put Buck in danger. The whole idea was irrational and I tried to ignore my growing fears, but at the fringes of my memory there was…something—a garbled vignette of a terrifying experience in a similar context, an image of a child screaming. But that made no sense and I knew it.

I took one deep breath after another and tried to clear my head of the growing sense that I'd seen this before.

Buck was calling Eve's name now. There was no sound coming from the darkness behind the wine vault, except for the faint hum of its cooling system. He called her again and then looked over at me and said, "Maybe I should just go back there real fast and grab her—and your flashlight." He spoke without conviction.

I didn't answer immediately.

Buck started fidgeting beside me, picking at balls of fuzz in the carpet. Then he said, "Dad, I don't want to do this. I'm really scared."

Chapter 11

Saturday evening, Grace asked me to help find our dog Daisy. It wasn't uncommon for Daisy to ignore us when we called her. She was that kind of dog. When she felt like sleeping or when the weather was hot, she often disappeared for hours to a secluded spot in the backyard or in the garage that was shady and cool, and she returned to our backdoor when she was ready. But she'd been ignoring Grace's call for hours and hadn't come to the house at all for breakfast. Her food bowl had been full all day. That never happened. Grace looked all around the backyard, checking all the damp places under the bushes along the back fence where Daisy had been barking so loudly during the night. I looked under the gazebo and in the garage. Neither of us found her. The gates were closed, and we saw no rotten places in the fence big enough for a dog to crawl through. We were standing in the twilight, in the middle of the backyard, wondering what to do next, when it occurred to me to ask, "Did you look in her doghouse?"

"No, why would I—I mean, she never goes in there." Grace stared at me for an instant and then turned and trotted toward the cluster of trees under which the old doghouse sat. I was close behind. We saw, in the dark shadows inside, Daisy's head resting on her crossed front paws, as if she were asleep. But she was dead. The vet later said that she'd been bitten by a snake, probably a water moccasin.

She wasn't a young dog, but it was too soon. She enjoyed her life and should have had some good years left. Her death—killed by a snake after a good day barking at squirrels—was more evidence, if any was needed, that there's a random pattern to life's important moments.

I took Buck out for donuts the next morning. Nothing is better for creating an atmosphere where a father and son can have an open, free-flowing discussion than going to the donut shop. Paradise Donuts was only a few minutes from where we lived. The women who worked there knew us well, from our frequent visits on so many Sunday mornings. Sometimes they set aside a strawberry frosted donut for Buck, because that was his favorite, and his face always fell if they'd sold out before we got there. One of the women named Ida came to Thomas' funeral. I guess she saw the announcement in the newspaper obituaries. We didn't talk at the funeral and I never exactly got around to thanking her later, but it meant a lot to see her there. It was evidence that for at least a short time, Thomas was a living, breathing little boy who had ordinary moments of pleasure.

We hadn't told Buck yet about Daisy's death. It didn't seem like a good idea to tell him just before bedtime—he was at an age where nightmares were increasingly common—and so Grace suggested that we deal with it the following morning. Then, after thinking about it a few more minutes, she said, "But without me around. It'll make me cry—I'm sorry. Could you do it without me?" I said okay. Normally, Buck goes to church with Grace on Sunday mornings, but instead, she went alone, so that Buck and I could have enough time for our talk.

After paying for our donuts, Buck and I took them to a table in the corner. Neither of us spoke for a minute. It had seemed to me on the drive over that Buck was unusually quiet. When I'd asked, "Everything okay?" he'd nodded slowly as though he wasn't really sure. I began to think that he already knew about Daisy, that maybe he'd overheard Grace and me talking about it. So I'd rehearsed in my mind a short pep talk about sadness being a healthy human reaction to loss. That's what dads do.

After we'd each finished one of our donuts, I said, "So…Daisy died yesterday." He seemed surprised, but he didn't have a lot to say in response, didn't ask how she'd died. Buck liked Daisy, but I think he was also a little scared of her, the way she jumped around him and got in his face. I told him that death is part of life, but that it's okay to be sad about it.

He interrupted me. "How do bad dreams work?" He looked into my eyes as he spoke, hopefully, as if I were capable of understanding and explaining all the mysteries of existence. "I mean, when you have a bad dream, do you sometimes forget that it was just a dream or… forget exactly where the dream came from?"

"I guess." I didn't quite understand his question, but that didn't stop me from offering an answer. "Sometimes when I have a bad dream at night, I can't remember the details when I get up the next morning. Is that what you mean?"

"No." He looked down at the uneaten strawberry donut on his napkin. "I had some kind of bad dream about the monkey hurting me in the closet."

"Last night?"

"No. I don't remember *actually having* any kind of bad dream. But I remember the dream—what happened in it. I was crawling into the back of the closet and Eve hurt me…real bad. Yesterday morning. When you made me come downstairs and help you."

I didn't say anything at first. His words made me remember… something. In those last moments when we were in the closet together, talking about him crawling behind the wine refrigerator to get my flashlight, I'd had an overwhelming sense of déjà vu—and also, like Buck, an image of him being injured. Disfigured. Bleeding. But those horrible images were almost beyond my ability to recall now. If Buck hadn't mentioned having a dream about Eve hurting him, I don't think I'd have remembered them at all.

He continued. "It was like I'd been there before. But here's the thing…" He stopped talking and waited for me to give him some indication that it was okay for him to keep going with what he was saying.

I said, "Go on."

He took a deep breath and then let it out slowly. "Thomas was there."

I didn't say anything at first, and he must have thought that I didn't know who he was talking about.

He said, "My brother. Thomas. You know…" Then he looked over his shoulder as if he was worried about other people overhearing what he was about to say. "And it's weird. It's like he had socks hanging down from his ears. It was stupid."

A fleeting image came back to me, as if of a distant memory. "Red and white striped socks, right?"

"I think." Buck looked surprised. "How did you know?"

I held up my hand to stop Buck from asking me anything else, to give me a chance to think, to try to see it in my mind. I was trying to remember more, straining to find more details in that image—a glimpse of Thomas' face, his unruly brown hair, something…but it was gone. Just like that. I saw it in my mind for an instant, and then it was lost, as though it had never been there.

Buck picked up his donut, then immediately set it back down and pushed it away. "So seeing Thomas was just a stupid dream?"

Chapter 12

Things aren't always what they seem at the time or the way you try to remember them later. I apologize—sometimes I repeat myself, not remembering if a thought that has replayed itself a thousand times in my mind has ever been spoken aloud. But some revelations—perhaps it would be less grandiose to refer to them as "intuitions" or even "thoughts"—refuse to be articulated. The more you try to frame them in words, the less you're able to grasp. Focus dissipates some underlying truths, as sunlight does a delicate morning mist.

Buck wanted answers from me, and I didn't have them to give. Not yet, anyway.

I didn't know what to tell him about his realization that he'd seen—that we'd *both* seen—Thomas in a shared dream or vision or in some type of shared déjà vu. In that moment at the donut shop when Buck told me about having seen his brother Thomas and about the premonitions he'd had of being in danger, I was certain that I had experienced exactly the same thing along with him. For me, there was also a tantalizing memory associated with it, a memory that had to do with Grace—of a different kind of love between us, of a warmth and a sense of shared happiness. But within minutes, all those memories were gone, and in place of them I only had an unsettling sensation of knowledge being just beyond my grasp. All those memories had faded. I didn't know how to explain any of that to Buck.

In recent years I have taken refuge in an open acknowledgement that there are certain fundamentally important questions to which I don't know the answer. When I'm pressed to tell someone what I think about some religious or metaphysical quandary, I'll often preface my opinion by saying that, of course, I don't know.

Once Grace asked me if I ever talk to Thomas, even though he's dead, and I said yes. I talk to him frequently, when I'm alone. Grace said that she does too, and then she asked me if I think he can hear us. I said, "I don't know." It would have been far kinder for me to have said, "Yes, I believe that in some way Thomas is aware of the things we say." I actually *do* think that, but I don't know it to be true.

Other people *know* things. Scientists, engineers and doctors have an air of certainty about things that they believe. They may change their opinion occasionally, but they believe what they believe with confidence. Things for them are black and white. Maybe law school hardwired into my brain a style of thinking that forces me to live in the gray areas, to see both sides of arguments as having validity, to see unwarranted confidence as intellectually sloppy, if not dishonest.

It's also a form of cowardice. Refusing to acknowledge what your gut tells you is true is caused by fear—fear that you are building your peace and hope on something that will desert you.

When Thomas was dying—during that last few weeks of his life— I dreamed more than once about traveling with Thomas and losing him. The dreams were far more vivid and focused than what is typical for me. In one dream, we were walking down a cavernous, long corridor, with brightly lit shops on either side, with people milling around on all sides of us. And in the distance was a carnival, and an elephant lumbered into view, but the elephant was huge, so huge that in the dream I knew that he was a hundred feet tall. The walls and ceiling of the corridor narrowed, and so I could never see the entire elephant, but I could see his side, which was draped with brightly colored fabrics and one of his pierced ears, which had loops of gold hanging from it, and his massive legs and feet. I had no sense of danger, just fascination for what lay ahead, but Thomas slipped into the crowd ahead of me and I could no longer see him.

The dream with the elephant is the one I remember the best, but there were other similar dreams in which I lost Thomas—almost always because he had gotten ahead of me, which was interesting, because in reality Thomas would never have left my side in a crowd. He was almost six when he died and was cautious, almost clingy when we were out in public. He told Grace once that he wasn't very afraid of dying, but he was afraid of how it was going to work, to be separated from us after he'd died. He'd said, "Who's going to take care of me—talk to me, that kind of stuff?"

There was no really good answer for that question, but we told him about heaven being a place where there was no more sickness and fear—and no sense of time, so that when we were all reunited, it would seem to him like only moments had passed. What else could we say?

Thomas had interesting dreams too. He liked to tell them to me in the morning, when I was getting ready to go to work. In one of them, he walked into a sparkling lake and an angelic figured baptized him, and then a voice from the sky said, "Good job, son."

Those were words I often used to praise him. I asked him, if it was me talking in the dream, and he said, no, that it was God, and then he got embarrassed and didn't want to talk about it any more. And I didn't push it, but, of course, in the dream, Thomas was Jesus. That was how Jesus was baptized, more or less, and Thomas knew the story very well. The picture book about Jesus' baptism that Grace often read to the monkey was a book that Thomas liked too.

I mentioned Thomas' baptism dream to our friend Elaine, and she said that it was an *archetypal* dream. As a psychologist, she's very interested in dreams. She said that as people go through life, some develop an intuitive awareness of spiritual things and that their intuitions are reinforced by powerful dreams, dreams that contain personalized versions of well known myths and Bible stories. Jungian psychologists call them archetypal dreams. She said that it was very unusual for someone Thomas' age to be having such a dream, but his circumstances were different—as we all knew. His dream was a revelation—coming from the *inside* rather than the outside—of the essence of his own spiritual nature. That's what Elaine said: the essence of his own spiritual nature.

Elaine told me several years later that she'd had to struggle not to be envious of Thomas, that his natural, childlike intuitions about the things underlying his dreams were beyond anything she'd experienced personally. I was proud for him, but bitter too. I said, "What's the point of revelation—if that's what it is—if all that comes afterwards is that you die?"

She said, "That *is* the point. Living is a journey that ends in death for everyone. Awareness—the kind that Thomas had—doesn't change that, it just puts things in perspective before you die."

And so I imagined Thomas as being unusually full of grace—and it helped me deal with losing him. His dreams had made him special.

Several hours after Buck and I returned from our trip to the donut shop, Bonnie Norton showed up at our front door. I said, "Well, this is a surprise."

She dropped a lit cigarette butt on my front step and ground it out with the sole of her shoe. She took a long breath, inhaling through her nose. I could hear the sound of air being forced through congested sinuses. She seemed uncertain, at first, as to what she wanted to say, but after a few seconds she said, "So you just let them do it."

"Let them do what?"

She took a step toward me and stood on the threshold of my front door, clenching her fists. "Kill her."

I didn't think Bonnie was going to take a swing at me, but I took a step back anyway. "No."

"They told me she died." The words were tinged with sarcasm. "Natural causes. Unrelated to the drug tests."

"Who told you?"

"Gina." She was another grad student on the team. "I could tell she was lying." Her voice got louder. "You didn't do anything, anything at all…to stop them." She took another step toward me. This time I stood my ground, to keep her from coming further into the house, and so now her face was only inches away from mine.

I let my voice get louder too, to match hers, to make her listen to what I was trying to tell her. "Yes, I did—"

"A lot of good it did then, huh?" She abruptly turned away, intentionally jostling me with her shoulder. "A lot of fucking good."

I asked, "Would you like to see her?"

She looked back at me and stared, without answering, as if I were asking her a trick question.

"She's living here now…with us." I waited for a second to see if my words were registering with her. "I took her."

"This is a joke?"

"No. She's here."

"You're really not joking?"

"No. I took her the night you left. I decided that I couldn't leave her there to die."

Without warning, Bonnie grabbed me and threw her arms around me, hugging me with my arms pinned against my side. Then she let go, took a couple of steps back onto the front step and said, "I'm so sorry I was always mean to you."

"It's okay."

"I was always such a bitch." She looked down at the cigarette butt she'd dropped on my porch and squatted down to pick it up, slipping it into her pocket as she stood up.

"It's okay."

"I'm sorry. I'm so sorry." By now her words were just nervous rambling.

I heard Buck calling me from the kitchen, complaining that he was hungry.

I ignored him and held up my hand, gesturing for Bonnie to stop talking. "It's okay. Really, it's okay."

Buck continued to yell from the kitchen, louder now, asking if he could have a snack. In other circumstances I would have stormed in there and given him a stern lecture about not bothering me when I trying to talk to someone, but at the moment I just wanted to finish my conversation with Bonnie, free from interruption. So I called back, "Yeah, but eat it in there."

Bonnie said, "So…can I see her?"

I gestured for her to come into the house. "Yes, but there's something I want to ask you first. Was what the article in the newspaper said true?"

"Yeah. I was their snatch…I guess you'd say."

"Snitch. You were the *snitch*."

"Snitch…whatever."

"And so Eve is one of those monkeys? The ones that have human junk DNA in their chromosomes?"

"Well, yeah. Didn't you read the files I left you?"

"I tried." I led her through the entryway toward the den.

She continued, "The grad students who were doing the monkey embryos—Gina and somebody else—and Dr. Hermann—they wanted to see what would happen—what implanting those extra strands of would DNA do."

I stopped and turned around so suddenly that Bonnie ran into me. "So…*what do they do?*"

Bonnie stood on her tiptoes, looking past me, trying to catch a glimpse of the monkey. Then she looked at me and blurted out, "Maybe it causes some kind of—I don't know—elevated form of alienation? Does that make sense?" She walked around me, not waiting for me to answer. As she went into the den, I heard her whisper, "Evie."

The monkey was asleep on the couch, nestled among pillows at one end, with her face turned in our direction. Her eyes twitched under her closed eyelids and her lips moved as though she was making monkey conversation. For an instant her face seemed to register anxiety, and then it was gone, and a placid expression replaced it.

Bonnie whispered, "Look, she's having a dream."

Grace and I sometimes used to talk about our cat Porky dreaming, because his face would twitch while he was sleeping, but I don't know if he really was dreaming. I was curious. Most of what I knew about monkeys, I'd learned from having Eve around, but Bonnie had actually studied primates. I asked her, "Do monkeys really have dreams?"

"Of course."

"But what would they dream about?"

She frowned. "I don't know. Adventure. Danger. Sex. The same things we dream about. That's what the research says." Bonnie sat down gently next to Eve and began to stroke the coarse amber fur on the top of her head. Monkeys don't smile, but if you're around them enough you begin to recognize changes in their facial expressions that register enjoyment. I could see that Eve, even in her sleep, enjoyed the sensation of being petted.

Bonnie took Eve's tiny hand in hers and squeezed it. Eve opened her eyes and looked up at Bonnie, then slid over into Bonnie's lap. She lowered her head into the crook of Bonnie's elbow and then closed her eyes again.

Bonnie rubbed Eve's back lightly and said, "Are you having a hard time waking up, girlie?"

Eve slowly sat up and looked at me, sought eye contact with me, with her angular, dark brown monkey eyes. It was one of the looks that she sometimes gave me that signified...something. The eye contact was purposeful, but she was a monkey, concerned about monkey things, and I had no clear idea what she wanted me to understand.

Eve slid out of Bonnie's lap and bounded over to our bookcase. From the lower shelf where we keep the children's books, she pulled out John the Baptist and carried it back to Bonnie.

I said, "That's her favorite book."

Bonnie smiled until she saw the cover of the book. "You're kidding me, right?"

"No. She wants you to read it to her."

"She's found Jesus?" Bonnie rolled her eyes. "Oh, my God."

I just smiled. Bonnie didn't understand.

Eve climbed back up on the couch next to Bonnie.

"Okay...whatever." Bonnie opened the book to the first page and began to read the words that described John as being a man who wore animal skins and ate locusts and honey in the wilderness. Eve pulled the book away and, with a hand that shook both from Parkinson's and a sense of urgency, she flipped past pages and then pointed at an image near the end of the book. She looked away from the book, wrinkled her nose and sniffed, and then looked down into the gap between the couch cushions and pulled out an old, stale kernel of popcorn—something Grace had probably dropped days earlier. She popped it into her mouth and then pointed again at the image on the page.

Bonnie looked at me. "What does she want?"

I sat down on the couch on the other side of Eve to look. Eve had opened the book to the page on which John the Baptist is lifting a wet Jesus out of the river Jordan.

Eve lifted her hand, formed it loosely into a fist and hit her chest with it, just once.

Bonnie said, "I don't get what's going on here."

Eve looked up at me, as if I was supposed to understand. And I did. She'd had a dream. A dream about being baptized.

And what came into my head next was the treasured memory of my son Thomas waking up and telling me that *he'd had a dream* in which he was Jesus being baptized. Elaine had said it was a rare and meaningful dream. I didn't like the idea of a monkey having a similar experience. It trivialized what had happened to Thomas, made it all some kind of joke.

I flipped the book shut, stood up and turned away. I might have been wrong about the exact connection between the picture in the book and Eve's dream—it was absurd to consider the possibility that a monkey would comprehend and identify with some kind of archetypal Jesus—or the fundamental idea of baptism. But those were the connections in my head and I couldn't pull together my thoughts at the moment to deal with it in any other way—and it frustrated me. And made me angry with myself. . I felt the rational part of my brain shutting down, too overwhelmed to keep trying.

Bonnie looked at me, puzzled at my sudden mood swing. "Is something wrong?"

"No." I stared at her for a minute and then changed my answer. "Yes."

I didn't know her well enough to talk openly about my problems of faith or my financial problems or my growing marital problems. And so she took a guess as to what was on my mind and made an impulsive offer. "I can take her," she said. "I don't have my own place yet, but I could make it work."

"Where are you living?"

She hesitated. "With friends. Until I find my own place—but I'm going to have my own place soon. And anyway, she'd live at the new college where I'm going to be…going."

It wasn't a response that instilled confidence—but, even so, I considered it. Getting rid of the monkey would have made Grace happier and removed an area of conflict between us…probably. But maybe not. The more I thought about it, the more I could picture Grace questioning my judgment. She would have questioned the idea of me giving Eve—or any animal—to someone incapable of providing it with a stable home environment. That was a fundamental tenet of animal rescue groups, hers included. I'd heard her say so. And Buck would have been upset. Surprisingly, the "bad dream" he'd described to me the earlier in the day hadn't diminished his enthusiasm for horseplay with the monkey. I'd already put a stop to one game of toss the monkey.

So I said, "Maybe we should wait—you know…wait until you know more about your situation. Then we can talk about it."

She gave me a puzzled look and said, "You just said that."

"No, I didn't. Did I?" Now that she'd put me on the spot, I couldn't remember if I'd said it or just thought it.

"Yes. You already said it."

Eve slid off the couch and scampered over to the window. She glanced in our direction and then climbed up the curtains. Her weight made the fabric come loose from several of the curtain rings, but Eve hung on and swung to the top where she sat on the brass curtain rod, with her head touching the ceiling.

Bonnie frowned. "Look at her. A monkey doesn't belong in a nice place like you've got here."

I looked up at Eve, still perched on the curtain rod. Beneath her poker face, I could detect growing anxiety. She began to whimper.

Bonnie said, "Anyway, she wouldn't be living in an apartment for long at all. The new college I mentioned…I'm talking to them about finishing up my Ph.D. there. And they've got a great lab where she could live. I've seen it."

"What college?"

She looked away. "Actually, there's a couple that I'm talking to. Well…three now. I haven't made my decision yet, but I'm thinking…about one, in particular, that has a lab that just studies monkey behavior—no drug tests like they were doing at UTH. Oh! And your name would never have to come up—were you worried about that? No one would ever know that you took her."

I had the powerful sensation that Bonnie had said those same words to me before. But I knew better. I played back our last few minutes of conversation in my head, and I was certain that she had not repeated herself. I wondered if somehow I had simply known what Bonnie was going to say about protecting me—keeping my name secret—by intuition. It was possible. I also wondered if I was losing my mind—if these déjà vu episodes were a symptom of something that was wrong with me. And getting worse.

Bonnie stood up. "I could take her today. Right now."

Despite all my reservations, I was tempted to let Bonnie have her. Very tempted. I had the sudden irrational thought that it might be the monkey that was the source of all of my problems—my growing distractibility and all these strange new sensations of time repeating itself. How could I land a job—and how could I get my marriage back on track, if I was somehow becoming…whatever it was that I was becoming?

Before I could answer, I noticed that Buck was in the doorway. He had a bag of Cheetos in one hand and was gripping a Dr. Pepper bottle with the other. He shook his head from side to side. I said, "What?"

"Please don't. Please."

I looked back and forth between Buck and Bonnie. "Buck, this is an old friend of Eve's…and of mine."

Eve began to chatter frantically from her perch on the curtain rod.

Buck shifted from foot to foot. Tears began to fill his eyes. "Don't. Dad, please."

Chapter 13

Buck took a bite of Cheerios and, as he chewed them, said, "It happened again, Dad, didn't it? Yesterday, when that woman was here, trying to take Eve."

I was at the table across from him, eating a toasted bagel. "*What* happened again, buddy?"

"I had another one of those…dreams, you know? You let that woman take Eve and I cried and you let her anyway. And then you didn't. You know what I mean." He waited for me to say something.

"You dreamed it? Last night?"

"No. It was just like it happened before—to you and me—like on Saturday morning when you wanted me to crawl into the back of the coat closet. First everything happened one way, and then it happened all over again—but different."

I now understood what Buck was saying, but I didn't remember anything out of the ordinary happening when Bonnie had come by on Sunday. I'd let her see the monkey. She offered to take her. I'd said no—I'd thought about it, but I'd said no. Buck was there, listening in on our conversation, and he'd obviously been afraid that I was going to let Bonnie take Eve. But I'd said no.

While I was busy thinking, rather than talking, Buck was repeating his explanation. His voice quivered as he talked. "You were about to do it. I could tell, and I said, 'Please don't. Please don't let her.' And finally you told her no. But before you told her, it was like I could see you saying yes—but it was in my head, like a dream or something. And I could see myself crying and grabbing Eve away from that woman and running and—"

Grace came into the kitchen, yawning as she walked. Her eyes were a little puffy from sleep. A couple of strands of chestnut colored hair were hanging down over her face. She had put highlights in her dark brown hair. I hadn't noticed before. I was afraid to compliment her on her new look, for fear that it wasn't all that new.

She waved lethargically and said, "Good morning. Where's the coffee?"

Buck lowered his voice to a whisper. "It was the exact same kind of thing we talked about at the donut place yesterday, you know?"

I nodded.

Grace looked over from where she was pouring coffee. "Where's the newspaper, guys?"

"Still outside. Want Buck to go get it for you?"

"No, I need the exercise."

Neither of us responded quickly enough.

She said, "Hey, when a woman says 'I need to exercise'—implying that she needs to lose weight—what response is required from the gentlemen in the room?"

I said, "No, sweetie, you look wonderful."

"Buck?"

"Mom, you're not fat."

"Thank you. Thank you both. Now, if you'll excuse me, I'm going to get the newspaper, because I need the exercise. I'll be right back." She smiled, but her smile was forced—I could tell. She was putting on a brave face that morning to hide her unhappiness about…something. I wasn't certain what. She was taking the new anti-depressants her doctor had prescribed. I wasn't sure they were working. They didn't keep her from being unhappy, but her immediate source of unhappiness changed from day to day. At the moment, it was—quite appropriately—that I didn't have a job, and we would be dipping into our savings, if I didn't find something soon. But sometimes her bouts of depression were triggered by small things, such as a bad haircut, or a thoughtless phone call from a good friend, or too many days of overcast skies.

As soon as she left the kitchen, Buck added, "But it was like I could see things from a totally different direction. I don't know how to say it. Up, down, sideways and…and sort of from inside out. Does that make sense?"

He maintained eye contact with me, waiting for me to acknowledge that I'd experienced the same thing he had, when Bonnie had been in our house. But I hadn't. And I had no idea what he meant when he said he could see things from a totally different direction.

I said, "Was Thomas there?"

Buck shook his head from side to side and said, "No. And in the middle of things, I wasn't there either. I just wasn't there—I disappeared. It was scary. Are you doing it? Are you making all this happen? So you can see Thomas again?"

I was astonished, but I should have expected the question. Buck and I were a part of something unexplainable. And, like any child of that age, he thought I was in charge—somehow totally in control of things.

Grace came back into the kitchen and sat down beside me with a cup of coffee, but she left the newspaper folded on the table in front of her. I could tell she had something on her mind, but she didn't say anything at first. Then she cupped her hand around my ear and whispered, "Muffin is dead. Does Buck know yet?"

Buck had returned his attention to his cereal. He was chasing remnant Cheerios around the rim of the bowl with his spoon.

I said, "I don't think so." Muffin was one of Buck's two pet gerbils. He'd been lethargic lately, and so it wasn't a big surprise. Muffin and his brother Pinkie lived in Buck's room in a small terrarium with a screen lid. They didn't crave a lot of human interaction, but got quite a bit anyway. Buck liked to build mazes out of blocks and let them wander around inside of them. Or he'd build cities with Legos and narrate adventures as the gerbils stumbled around, knocking over Lego characters. We never let Eve in Buck's room when Buck had the gerbils out of their terrarium. We weren't sure what she'd do—whether she'd want to play with the gerbils too or try to eat them.

Grace spoke now without whispering, but used deliberately vague language, in case Buck was paying attention to what she was saying. "I looked in…there…and you could just tell. Do you want to…?"

Buck looked up from his cereal bowl and said, "Muffin died?"

Grace reached across the table to squeeze his hand. "I'm sorry, sweetie. He was pretty old, you know?"

"I know." He nodded. "He'd been real tired." There was resignation in his voice, very much at odds with the childish enthusiasm he usually had for everything that came his way. "How long until his brother dies too?"

I shrugged. "I don't know. Maybe a year or so." They were from the same litter.

He started to lift his bowl to his lips, to drink the sugar-sweetened milk that was in it. Then he set it down, without drinking, and looked back and forth at me and Grace. "How do you know I'm not going to get leukemia like Thomas did and die too?"

Grace dropped the spoon she was using to stir the cream that was in her coffee. "Buck."

"Like Thomas did. How do you know?"

She said, "What an awful thing to say. You're not going to get leukemia."

"How do you know?"

I tried to think of an answer that wasn't a lie or a knee-jerk abdication to God's grace. I did the best I could and said, "Buck, when your brother was sick, we were at the hospital all the time. We met lots of families with a little boy or little girl who had come down with leukemia. Not once—not once—did any of those families have two children who had it. In fact, I've never heard of two brothers both getting leukemia." I looked at Grace to see if she would back me up on my seat-of-the-pants logic.

She nodded vigorously. "Your dad's right." She pushed her coffee away, toward the middle of the table.

Buck stirred the milk in his cereal bowl with his finger and spoke without looking up. "I want to get baptized, just in case."

I couldn't stop myself from clarifying things. "Buck, baptism doesn't protect you from—"

Grace interrupted me. "He knows.

"And it's not like a requirement for—"

"He knows." She glared at me and I stopped talking.

At the age of five, a person's thoughts on death should be almost totally abstract, but that wasn't the case for Buck. He was less than a year old when Thomas died, so he had no memory of that exact time, but since before he could remember, the reality and immediacy of death were a concrete part of his life. Thomas' pictures were throughout our house, including one taken in his last month at his birthday party in which he looked genuinely happy and overwhelmingly tired. Thomas was Buck's only brother, and Thomas died when he was Buck's age. It was no wonder that Buck had anxiety about death. Plus, our dog had just died and now his gerbil. It must have seemed to him as if death was rampant and closing in on him.

"The two things aren't connected—baptism and...you know," Grace said. "You *do* know that, don't you?"

He nodded, looking down at his cereal bowl.

She continued, "But if you're ready to be baptized, then...I think you should do it."

He looked startled, apparently surprised that he was going to be allowed to do what he wanted without further negotiation. "I'm ready."

Grace nodded. "Of course, you'll need to talk with Dr. Thorn first, to tell him you want to be saved...you know."

Buck frowned. He'd told us a number of times before that he didn't really like Dr. Thorn.

Dr. Thorn was probably in his mid-seventies. He'd been the pastor of Spring Road Baptist Church since I was a kid. He was sincere in his beliefs and well-intentioned, but over the years he'd become pretty inflexible about a variety of things, including horseplay in the church. Buck had been the recipient of one of his angry lectures on treating God's house with respect, and Buck had never forgiven him for it. As Buck told us later, "The door just knocked me backwards. That's what started everything."

97

Buck said, "Could Barry do it? He's a preacher. He could baptize me, couldn't he?"

We didn't encourage Buck to call grown-ups by their first name, but, in this case, that was the only name he knew. He'd heard us talk about Elaine and Barry all his life and had probably never even heard us mention their last name.

I could see in Grace's face that she didn't like that idea. I'm sure Barry would have been honored and delighted to baptize Buck, but Presbyterians don't baptize people by immersing them in water. They sprinkle them with water, and they typically do it when a person is an infant. Southern Baptists have complete distain for such a non-literal approach to baptism—it wasn't how Jesus did it. Before Grace could say no, I said, "Why don't we figure that part out later?"

Chapter 14

Our monkey had concerns about death too. When we brought Muffin downstairs, the stiff, little gerbil was wrapped in an old washcloth. Eve came over quietly and, before I could lift the tiny bundle out of reach, she began to smell it. She wrinkled her nose and cheeks as she sniffed it, and then she scampered over to the window where our cat Porky was sleeping, and she began to smell him—and then to poke him. Was there some smell of death wafting up from Porky too? Maybe, but Porky was still alive and a bit annoyed at being poked while he was trying to sleep. He stood up slowly, arched his back in a languid stretching movement, and then walked to the backdoor and waited for me to open it and let him outside.

Porky had always demanded the right to come and go as he wished. Although his final weeks with us were typically spent sleeping inside the house in a sunny spot under a window, he often wanted to go outside in the evenings to sharpen his claws on a tree or roam the neighborhood. With orange fur and one missing leg, he was easy to recognize, and we had friends in the neighborhood who would report to us that they'd seen Porky strolling across their front yards. I saw him once when I was coming home from the grocery store, and I sat in my car and watched him walking. Even as an old cat, he seemed to savor the feel of the grass under his feet and the suburban Houston smells that greeted him along his path. He walked slowly, with the limp in his gait that came from only having three legs, but he walked proudly, with his tail erect. I wondered if he had any sense of the passing of time, of the cycle of a cat's existence. Did smells that he encountered on his walks trigger memories? When he chanced upon a young female in heat, did he remember having once been in that season of his life? And did the memories give him pleasure or did they possibly even contain a sense of satiated completeness: done…well done.

One night several days later, Porky stood at the door meowing, and I let him out. I last saw him walking through the twilight in the direction of the creek bed behind the houses at the end of the culvert.

No one ever found his body, but we know that he died. Maybe he was bitten by a water moccasin—like Daisy—or maybe he just lay down and died, because he was ready. Grace and I shed a few tears for Porky, but Buck didn't—he stonewalled our questions about how he was feeling about things. All he said was, "I don't want to get any more pets." Only the old gerbil Pinkie was left—except for Evie, of course.

Eve continued to feed Porky. She seemed to think that he still needed to be fed, even though he was gone, so she kept his bowl full.

We dumped out the food from his bowl every few days, so the mice or rats wouldn't make our laundry room into their regular hangout. When the bag of dry cat food was empty, we put Porky's bowls in the garage and bought a new rug to go in front of the dryer.

It was hard for Eve to let go of Porky, and I think that in her own mind, she believed that we didn't understand Porky's death correctly. Pretty soon we began to find one of our plates sitting on the floor where Porky's food bowl had been. Eve was getting dirty plates out of the sink or the dishwasher and putting them on the floor for Porky. We couldn't make her stop.

Grace was concerned about the possibility that Eve would break one of our dessert plates, leaving us with only eleven, an incomplete set. I was more philosophical about it, but it worried her—a lot. We were lying in bed one night, and she couldn't stop talking about it. It made her angry that, as she put it, the "whole set of dishes will be ruined." So I got out of bed, went into the garage and got Porky's old dish and brought it back into the laundry room and set it on the floor where it had been throughout recent years.

Concern over our set of dishes was not the only thing we'd been dealing with. Grace had become obsessive about keeping everything in the kitchen organized. In a sense, that was understandable. The kitchen was her domain. She did almost all the cooking. She had selected all the appliances and gadgets, except for the ones that we'd bought her for Mother's Day—and even those purchases were with her explicit instructions. But her new fixation on getting the kitchen completely organized worried me. It was as if she was getting things organized so that we could find things without her. She began writing down Buck's favorite recipes and telling me where to find things. Her most recent cooking magazines were in a stack, unread.

I wasn't stupid or oblivious to what was going on. But some things are hard to say—I don't know why that's true. Maybe people have an ingrained belief that when you put your worries into words, it gives them a life of their own. After you voice them, they're free from your control—to find their own way—or to run amok if that's in their nature.

When I got back to the bedroom, the light was off. As I slid under the covers, I said, "I found Porky's old bowl."

She said, from her corner of the bed, "Was one of my plates on the floor?"

I slid my arm under her neck and put my other arm around her waist. "Yes, but it's in the dishwasher now. Eve won't take any more of your dishes."

She scooted against me, letting her back find a comfortable place, nestled against my chest. "Thanks."

I said in a low voice, "Grace…"

"Yes?"

"Buck needs you to be here."

She didn't answer. I felt the tempo of her breathing change to something stiff and regular, as if she was forcing herself to breath quietly.

I repeated myself. "Buck needs a mother."

"Does he really? Someone like me?"

"Yes."

A week later I heard Grace singing on the front porch. I had my gray pinstripe suit on, since I was about to leave for a job interview, with a small law firm that specialized in employment law. My old boss Bob had called me about the opportunity and had recommended me to one of the partners there who was an old friend of his.

Grace was on her knees, planting some crisp, white gardenias in a pot that had previously held a ratty-looking variegated ivy of some kind. She had pulled the ivy up by the roots and tossed it out into the yard. She smiled up at me, gestured to the new flowers as if she were a magician and said, "Presto change-o."

I said, "Looks nice."

She wiped sweat off of her forehead with the back of her hand, looked back down at her work and said, "I'm thinking about a trip to Rockport. Maybe do a little sailing."

I said, "I don't know." I thought she was talking about a family vacation, and I wasn't sure that was a good idea, for a variety of reasons. "Buck's not that strong a swimmer yet. Maybe next year would be better."

She patted the potting soil around the gardenias, still not looking up at me. "Well...I'm thinking about going, just by myself."

"Right now, money's kind of tight, don't you think?" That was certainly the biggest obstacle, but I was surprised and not completely enthusiastic about the idea of Grace going on a vacation alone. I felt as if she needed me around her, to keep her spirits up. Buck and I had taken a fishing trip a few months earlier, and when we got back I discovered that she'd hardly gotten out of bed the whole time we were out of town. Her only explanation had been that she didn't feel like it.

She looked up quickly and spoke with almost childlike earnestness. "Daddy said he'd pay for it. He said it would make me feel better. He said, maybe I just need a little time away from everything around here."

That imbecile. Her dad meant well—of course, he meant well, but why hadn't he talked with me about it? All I could see in my mind's eye was the dark, inviting water of the gulf—Grace in the darkness alone, slipping silently into peaceful, dark water. I wasn't certain of her intent. Grace probably wasn't fully aware of her own intent. But I was afraid for her—and us.

Grace had never said anything that implied a desire to be dead, to commit suicide. But she didn't have to say the words out loud for me to understand what she was capable of doing.

As I was driving to the interview, I called Elaine. I wanted to confide in someone who really knew Grace, but who wouldn't blab about private things to all our friends. The other parents of the kids in Buck's kindergarten class were our friends. They were genuine friends, but it was like a big family. Among the parents—like in most families— no secrets were kept for long.

Elaine suggested that we meet for lunch at a café not too far from where I was having the job interview. We were both a few minutes late and arrived in the parking lot at about the same time. She hadn't seemed surprised when I'd called for a last minute lunch date. All I'd said was that there were a couple of things I needed to talk with her about, and she'd said, "Sure."

The host first offered us spots side by side in a booth, which would have been awkward, so I asked for a regular table in the corner instead. He said, defensively, "I thought maybe you wanted…." And let his words trail off.

Elaine thought it was funny—the waiter's assumption that the two of us were meeting for a private, romantic lunch. As we stood by the new table, waiting for our waiter to organize it for us, she winked at me and said, "We should do this more often."

I asked her about her kids, and she said she was a single parent for the week. Barry was at some kind of national Presbyterian gathering, where he was giving a report on the work of some task force on social justice that he'd led. The task force's work was controversial, particularly with the conservative churches in the South. She said, "I hope he doesn't get himself fired too."

After a brief, but awkward silence, she asked me about my job interview. I told her that it had gone okay. The salary was better and the hours were worse than what I'd gotten used to at the university. They had said that they were looking at several candidates and would decide before the end of April.

After we ordered lunch, I brought up my concerns about Grace. Our conversation about that was shorter than I expected or wanted. When I told Elaine that Grace was suicidal, Elaine nodded and said, "I know."

"You know?" I waited for a more detailed explanation and some assurance that things were okay, despite appearances to the contrary.

"Yes." She nodded and searched my eyes, as if it were me and my state of mind that was the subject of discussion, rather than Grace's. "But I think Grace is doing okay right now. How are *you* holding up?"

It was obvious that Grace and Elaine had talked about Grace's depression in detail, enough that Elaine registered no surprise whatsoever at hearing from me that Grace might be planning to kill herself. I shouldn't have been surprised. There's probably little they hadn't talked about, little or nothing. I said, "Okay, I guess."

"Do you have someone *you* can talk to? You don't have to be strong *all* the time."

I chuckled. I didn't view myself as being particularly strong.

She said, "I'm serious," and stared at me with her pale green eyes, searching for at least a non-verbal response that was honest.

"I know."

"You need a place where you can take all the space you want—you know what I mean? Where you can just be whatever you are…happy, sad, angry—your choice. I worry that Grace is taking up all the emotional space in your lives."

I asked, "Do you know about the trip she's planning to Rockport?"

At that, Elaine flipped open her pocket calendar, as if she was checking it for an answer. A couple of dog-eared, yellow slips of paper and credit card receipts fell out. "No. I don't think so. When is she going?"

I told her what I knew and also explained my worries about the whole idea of Grace being alone there for days.

She nodded and said, "I'll make a new pact with her. We have a rolling thirty day pact. Grace promises me every month—*promises*—that she won't do anything to harm herself for at least another thirty days."

I thought over what she was telling me. It seemed to provide pretty skimpy assurances that nothing bad was going to happen. I said "A promise. Thirty days? That's it?"

She smiled. I know she didn't mean for the smile to come across as condescending, but that's how it felt, as if she were talking to an attentive, but simpleminded child, someone who could only comprehend watered down explanations. She reached over and touched the back of my hand with her fingertips. "It's the impulsive behavior that we have to worry about the most. If I can get a firm commitment from her that she won't do anything for even thirty days, it takes away the risk of her doing something impulsive."

I was having a hard time believing that a genuine strategy could be so cut and dried. "So you're not worried?"

She let her guard down for a few moments and her eyes became clouded with a few escaping tears. "Of course I'm worried. Of course I am. I don't know how I would make it, if she was…gone."

I nodded. "Yeah."

"But she's in so much pain."

"Yeah." I couldn't help adding, "But she's not alone." I'd *also* lost a son.

"I know." She wasn't Grace's therapist, but she was her best friend, and she clearly wasn't comfortable talking with me about Grace's secrets. So she changed the subject again. "And how's Buck holding up?"

"I don't know." I told her about the back-to-back deaths of family pets—Daisy, Muffin and then Porky—and about Buck's sudden interest in being baptized.

She said, "That sounds like a perfect response." She talked about the symbolism in it, the symbolism of rebirth, the symbolism of an awakening. She said, "Don't think about it as just some Baptist thing. It's a universal ritual—you know what I mean? It resonates with people of all faiths in the way it celebrates awakening."

The word "awakening" made me think of dreaming, which made me think of the dream-like experiences that Buck—and I—had been having. Elaine knew so much about dreaming that I decided to tell her about our experiences to see what she would have to say. I told her about the most recent episode first—when Bonnie wanted to take the monkey. Then I told her about the episode involving the closet under the stairs, where we both initially had vivid memories of having seen Thomas. And, finally, I repeated what Buck had said about *being able to see things inside out*—like maybe it was some kind of psychedelic experience—and that he'd disappeared in the dream…if that's what it was.

She stared at me for a few seconds after I had stopped talking. At first I thought she was waiting for me to say more, to explain everything more clearly, but as I opened my mouth to begin talking again, she held up her hand and said, "I'm trying to process what you said. Shared nighttime dreams are not uncommon, but shared lucid dreams…I don't know. I don't have any experience with that."

"Oh well." I was disappointed.

"There's a book—fiction—it's not particularly well-written, but what you said made it pop into my head. It's about William James— you know…the philosopher?"

I'd probably heard of him, but couldn't say that I knew much of anything about him.

She continued. "It's kind of a silly mystery-thriller-historical mash-up. In the book he discovers that there are alternate realities. In real life, James came up with the word 'Multiverse,' and this book…kind of takes it from there."

"How?"

"I only read part of it. Like I said, it was kind of silly. Since the main character was *William James*, I thought there was going to be a psychological-theological subtext, right?" She obviously thought I knew more about the man than I actually did. "And there kind of was, but it was mostly parallel universe gobbledygook."

"And that makes you think I ought to read it?"

She frowned, lost in thought again, and then said, "I don't know. Maybe. Not as a book that explains things, but maybe as a tool to help you get in touch with what you're feeling about the…experiences you and Buck had."

"Okay."

"I gave my copy away. Otherwise you could have it. I think it's called <u>Reflections from the Multiverse</u> or something like that. It wasn't a best seller or anything. Some university press published it. I can't remember which one. Maybe SMU? You could check."

"Okay."

"Sorry, I can't even remember the author's name. I'm not sure he's published anything else."

"I'm sure I can find it."

"He's lives around here, I think. Maybe Galveston."

Chapter 15

Eve was on a spiritual journey. That sounds silly, even crazy, to say.

How did I know? I just knew. She had a sense of self-awareness that animals aren't supposed to have. I saw a glimmer of it each time we made eye contact, but I felt it strongly—overwhelmingly—on those occasions when she was troubled by something. She would stare into my eyes without looking away. And I would know...*something*. I wouldn't be able to put into words exactly what I knew, but the sensation was powerful that she perceived things beyond what was driven by ordinary animal instincts. Was that because of the human DNA that she carried? It must have been. What else could have caused it? What did it mean? I didn't know.

As the weeks and months passed since the day she came to live with us, I began to notice peculiar behavioral patterns—even obsessions—that she seemed to have. I've already mentioned her obsession with thunderstorms. Some other things: I noticed that she was spending time alone in silence, in the closet under the stairs, in the nook behind my wine refrigerator—almost daily. And almost every day, she spent time looking at the pages in the book about John the Baptist where John tells the crowd that Jesus has come to baptize men with fire and then proceeds to baptize Jesus in the swirling current of the Jordan River. She always made sure that something was in Porky's food bowl—maybe a piece of fruit, or a wad of colored paper, or one of Buck's small toys.

And she began crying again—for no apparent reason—sometimes at the end of the day. Not every day, but frequently. Maybe she was lonely. Maybe she longed to have a mate and offspring. Maybe she was frustrated by the worsening symptoms of her Parkinson's. She cried because she could and because she wanted to.

I sometimes found her—or Buck or Grace did—sitting alone and crying, making quiet monkey sounds between quiet sobs. It was as if she was giving a voice to her suffering. That was Grace's observation, and I think she was probably right. It was as if Eve's suffering, in whatever simple, primitive form it could be experienced by a monkey, *had to be* given a voice. Alone, in the stillness of whatever place we found her. A kind of prayer, an honest outpouring of her wants and needs.

I toyed with that idea one night in my head, the idea that Eve was praying. And thought, how many days, weeks, years would a monkey continue to pray before abandoning the effort? Because a monkey would have little ability to imagine intervention from a higher power, maybe its expectations would never be unsatisfied. Maybe a monkey's faith would never falter—the monkey, like a child, capable of effortless, honest belief in things that can't be seen, capable of giving voice to suffering without being conscious of the possibility that there is no one there to hear. What miracles could such a faith achieve? God only knows what power such a primal, blunt-edged faith could have.

Buck didn't forget about the idea of being baptized. He brought it up frequently at meal time, when we were all there, to get the benefits of Grace's unconditional support for the idea, along with my flexibility on implementation. He didn't back down on his strategy of getting our friend Barry to perform the baptism, rather than the wizened, humorless minister of the Baptist church that Grace attended. Finally, one night Grace relented, in a moment of weakness, and said, "Fine. Let's make an appointment with Barry. We'll talk to him. If he's willing to come to our church to perform the baptism, then….okay. Okay?"

Buck bounced up and down in his chair, which jiggled the table as his elbows made contact, which made milk slosh out of his cup. "Thanks, Mom. Thanks, Mom."

She handed him her napkin. "Stop jumping around."

He looked at each of us with innocent, childish optimism. "I've got a great idea. We'll get him to baptize Eve too."

We answered him in unison. "No."

"But that's what she wants. She wants to be baptized too."

Grace leaned in his direction and wagged her finger to punctuate her clearly articulated words. "Listen to me. No. Eve is a monkey. It is sacrilegious to even talk about—do you know what that word means? Sacrilegious?"

"No." Buck looked at me for guidance.

I said, "It means being disrespectful."

"Worse than that." The very idea of it made Grace angry. "Baptism is for believers. We do it to follow the example of our lord and savior, Jesus Christ. You know that. Eve does not have a soul—"

He looked at her with skepticism. "How do *you* know?"

Old churches have their own unique smell, comprised of musty old books, floor wax and the damp, rusty odor of air pushed from ancient air conditioning systems. Barry greeted us at the door of his office in his church. I don't think I'd ever seen his office before. It was part of a wing in the church which had been remodeled in anticipation of hiring Barry when he was a young, hip preacher, almost ten years earlier. It was nice, with built-in bookshelves across two walls and matching oak furniture. There were seascapes on the wall—one with Jesus and his disciples returning to land and the rest with images of the Gulf of Mexico near Padre Island, where Barry had been born. He knew why we were there, but to get Buck talking, Barry leaned down, held out his hand to Buck, and said, "What's going on, big guy?"

Buck took Barry's hand with hesitation, then shook it twice and said, "We just wanted to talk with you about...some stuff."

"Well, come on in."

Buck looked around the room. His gaze stopped on what appeared to be an aging on/off switch, the type that is usually found, along with twenty or so similar switches, in a fuse box. It was on the wall behind Barry's desk. There was a small, empty gilded wooden frame that hung on the wall over it, crudely framing the switch, as if it were modern art. I assumed the frame was a joke of sorts—Barry's or by somebody on the church staff.

Buck said, "What's that do?"

"Excellent question." Barry looked at me. "It's an old circuit breaker...obviously. It's been in that spot, probably, since the church was built, but nobody knows anymore what it does. The building committee doesn't want to take it out, because it may actually do something important."

"Cool." Buck nodded admiringly. "Can I flip it?"

"Nope. It *might* do something we wouldn't like."

Barry had a marvelous, dry sense of humor. Even after knowing him for twenty years, I couldn't always tell when he was kidding. So I played the straight guy. "Really?"

He nodded. "Really. My first day here, they told me to leave it alone. And I have."

That made me want ask if I could flip the switch too, but I decided to be a good example for Buck and keep my mouth shut.

Barry gave Grace a gentle pat on the back. "Why don't we all sit down?"

The sitting area in Barry's office had a small tweed couch, a small matching chair and, next to a lamp table stacked high with books, an oversized soft leather high-backed chair. It looked comfortable. That chair was where Barry probably intended to sit—probably where he always sat when he was reading and preparing for his sermons—but Buck hurried and sat there first, as if competing at a game of musical chairs. Grace said, "Buck, get up. Let him have his chair."

Barry held his hand up to stop the discussion and said, "No, it's fine." He sat down in the small chair, leaving the couch for me and Grace, but then immediately jumped up, which startled all of us. He took a step toward his desk, picked up a book with a gaudy-colored dust jacket, and handed it to me. "Elaine said to give this to you. She said to tell you that she thought she'd given it away, but she hadn't. So…here you go."

I took it. It was the book she'd mentioned at lunch, <u>Reflections from the Multiverse</u>. I held it in my lap, but turned it over, so that its bold pink, purple and green lettering and graphics wouldn't distract me. There was a picture of the author on the back, a fat guy with a white hair and a goatee.

Grace was curious. "What's that?"

"A really bad book that Elaine told me I should read."

She frowned at me, thinking that I was making fun of Elaine in front of her husband.

But Barry wasn't interested in talking further about Elaine or the book. He turned to Buck and said, "So…I hear there are some important things we need to talk about."

Grace and I turned toward Buck too and signaled for him to respond. We had been coaching Buck a bit as to what he should say, but he ignored or forgot our advice about giving Barry relevant background information on his church-going history. Instead, Buck simply said, "I need to get baptized, but I want to be dunked, not sprinkled."

"Okay." Barry nodded and leaned back in his chair. "Tell me more. Why do you—let me start over—why does *anybody* want to get baptized?"

"It's like having an itch that you need to scratch."

It was an interesting answer, but not at all what we'd coached Buck to say. No one said anything for minute, and then Barry said, "Help me understand that."

Buck shrugged and said, "Every time you go to church they talk and they sing about being lost and about getting found, until I'm like, 'Hey, I get it, all right?' Like…who doesn't want that? It gets in your head. And once it's there, you just *want* it. I saw a commercial on TV where a guy with his arms straight out like Jesus falls backwards into a lake or something and comes up smiling and relaxed. And I think, 'I want that.'"

Barry nodded. "In the Presbyterian tradition, we often think about it a little differently."

"Yeah?" Buck slumped in his chair, waiting for the boring monologue that he assumed would be coming next.

But instead, Barry loosened his tie a little, leaned forward and asked, "But I'm interested in what *you* think. Tell me a little bit more about being lost. Is that something that worries you?"

"Well, yeah! When I finally got what they were talking about—what it really means—I was like, 'Whoa, I don't want to be lost.'" Buck looked at me as if I would understand perfectly the significance of what he was saying and repeated with more urgency: "I don't want to be lost, if I were to…die…now."

Barry's voice resonated with warmth, but I detected a hint of anger, "You're a child of God, Buck. You don't have to worry about being lost. God loves you. He isn't going to abandon you. Who's telling you these things?"

Grace interrupted. "There's a moment when a young person reaches the age of accountability and at that point in his spiritual life, he needs to make a personal decision to follow Jesus, and if he doesn't, he *is* lost."

Barry grimaced. "I disagree." He paused, searching for diplomatic words. "I think that some denominations get way too hung up on the idea of condemnation."

Grace said, defensively, "That's what the Bible tells us."

Barry shook his head. "The Bible tells us about love. Love."

Buck slid forward, so that he was sitting on the edge of the chair. His feet barely touched the floor. "I'm talking about *really* being lost. Like in time travel TV shows where people just flat disappear—you know, how the air gets all blurry around them, they get this stupid look on their face, and then they disappear? I've been having these dreams—or something—and it was like one second I was right there with a Dr. Pepper in my hand, and then all of a sudden I'm out of there. Gone. Like somebody flipped a switch and the lights go off and the sound stops. I'm just gone." Buck's eyes drifted toward the circuit breaker above Barry's desk. "Like God accidentally hit his elbow on some kind of *off* switch."

Chapter 16

The small law firm where I had been interviewing made me an offer, not an offer to join the firm as a full partner, but a reasonable, even generous offer, under the circumstances. They proposed an arrangement where I would handle a caseload of between twenty and thirty lawsuits—some of which would be important, high dollar cases and some of which would be "dogs." They offered a salary that matched exactly what I had been paid by the university, with a potentially lucrative bonus formula that was based on the amount of legal fees collected from the cases I handled. They said that they would consider me for partner after two years and saw no reason why I wouldn't make it.

When I told Grace about the job offer, I already knew that I was planning to turn it down. Picturing myself as a relatively highly paid state court trial lawyer gave me the strange sensation of being an imposter, a bad actor struggling to find the motivation for his role. I could envision the essence of what I am withering away. It was a more compelling explanation when it was repeating itself non-stop in my head than it was when I tried to articulate it for Grace. We were both sitting on the edge of the bed, getting ready for the day.

Her first words were, "You didn't used to be like this," which was probably true, but to my way of thinking, not an altogether bad thing.

I said, "You didn't either. You used to be happy...most of the time–a reasonable amount of the time."

"Reasonable? You want me to be reasonable in how I feel—after what we've gone through? And just put on my happy face? I can't do it. I'm in pain and I feel it all the time."

It sounded as if she was accusing me of being a Pollyanna. "You think I don't feel anything, that I don't miss Thomas too?" She didn't answer. "But I'm dealing with it. For Buck's sake. For our sake too, you know?"

She nodded. "You're right. And Buck is lucky to have you. I watch you and I see how you've managed to carry on after...everything. And there's a part of me that respects you for it. And there's a part of me that despises you for it."

I obviously looked startled.

She smiled sadly. "It's the truth. Sort of." The muscles in her face tightened. She was fighting back tears. "So...."

"Yeah." I had the familiar wish that I was a thousand miles away. But unexpectedly, a more vital wish intruded, the wish that Grace could somehow become the woman I'd seen and touched in my déjà vu dream, a woman who had an open, uncomplicated love for me and who brought out in me out similar reciprocal feelings. Maybe if our lives had unfolded differently, if Thomas had lived—or had never been born–that's how things would be.

Grace put her arm around me and leaned her head on my shoulder. She said, "I'm sorry I make you so unhappy."

This was my reality, this very sad place and time. And I was at a loss for words. I reached over and patted her leg and then squeezed it lightly.

She said, "I don't want you to take a job that makes you miserable. But we've got to live. Pay for things."

"I've been thinking about selling real estate. I would be pretty good at it, I think."

She spoke slowly now, carefully choosing her words. "Is that something you'd enjoy?"

"I'm not sure."

"What is it that you want to be?"

It was interesting that Grace chose the word "be." What do you want to *be?* Rather than asking me what I wanted to *do.*

"A philosopher."

"What?"

"Or a quantum physicist."

"Be serious."

"Or a philosopher-physicist."

"Stop." She closed her eyes and turned her face away.

Haven't you ever wanted to be one of the interesting characters in a novel you're reading? I think we all have. I'd read the first chapter of the novel that Elaine had asked Barry to give me, <u>Reflections from the Multiverse</u>—and skimmed the next fifty pages. Its protagonist was a philosopher-quantum physicist—hence my sudden interest in that field as a possible new calling. The book was, as Elaine had said, a pretty silly novel, but it had caught my interest. It was about parallel dimensions. And God. The author's style of writing was jarring and manic, as though everything said was confusing, but completely real to him. That's what you expect from good writing, I suppose, but this was more than just a normal author speaking through a fictional narrator. You could tell.

Grace stood up. "Let me know when you're ready to have a serious conversation."

I was being serious, but I wasn't being practical, and I knew it. "Do you think I should take the job with the law firm? I haven't told them no yet."

She shrugged. "Don't do it for me."

Chapter 17

Circa 76 C.E.

The Master asked Cephas, John and James to come with him for a walk. He led them up the side of a mountain, past a lush vineyard, to a barren spot near the peak. Clouds were forming along the horizon, softening the harsh glare of the afternoon sun. The Master said, "Pray with me."

Cephas knew more than a few ritual prayers, some that were only used in ceremonies on holy days and some that were appropriate for daily use. The words that the Master used in prayer were of neither kind. Cephas was not confident in his understanding of such things, and so he sat somewhat away from the others and watched the Master praying and listened to the Master's quiet words. John and James reclined beside the Master with their eyes closed, praying too or dozing. The three of them were in the dappled shade of a small, crooked tree that grew out of the rocks. The breeze made its leaves flutter and caused the shadows that fell on them to deepen and then dissipate, caused the sunlight on the Master's countenance to fade and then to glow brightly. There was a simple beauty in such things.

Broken clouds began to form over them. The smell of rain blended with the smell of dust. Cephas saw that, despite the thickening clouds overhead, the light that fell on the Master grew brighter. The curious appearance of his homespun, dingy robe shining brightly out of the deepening shadows was like the glow of lightning within dark storm clouds. It was fitting. Cephas closed his eyes to pray.

His prayers were interrupted by the sound of quiet voices. When he opened his eyes, he saw two men, standing and talking with the Master. These were not ordinary men. They had flowing white hair and were dressed in brilliant white garb, trimmed in rare colors—such fine clothing as archangels would wear. They were talking to the Master about things that were yet to come, such as his departure in the coming days. In the company of these splendid messengers, the Master was transformed.

Chapter 18

The cover of <u>Reflections from the Multiverse</u> had the kind of pseudo-computer typeface that used to be synonymous with futuristic themes, blocked letters with blunt, thick horizontal lines. The cover had ambiguous silver faces, like reverse images in a black and white photograph, against a background of garish colors cut into angular shapes. The author's name was Dr. Anthony Brock. There was a detailed bio on the final page of the book. He had been a physics professor at several well-known universities over a short span of time—indicating to me, as a former university lawyer, a problem staying on tenure track--where, according to the bio, he was "engaged in research on the cutting edge of atomic particle theory". The back cover included an internet address for his institute, but the web site was under construction and had little content other than excerpts from the book and a street address in Galveston.

I tried several mornings in a row after Buck left for school to sit down and read the book. It was not easy reading. I found myself flipping pages, skimming passages at random, many of which presumed a preexisting knowledge of quantum physics that I didn't have. The fictional narrator, Hubert Ingersol, was a middle-aged physicist who, in his youth, had met the dying philosopher William James and had been entrusted with James' most precious, unpublished journals—journals which described, in the worshipful words of a theologian, parallel, co-existing universes: the so-called Multiverse. Of course, William James is a *genuine* historical figure, famous for his writings on the varieties of religious experience. I think he really did come up with the idea of a Multiverse, but in reality, he didn't leave behind any illuminating writings on the topic. There were no journals. A lot of novelists these days are shoe-horning famous people into farfetched fictional plots. Sometimes they're fun to read.

Reflections from the Multiverse was a fictional account of Ingersol's research into the behavior of subatomic particles and—enlightened by William James' journals—Ingersoll's discovery of parallel dimensions. The premise was quite interesting to me, as Elaine had thought it would be, but as literature, the writing was ham-fisted and melodramatic. The characters had painfully long dialogues in which they became passionate about controversial measurement anomalies. They shouted a lot and frequently had to wipe tears from the eyepieces of their scientific instruments. It was a really bad book—bad, but not stupid. As I flipped pages, I found many sentences that were intriguing, even taken out of context. In one short chapter near the end of the book, I was drawn in but thoroughly confused by ruminations of the fictional Hubert Ingersol on the possibility that the truly random and mathematically unpredictable behavior of electrons is proof that *parallel dimensions exist in which the entire course of history deviates slightly from our reality in seemingly random ways.*

Enigmas are best contemplated after dark. I don't know why that is, exactly. Something about the solitude of nighttime fills me with the sensation that a coy awareness lurks in the infinite black depths overhead, whispering...something really useful.

One evening, a couple of weeks after I'd brought the book home, I told Grace that I was going to read for a while before coming to bed, and I took Brock's book and a double espresso with me into a small room upstairs that I'd converted into an office. A plush wingback chair and matching ottoman that used to be in our den were now in the corner of the room, sandwiched between tall bookshelves.

Espresso helps me focus. I needed focus, because I wanted to read and understand enough of the book to decide if the ideas behind it were bullshit. I reread the first chapters of the book along with a number of long passages that I'd marked and then I skipped to the end of the book and read the last few chapters carefully.

When I was finished, I set the book down and tried to put my jumble of ideas into simple words.

What if experiences of déjà vu—the kind that Buck and I had—fleeting memories of alternative realities—were a kind of glimpse into nearby branches of the Multiverse? That was the idea behind the book: intersecting alternative universes. How would that work? How *could* that work? Did William James really believe in such a thing? Did Anthony Brock, the highly educated physicist author? Did it matter if they did or didn't believe? And most importantly, what would it mean if it were true?

It gave me a glimpse of something…that might explain everything, and so I decided to drive to the Galveston address that was in Brock's web site, to meet him, to hear what he had to say about the scientific theories underlying his book. I wanted to understand. If it had been a longer drive, I would have left right then, but Galveston was only an hour away. It would have done me no good to arrive at Brock's house at two o'clock in the morning. So I took my clothes off, quietly slipped into my bedroom and into bed, intending to sleep for a few hours before getting up and heading out to Galveston.

I was taking action, and that made me feel good. I pulled the covers up under my armpits and lay in bed waiting for sleep to come. I thought that I was being courteously quiet, but Grace turned in my direction, sighed and said, "How many times are you going to say, 'Hmmmm'?"

"I wasn't saying anything. I was being quiet so I wouldn't wake you up."

"No. You were going, 'Hmmm,' like you'd just finished Thanksgiving dinner."

"I don't think so."

"Yes."

I thought about it and couldn't confirm or deny her allegation. "Are you awake?"

There was a stunned silence and then she said, "Guess."

The room was completely dark. I couldn't see her, but I could hear her breathing and feel the tremors in the mattress when she moved around. I said, "I'm going to Galveston tomorrow. Early. Would you feed Eve when you wake up? And Buck. Buck too. And take him to school."

"Why are you doing this?"

"Going to Galveston?"

"Punishing me."

I reached over to put my arm around her. She batted my hand away. She said, "It's two o'clock."

"No, it's not."

"Yes, it is,"

"I'm going to Galveston tomorrow."

"You already said that. Why are you so happy? Do you have a girlfriend there?"

"No." I thought about it. "Maybe the gentle buzz from the espresso I drank hasn't worn off yet."

"You drank espresso at bedtime?"

It was more of a criticism than a question, so I didn't answer right away. My mind was drifting to other topics—such as the route I would take to Galveston when I got up. And what I would say when I met Brock. Then I realized I hadn't actually answered her question, which under normal circumstances irritates Grace, so I said, "Yes."

In a faint voice, she said, "Yes? Yes, what?"

This, too, was more of a criticism than a true question, so I didn't feel compelled to answer. I heard our bird clock chiming in the den. It *was* indeed two o'clock, because the doves were cooing. If it had been one o'clock, the whippoorwills would have been going, "Whippoorwill." Or whatever. I was feeling hyper, but was lying completely still so I wouldn't keep Grace awake any longer.

Grace said, "Are you dead?"

"Why?"

"It's like you're holding your breath. I can't even hear you breathing."

"Have you ever heard of Anthony Brock?"

"Do we still keep a baseball bat under the bed?"

The address in Anthony Brock's web site was of a house on the far west side of Galveston Island. To get there, I drove past several long expanses of muddy beaches, past campsites with small tents and parked cars clustered around picnic tables and large metal trash barrels. It was a little after eight o'clock in the morning as I drove past. A few people were cooking breakfast over small fires—some of them looked like college students, others were probably vagrants.

The house had been built in the forties, with yellow wood siding. It had a trellis on one side of the front porch with thick vines covered in white tropical flowers. A thin, old woman with short white hair was sitting on the front steps, smoking a cigarette. She noticed me slowing down in front of the house, reading the number on the mailbox at the curb, and she lifted her hand and pointed her index finger at me—an ambiguous, not particularly friendly gesture that could have meant a variety of things.

I parked my car and locked it and walked up to the steps where she was sitting. I had my copy of <u>Reflections from the Multiverse</u> in a canvass satchel that Grace had given me for father's day. I said hello.

The woman looked at me and said, "You one of them?"

"One of who?" I looked past her, in the direction of the screen door. I could see lights on inside the house. I thought I could also hear footsteps inside the house, the sound of someone heavy walking across a creaking wooden floor.

"One of *them*." She twisted her lips to one side and blew out a thin stream of smoke. "From the hospital."

I thought it better to ignore her question. "Is this where Anthony Brock lives?"

"Could be."

"I've been reading his book." I pulled my copy of his book out of my satchel for her to see.

"Oh…so you read his book?"

"Well, I'm in the process."

"In the process?"

"Yeah."

"Well, I'm in the process of trying to smoke a goddamned cigarette in peace. Or was."

I noticed the silhouette inside the screen door of a very short, round man, someone who was maybe five feet tall and nearly as wide. I pointed toward the doorway and said, "Is that…?"

She swiveled around on the top step, sighed and said, "Yep. That's him all right." With a quick glance back at me, she called out, "Son, you have a fan out here. Or so he says."

"Hello?" He had a high pitched, melodic voice. I could imagine him being the guy who sings tenor in a gospel quartet.

I went up the steps and stood on the porch. "Hi, I'm Jim Drewry."

The woman said, "Is he one of them?"

He opened the screen door and came out to shake my hand, smiling broadly. He had a boyish air about him, but prematurely gray hair. His hair was short and disheveled—nearly white in color—and he had a matching white mustache and goatee.

I said, "A friend gave me your book and I wanted to come meet you and talk to you. Is it too early?"

"No, not at all." He held the door open for me and gave me a friendly pat on the back as I came in their house. "Come on in. I'll make some fresh coffee. Want some?"

"Yes, thanks."

He led me into the kitchen. He was barefooted, but wearing pressed and creased blue jeans and a Rice University tee-shirt that was stretched tightly over his bulging stomach. He talked as he ground coffee beans. "How did you find out where I live?"

"It was on your web site."

"Of course." He carefully measured water in a large, clear measuring cup, holding it up to the light to sight along the red measurement lines on its side. "That makes sense." He poured water into an odd-looking coffee maker.

I looked around the kitchen. There was a computer on the table, which was connected to a printer on a chair. A built-in china cabinet in one corner was filled with physics texts and other thick books with titles that were in typefaces too small to read from where I stood. The bottom shelf had nothing but ten or twelve copies of Brock's novel. There were three identical large, unopened boxes stacked beside the refrigerator. My guess was that they held scores of copies of his novel.

"I use this as my office. It's not as if Mother ever uses it for cooking." He poured two cups of coffee. He waited for me to sit down and then sat down on the opposite side of the table, facing me. He smiled and said, "So...."

Good manners required that I say something positive about his book. "I'm glad I discovered your novel. It's very interesting—"

"How did you hear about it?"

"A friend of mine had been reading it. She thought I'd—"

"I wonder how she heard about it. Do you know? Sorry for all the questions. I'm trying to figure this out—the marketing part. I can't get newspapers to review it. Philistines! I can't get bloggers to say anything 'nice' about it. I can't get chain bookstores to let me do readings. Fucking philistines. Whose turf are *they* protecting?"

"Right." He was talking too fast, making it hard for me to follow.

He smiled. He had remarkably blue eyes that glittered unnaturally as if there was a fire raging inside of them. "So...how'd you hear about my book?"

I was confused, since I'd just answered that question. I shifted the subject of the conversation. "Some of the science in your novel is hard for me to understand, like—."

"Really?"

"Yeah." I opened my copy of his novel to a page I'd marked in the third chapter. I'd marked the passage with a yellow peel-off tab. "Right here. I can't follow what the connection is between sub-atomic particles and the idea of other parallel dimensions."

"Oh...well, that's explained in Chapter 8. Here, let me show you." He flipped ahead in the book. "In the fifties, when physicists first developed tools to measure the behavior of electrons, they made a startling discovery. Mathematical formulas could only give *a good guess* as to the location of electrons. Up until then, every known aspect of our universe seemed to function with mathematical precision. But here, at the sub-atomic level, it was discovered that electrons don't behave according to any consistent mathematical principals. An electron's actual 'location' is always different—each and every time a measurement is made. Just a measurement anomaly anomaly, right?" He looked at me with anticipation. "An anomaly anomaly...anomaly?"

He began to laugh, with such enthusiasm that tears came to his eyes. After a few seconds, he looked at me and said, "Sorry. Nerd humor alert!" Then he began laughing again, quietly, to himself.

He was making me uncomfortable, but I didn't want to leave until I'd asked all my questions, so I chuckled along with him and waited.

His mother called out from the front of the house, "Y'all sure are having a good ole time in there." She'd come inside, probably curious as to who I was and what we were talking about.

He stopped laughing abruptly and said, "Mother? Please."

She didn't answer. He rolled his eyes and continued with his explanation. "At least one very prominent physicist at the time—and people like me—believe that for every seemingly random location that an electron inhabits, a totally separate dimension exists—a fucking *parallel* dimension. That occupies the same space and 'time.' Time is just another dimension, right? You knew that, right? Right?"

I nodded.

"Of course. But somehow, as we attempt to measure the behavior of sub-atomic particles, we're able to see and measure atoms in *all of the dimensions* that occupy our 'space' but every measurement reflects different electron locations, because these electrons are affixed to atoms from different parallel dimensions—each dimension slightly different somehow."

I was barely keeping up. I asked, "Different, how?"

"It's an anomaly anomaly. Sorry, that's just fun to say out loud." He smiled as if posing for a camera. "Way different. And that's the amazing thing about William James. He came up with the idea of the Multiverse, came up with the name. He was a philosopher doing his thing around 1900. And in his gut he knows something that the scientists didn't figure out for half a century. How'd you like the part where he gives the big lecture?"

I wasn't sure what he was talking about.

He didn't give me much time to answer. "In the book. Where he talks about justice existing only if you consider the Multiverse *as a whole?*"

"I don't think I've gotten to that part." I decided to give up with the pretense that I'd read the whole book. "I haven't finished. I'm having too much trouble understanding it."

My admission didn't faze him. In fact, he didn't act as if he'd heard me say anything. He continued, "...which is a pretty damn amazing concept to get your head around. Think of it like this: if a hundred ton slab of rock buried out in the Gulf is a half an ounce lighter in other parallel dimensions, who cares? And what if that made the water level in the whole Gulf of Mexico a micron lower, who the fuck would care? Right? What if my DNA has markers for tendonitis in this dimension but not in other dimensions? What if the water in our coffee had a trace more calcium than in some other dimensions? But maybe less sodium chloride? There are billions upon billions—trillions upon trillions of minute differences in the sub-atomic particles in the world around us—if you were going around comparing one dimension to another—and most of them would be undetectable, except by scientists. Does it matter? Fuck, yes, and it's all in my book—right there in my book! And that's why all the guardians of truth in the scientific high church are getting so pissed off. Fucking Philistines."

Every time he said the word Philistines, he shuddered as if he had a chill. His words made sense, but his energy level seemed out of place, like a politician yelling out a campaign speech to an audience of five. He seemed to be waiting for me to say something, so I said, "Keep going."

He smiled and then he continued. "So...in the Multiverse, history is different in every dimension—maybe just a little different, maybe more than a little. But *different*. That was William James' big fucking revelation. Why, you ask?"

From the other room his mother yelled, "Do you have to use that kind of gutter language all the time?"

He stood up and walked over to the doorway. "Mother, don't you need another cigarette?" He sat back down and spoke in a loud voice. "I've been thinking about getting my own place."

"Wouldn't that be nice? Wouldn't that be really nice." Her voice trailed off. The screen door slammed. She'd gone back outside.

He said, "You can see why my friends don't come over any more."

I shrugged.

"But I've got a fan club from the hospital—they haven't forgotten me."

He smiled cheerfully, maintaining eye contact with me for so long that it was awkward for me, making it seem as if he were waiting for me to say something. So I said, "Did you have surgery—or some kind of...procedure?"

"No. I just went in for the deluxe spa treatment package." He tilted his head back, let his face go slack, and shook his body as if he were being shocked—then stopped suddenly. "Just kidding. It was only play therapy. Nothing but play therapy."

He waited for me to respond. I had no idea what to say. Was he telling me that he'd had electroshock therapy? Or just making a joke about it? I wasn't sure.

He picked up the book, flipped to another spot and began jabbing at the words on the page with his finger. "So here's the thing: with all of these countless sub-atomic, undetectable differences in the physical world that have been occurring since the first moment of existence, the human experience in every dimension is going to have a different outcome. As a mathematical certainty. Not as a result of 'uncontrollable forces of nature.' Not as a result of human 'free will.' No...purely as result of chemistry at the molecular level and as a result of mathematics.

"If you trip on the rug when you walk out of this kitchen, is that a random accident? No. All occurrences in the physical world and every chemical reaction in every cell of every living creature since the beginning of time culminated in you tripping. When I asked you if you wanted coffee and you said yes, was that a 'choice'? No. All facts and circumstances since the beginning of time—and biochemical reactions stemming from your own unique DNA—resulted in brain activity at that instant that resulted in you saying the word, 'Yes.'"

I was out of my element. I didn't know all the language that scientists use. I didn't know much about the history of quantum physics. And I still wasn't following everything that Brock was saying. A part of me was intrigued by what he was saying. It resonated with me. But, at the same time, I had a growing sense that his thoughts and ideas were more than just unorthodox. They were either inspired—or they were insane. I said, "So…what is it that…makes all these tiny particles *do what they do*—makes them show up in more than one dimension…in random places?"

He looked around the room and over each shoulder, as though he thought there might be someone lurking there, who would be trying to listen in on our conversation. Then he lowered his voice and said, "You know what a random number generator is, don't you?"

I'd had my suspicions from the moment Anthony Brock first stepped up to greet me at his front door. Everything about him was just a little off-kilter—his awkward social skills, his childlike relationship with his mother, his paranoia—and then his incomprehensible comments about the hospital. But once he began talking to me in hushed tones about random number generators, I knew: he was crazy. There are more polite words and probably more accurate ones. Faulty brain chemistry. An unmedicated mental disability. His Theory of Everything which he reverently described for me, just before I left, postulated that the ultimate force that controls the behavior of subatomic particles—the smallest building blocks of matter that can possibly exist—is some kind of cosmic random number generator. The soul of the universe is a random number generator.

A random number generator is something that can spit out an infinite series of numbers in a completely random order—without any pattern whatsoever. Computers can be programmed to do that. In the physical world there are a few naturally occurring phenomenon like that. Pi, the numerical constant used to calculate the area of a circle, is a number that continues infinitely after the decimal point without pattern or repetition—and yet, the mathematical perfection of a circle is indisputable.

The soul of the universe is a random number generator—that was what Brock believed. The thing is: he might have been right, or he might have been *nearly* right, but he was crazy. I was there in desperate need of help in order to understand the waking dreams of alternate realities that my son Buck and I were having, and I had no patience for the rants of a crazy man—even a crazy genius. I had no ability to sift valuable nuggets of revealed truth from metaphysical garbage.

As I drove along the beach highway toward the bridge that led back to Houston, most of the tents and cars that had been there earlier were gone. In the distance I saw a tall column of fire shooting up out of one of the rusty, metal trash barrels that were set out along the beach near the picnic tables. The fire was more powerful than I would have expected from burning paper. It made me wonder whether someone had poured kerosene in the barrel, maybe the remnant from a five gallon can brought by campers to help start a bonfire with damp wood. I'd done the same thing at YMCA campouts. I slowed down and pulled off the road as I came near to the fire. The flame was bright orange and shot up, ten or fifteen feet into the air. Nothing appeared to be in danger. There were no cars around and no other structures. Several large Coors beer boxes—presumably empty now—were at the base of the trash barrel, turning gray from the heat and the ashes.

I looked down at Brock's book in the seat next to me. I didn't want it, couldn't stand to have it anywhere near me. It was now painful evidence of the futility of my efforts to gain understanding. Without thinking, I began to pray out loud—in a voice that was so loud it cracked. "God," I began. And then almost all words left me, all words except a couple of words that were fitting for the circumstances, fitting for what was in my heart. "*Damn* it."

I heard whimpering and a scratching sound and looked beside me at Eve, in her blue plastic animal carrier, sitting on the front seat near me. My yelling was upsetting to her. And a frantic voice from my son in the back seat: "Can we go home now? We need to get home. I'm worried about Mom."

I said, "I know."

I knew. I understood. I was filled with understanding—a somewhat superficial, but genuine understanding. About the monkey and our connections, what bound us, what separated us. Evie's *humanity*...strange word to use in connection with a smelly, little monkey. I could see, but not with my eyes, as though I was both distant from her and also inside of her cells at the same time. The monkey and I had become connected. Somehow.

And without turning around, I perceived my son. Perceived everything about him. And a prayer of thanksgiving began to form spontaneously in my mind, celebrating the elegant complexity of his existence, celebrating the untapped power in our capacity to love. I smiled and turned around and no one was there.

I looked down where Eve had been, in her cage, and nothing was there, except the book, the goddamned, crazy book.

It had happened again. A brief moment in an alternate reality. Pointless, this time, except for its haunting beauty. I would forget it—I knew it—almost immediately. I looked for something to write on, write with. I grabbed the book and tore the front pages out and began to write furiously with the pencil that had marked my place in the book. I wrote about the voice of my son, what he'd said: "We need to get home." He'd meant more by the word than simply the place where we sleep. Home. I was certain of it, and then suddenly I wasn't certain any more. Couldn't remember.

I grabbed the book, threw open the door to my car and got out onto the damp flat sand. My pencil fell to the ground. I could feel the heat on my face from the towering fire. I took a few steps toward the fire and then a few more, and I threw the book, meaning for it to go into the barrel, into the raging fire. To destroy it. But I missed. The book hit the side of the barrel and fell onto the sand at its base, open, amid beer boxes, wisps of black smoke and floating ash.

I was eight or ten feet away from the barrel. I noticed for the first time that there was a man standing on the other side of it. He'd been hidden from me by the smoke and fire. He was warming what might have been a small donut or a bagel on a white coat hanger wire. Despite the heat from the fire and the relatively balmy Galveston temperature, he was wearing a fleece-lined jacket over a dirty red striped tee-shirt. The skin on his whiskered face glistened with sweat. He looked at me and said, "Whatcha got there, son?"

I ignored him. I got down on my knees and crawled toward the book. The wet sand soaked through the fabric at the knees of my pants and felt cool against my skin. The fire was not intolerable if I stayed low to the ground, but I felt heat on the top of my head and my neck. I imagined it singeing my hair and lifted my hand, coated with damp sand to protect it. With my other hand I reached out and grabbed the book, rose up a little and lobbed it into the flames. As I watched it fly over the rim of the barrel, the breeze from the ocean blew smoke into my eyes, stinging them. I backed up on all fours, with my eyes clamped shut, until my path was interrupted by someone's feet and legs, someone who was blocking my path. I opened my eyes and looked up, and it was the man in the fleece coat. He had long, white hair that hung down around his face.

He didn't look as if he meant me any harm, but I was startled. He seemed to be aware my of discomfort, but didn't act as if it was an unusual thing to see someone like me crawling across the sand in order to throw a book into a towering trash fire. I stood up and took a step back from him.

His face took on a look of quiet contemplation and he said in a voice that I could barely hear, "I was famous, once upon a time."

Chapter 19

I was less than fifteen minutes from home when I got a call from Buck. He was calling me from his school. He said, "Can you come get me. Mom forgot or something."

"Did you call her?"

"Yeah, she's not answering the phone."

"Cell phone too?"

"Both."

At Buck's school, kindergarteners get out of school at noon on Wednesdays and at three o'clock on other days. I knew that it was possible that Grace had forgotten it was Wednesday and that she was outside working in her flower garden or running errands in a place where her cell phone couldn't get reception.

I told Buck that I'd be there as quickly as I could. I said, "Is that okay? Are you the only one left there?"

"No, it's okay. Moms are always late picking up kids around here. Dr. Perkus said she's tired of parents being irresponsible and so she's going to start charging money to—"

Buck's voice stopped abruptly and there was a brief rustling noise before someone else's voice came on the line. "Jim? Dr. Perkus here. Listen, Buck heard me say some things I probably shouldn't have said. Anyway...I wasn't talking about you and Grace."

Dr. Perkus was the head of the school. She was a tall, attractive woman who wore glasses with a red frame and big, round lens. We hadn't talked very often before. I said, "I'll be there in about ten minutes."

"Don't worry about it. Don't worry." Her voice trailed off as if she was about to change the subject and talk about something else, but an awkward pause followed in which she didn't say anything. Then she said, obviously to Buck and others in the office with her, "Why don't y'all wait outside on the sidewalk with Ms. Donna? Okay?" After another pause in which the background noise diminished, she said, "Is everything okay?" Her words had the gravitas of official concern, in the way that a simple question can, when spoken in the aftermath of a crisis. I'd been through that and understood the code. But Thomas' death had been years earlier and I didn't think she was inquiring about that. My guess was that she was inquiring about my jobless situation, and I was about to say that I had good opportunities that I was considering, but before I could answer, she said, "With Grace? I've been worried about her all morning. She wasn't herself."

I sped up and began changing lanes, passing cars that were in my way. I said, "How's that?"

"I like to help with carpool in the mornings, when I can. And I was watching Grace and Buck this morning. Something about the way she hugged him before she let him out of the car just struck me as... different. And then when she saw me, she rolled down the window and thanked me for what I do at the school. It's just—I don't know, maybe I'm making something out of nothing. I know this is a personal question, but are the two of you separating?"

"No," I said.

Dr. Perkus continued. "Or is she going into some kind of...program? I know she's been having a hard time, ever since...."

"No." I accelerated so that I could get around the slow car in the right lane. The driver honked at me as I swerved back in front of him and then hit the breaks so that I wouldn't lose control on the exit ramp. I repeated, "No. Nothing like that."

"I'm sorry if I'm intruding into–"

"It's okay." My car bounced as I sped through the intersection next to the overpass.

"Okay then." Her voice was flat.

"I'll be there in a few more minutes. I'm on Kuykendall."

"No hurry." She waited to see if I was going to say anything else and when I didn't, she hung up.

I shouldn't have said anything negative to Grace about the trip she was planning to Rockport, the trip her father had agreed to pay for so that she could have some time alone. She'd decided not to go after I'd brought up the topic at bedtime one night. I hadn't asked her to cancel her plans, but she could tell that I didn't like the idea. I'd been negative about it, because I was worried about her, but I'd wound up making things worse. She'd stopped trying. I should have kept my mouth shut.

The last few blocks to the school were stalled with heavy traffic. There was nothing I could do but wait in line with the other cars. I called our home phone and it rang until the voicemail message came on the line. Then I called Grace's cell phone and the same thing happened. I kept pushing re-dial. Dr. Perkus' words had scared me. As I sat in traffic, my fear grew. It was early when I'd gotten out of bed that morning, but Grace was awake. She called me back over to her side of the bed and hugged me. The words Dr. Perkus had used were good ones to describe the way she'd hugged me too—it was different. She'd clung to me for a few extra seconds before letting me go and said, "I love you. You know that, don't you?" Since it was dark in our bedroom, she couldn't see me nod and asked again, "Don't you?"

I should have known what she was planning to do. I should never have left her alone.

Grace's car was in the driveway. I parked behind her and ran to the front door. I unlocked the door and went in and called her name. The house was quiet—except for the sound of Eve whimpering somewhere. Over my shoulder, I told Buck to wait downstairs. He started arguing with me and I yelled, "Do what I tell you. Wait right here." And I ran into the den and called her name. The drapes were open. I couldn't see her in the backyard. The house was quiet. Now I couldn't hear Eve either. All the downstairs lights were off. The kitchen was clean. A lavender envelope was on the table under the pepper shaker.

I ran to the stairs. Buck said, "What's wrong?" His eyes were filled with tears. "Where's Mom?"

I said, "Wait *here*." And I started up the stairs. My steps slowed as I neared the top. I didn't have the courage for what we were about to go through. Words for a helpless, pointless prayer came into my head, unbidden, and made me angry. The idea of what Grace might have done to herself—to us—made me angry. The fact that no one would answer me made me angry. My instinct was to kick the bedroom door open—and I might have, but Eve was in my way, there at the bedroom door, whimpering and turning in circles, and then sniffing at the door, as if there was a smell coming from behind the closed door that disturbed her.

I turned the doorknob. It wasn't locked. I opened the door. Grace was lying on her back on a fully made bed. Her arms were limp and unnatural, one across her stomach and the other outstretched, at an odd angle near a small book that was lying open. There was a faint, but foul odor in the room.

This fragile, small woman was the love of my life. She was gone. Forever.

The sound of running was behind me. Buck burst past me screaming, "Mom," and bounded onto the bed. As the bed bounced, Grace's head fell in our direction. Her mouth hung open, slack.

I felt Eve's hands on my pants, as she was climbing up my leg. If she was whimpering or crying now, I couldn't hear it. All I could hear was the sound of rushing wind or falling water. My vision became distorted, as if I was falling—but not a slow motion sensation. The sense of movement and sound accelerated and then suddenly stopped, and my vision became clear again, perfect.

Grace was sitting up in bed, with our two sons on each side of her. Buck had his head in her lap, and Thomas leaned against her, with his arm loosely around her shoulders. He looked frail. Most of his hair was gone. Grace looked over at me. "Did you get your book signed?"

"What?" I couldn't make sense of the contradictory images that were in my head.

"Did Anthony Brock autograph his book for you?"

"No." I remembered a reality in which Grace was dead—she was dead—I remembered it vividly. This had happened to me before, an instant before. I took a couple of quick steps over to my bedside table, opened the drawer and looked for the notebook I kept there. I began rummaging around, spilling things out of it.

"What's wrong, Dad?" It was Thomas' tired voice.

"Jim?" In that single word, Grace conveyed a complete thought: what the hell is wrong with you...this time. There was a tiredness in her voice too, but a different kind of tiredness.

I found a pencil, but the lead was broken. I threw it on the ground and rummaged around for another pen or pencil.

"What are you looking for?"

"I need a pen."

"Here." Grace leaned over Thomas to hand me her pen. He groaned, as her weight pressed against his side. "Sorry, Thomas." Her eyes were full of worry—not for me—for Thomas. Yet, it was clear that my behavior was upsetting her. "Are you okay?"

I didn't answer. I needed to jot down my random memories before they faded. That's what they always did. My journal had several episodes like this, where things changed. Everything changed. If I wrote things down, I could almost keep myself from forgetting. But I didn't have my journal. Brock's novel was under my arm. I opened it and began writing frantically on a nearly blank page inside the front cover.

Her hands gripped my back. Her short fingernails dug into the flesh under my shoulder blades. I was lost in the glorious sensations of climax, kissing her open mouth, pausing for one last slow thrust. We sighed together, in unison, practiced. I relaxed my body and rested it on hers, felt the softness of her breasts and stomach, damp from perspiration. She moved her hand to my side and I felt the slight, gentle touch of her fingertips, letting me know that my weight was becoming a bit uncomfortable. I rolled off of her and lay on my back beside her.

In that instant, dark, dreamlike thoughts intruded…again. Death—her death—I could see it. I could almost hear Buck crying her name.

Grace slipped her arm under my neck and, turning on her side to face me, draped her leg over mine. After a moment of silence, she said, "Is something wrong?"

I turned my head. Our lips touched and I took that as an opportunity to kiss her again. Then I said, "Nothing, really."

She rose up on her elbow and studied my face, aware of the equivocation in my answer. "Are you thinking about Thomas too?"

"We agreed we wouldn't talk about that."

"I know." After a few moments of silence she sat up in bed. She arched her back, stretching it like a cat. "We don't want to waste all our time in Santa Fe lying around."

"Waste? That was a waste?"

"You know what I mean."

I did know what she meant. It was rare for us to have a chance to get away for a romantic weekend, away from our boys and the animals. It had been my idea, but her dad had offered to pay for it, had said that it would be good for us to get away—just the two of us. We'd agreed to leave our worries behind us and not to spend our short time away talking about the immediate problems in our life: Thomas' doctor bills, Buck's behavioral problems at school, and—of course—my job situation, all stress-inducing topics that we would inevitably talk about if we were at home.

The last forty-eight hours had been wonderful. There's a different way you talk to your spouse when you're relaxed and happy, a different way you think about love.

I sat up in bed too.

Grace turned so that her legs hung off the bed and her back was to me. "Would you rub my back?"

I sat behind her, cross-legged, and kneaded the muscles in her shoulders with my thumbs. There was a pleasant scent of cedar in the room. I tried to force my mind to block out a bleak vignette of tragedy in our bedroom in Houston that had intruded into my consciousness—that horrible image of Grace's dead body—along with the gut-wrenching feelings of loss that accompanied it.

I lay my head on her shoulder and said, "I don't want to lose you."

She put her hand on the side of my face. "Why would you say that?"

I didn't answer. Didn't want her to know. The medicine wasn't working any more. I closed my eyes, felt warm tears welling up.

———

Grace stood beside me with her arms crossed, tight against her body. "We have an appointment this afternoon."

We were in our bedroom—all of us. The boys were in our bed, watching us. Frightened.

Eve was in my arms, twisting around, upset too. She pulled at the collar of my shirt, trying to get closer to my face, and accidentally scratched my neck with her fingernails. It hurt, and I lost my temper and yanked her hands away and flung her onto the floor.

"Dad." Buck was admonishing me for being mean to the monkey, but knew better than to say more.

Grace touched me tentatively and whispered—discreetly, so that neither Thomas nor Buck could hear. "I called the doctor this morning. Thomas isn't–"

"Okay." I didn't let her finish the sentence. Things weren't getting better. I knew it without her having to say it. He was going to die. Again. I knew it. Without knowing how, I could see it clearly. I could see inner things—not actually *see* with my eyes, but perceive things and they were unbalanced, jarring. Thomas was going to die. And *she* was going to die…again. Grace too. I knew that too. But I would forget. It always happened that way, or if I didn't forget, the image would fade and I would no longer believe in it.

I couldn't do it, couldn't face it all. I couldn't. The thick book in which I'd been trying to write my alternate memories fell from my hands, and then I fell to my knees, limp and tired to my soul. I wanted

God to take me and leave them behind, healthy. Or maybe just take me first...just take me. I couldn't do it.

The monkey began screeching. I wondered if I'd hurt her when I'd fallen down onto my knees there on the floor. I didn't think so. Eve lifted her face and opened her mouth wide and screeched, and she wouldn't stop. Her shrill squeals were punctuated by short gasps each time she took a breath. I tried to sooth her and then I shook her, but she only screeched louder, more frantically. Thomas began to cry, covering his face with his hands. Grace said, "Get her out of here."

Buck began to shout over all the noise: "Dad. Dad. Dad."

I covered Eve's mouth with my hand and stood up. She was wearing one of the little dresses Grace had bought for her, the candy-cane striped one, so it was harder to get a tight grip on her. She struggled and bit me, not hard—not nearly as hard as she could, but it drew blood. I gripped her in a head lock and held her close to my body so that she couldn't twist around and bite me again. I stood up and turned, and in the relative silence heard Buck call my name one more time.

And then the room was quiet, quiet as though no one were even there. I turned around and saw Grace and Thomas asleep on the bed, on top of the covers. His arm was under her neck. His long brown hair half-covered his eyes. I said to no one in particular, "That boy needs a haircut again." I looked down. Eve was in my arms looking up at me quietly. I said, "Sorry. Did I wake you up?"

Our bedroom had the faint smell of cedar, something Grace kept in her drawer.

Then the awareness came to me suddenly, explosively, like a car wreck that you don't see coming, the realization of what had happened. My other son Buck no longer existed.

Chapter 20

Grace came into my study and shut the door behind her. She had something serious on her mind.

I was working at my desk. The monkey was there too, sitting on the floor next to my desk chair.

I took the note card on which I'd been writing and tacked it to the wall in front of me. It was one of my light blue cards. I'd decided to use only blue cards for notes and observations that related to my research on what it would mean for there to be more than one dimension for time. It had been Grace's idea originally for me to buy note cards in multiple colors to help me organize my thoughts, but she denied that now. What modesty that woman had.

She looked at the books that were stacked on my desk, almost completely covering its surface, and at the two spiral notebooks that were open on my lap and said, "You need a bigger desk, Jim."

"Yep."

"Or a job."

"Yep."

"How's that coming?"

"I think I owe some people a call."

"Owe some people a call?" Her voice didn't hide the frustration she was feeling with me.

It wasn't really a question, and so I didn't answer her. I still had a job offer with the employment law boutique—which I didn't want to accept, for obvious reasons—total lack of interest being the main one—and a chance at the number two position in the legal department at Rice University. That sounded more interesting. Rice had received international acclaim for its research on quantum geometry. One of the string theory books I was trying to read now was written by someone on the faculty there. But I hadn't had the time yet to do more than talk on the phone with the recruiter from Rice. I'd been too busy with my own research.

She lifted her hand and opened it. My new pill bottle was in it. She said, "You didn't take your pill this morning or yesterday."

"How do you know? Are you counting them?"

"Yes. What am I supposed to do? What else *can* I do?"

I didn't want to fight with Grace. She'd been patient with my job search. She'd been supportive of the research I was doing…for the most part. I made a mental note to take a pill out of the bottle every morning and evening, whether I intended to swallow the thing or not. Then I thought, no, I'm not going to be dishonest about it. I'm not going to pretend. Then I thought, what time does the mail come? The new books I ordered should be here today. I said, "What were we talking about?" But I was just joking—a joke I appreciated more than Grace did, because I knew—and she didn't—that my good ideas and random insights were crowding each other more than ever now, creating a kind of chaos, but also a genuine environment for revelation. It was about time. "Would you like me to take one now?" I asked.

"Yes."

I held out my hand. "Give it to me. I've got enough coffee here to wash it down. No problem."

She opened the pill bottle, turned it sideways over her hand and tapped it a few times with the fingernail of her index finger. A little white, round pill came out. She handed it to me. "Isn't that coffee cold? It's from this morning, isn't it?"

"No problem." I swallowed the pill and washed it down with what was left in my coffee cup.

Eve opened her mouth as if she expected us to give her one too. Maybe she thought it was a snack. Standing up straight, she sniffed the rim of my coffee cup and then snorted, blowing little drops of snot on the back of my hand.

Grace stood for a few minutes looking at us. I thought she was going to ask me whether or not I intended to go wash my hands, but instead, she said, "I saw your essay in the newspaper. I didn't even know you had gotten something published until my brother called me. Were you even going to tell me?"

"Really? I didn't know it was coming out this week. Please tell me they put it in the science section." It was the first of several essays I had planned to write.

"I'll get it for you. I left it in the kitchen." She smiled. "It's…um… interesting." Then she left the room without looking back.

I could hear her walking down the hall and then down the stairs. When she's mad at somebody, her footsteps are louder.

Evie nudged my elbow until I made room for her to climb into my lap. She looked up at me—with genuine love, I think. We were becoming inseparable. Then she looked away and became very still, surveying the things around us without much interest. She was becoming more and more lethargic as the weeks passed. I was afraid that it was a symptom of her developing Parkinson's. But there wasn't anything I could do about that.

Grace came back, glanced at the two of us, and dropped an open newspaper on my desk, on top of my stacks of note cards. There it was—my essay—printed at the bottom of the second page of the Houston Chronicle weekly science section, next to an advertisement for discount furniture.

Random Numbers
And the Mind of God

Science and religion have long had a complicated relationship—to say the least. Everyone knows about how scientists in centuries past were persecuted, put on trial and even executed by lackeys of the church hierarchy, when those scientists' theories were seemingly at odds with church dogma. It's less known, but also true, that the church's vision of a perfect creation inspired and put early physicists on the right track as they sought to discover the mathematical relationships that govern the workings of the universe. Math isn't always simple, but even complex mathematical formulas embody an elegant perfection that provides explanations of things that are as close as we can get to absolute truth.

As our knowledge increases, multiple fields of science have now collapsed into applied mathematics. Physics is little more than applied mathematics. As science develops better and better tools to understand molecules, atoms and sub-atomic particles, it has become clear that the essence of chemistry is physics--which is, in turn, math. Similarly, modern developments in biology—the molecular study of living things and the decoding and analysis of strands of DNA—have shown that biology is fundamentally chemistry, which is...math. As we learn more about human behavior, we find that our gene pool plays a dominant role in our behavior and even in our decision-making process. What seems to be free will or even creative thought may be a series of determinations generated by a brain that is governed by the laws of chemistry and physics—and the manner in which we think may be more like the binary calculations of a computer than we would like to believe.

How far up the chain of sciences and social sciences can we go, before we find something that is not fundamentally reducible to mathematics? If it is true that human behavior, including the random and seemingly arbitrary decisions borne out of our free will, is nothing more than the product of chemistry and mathematics...then what else is true? Do our dreams and myths come from the same source? Do our spiritual revelations?

If we go full circle, back to the sub-atomic level, we find more objectively random behavior there than exists at the human level. Physicists are intrigued and perplexed by the discovery that the tiniest sub-atomic particles that can be measured *do behave* in a random manner. Their exact location and other characteristics can only be imprecisely predicted. There is no math that governs the behavior of these particles of matter.

What does that mean? Possibly, that we simply haven't come up with the right mathematical formulas yet. Another possibility is that at the sub-atomic level there are more than three spatial dimensions, which complicates things immensely. A final possibility is that the particles that form the building blocks of all matter not only *seem* to be in more than one place at any given time, they are *in fact* in more than one place. That possibility has inspired physicists to theorize about the existence of multiple simultaneous realities.

What if the role of God in our physical universe is to instigate this random and mysterious behavior of sub-atomic particles? What if the mathematics that govern sub-atomic particles, and by extension everything else in our mathematically perfect universe, includes this random element, sacred random numbers, as the missing factor that makes the mathematical formulas work? The random numbers have to come from somewhere. God? What if the mind of God is the source? What if the mind of God is a random number generator?

Praise God from whom all blessings flow. Amen.

Jim Drewry is a lawyer and writer residing in Houston, Texas. He has long been an advocate for artists and writers with bi-polar disorder.

I lifted the newspaper and skimmed the article. It was all there, just as I had written it. I looked up at Grace. "What do you think?"

"Honestly?"

"Yes."

"The article was…well written, I suppose. But it says things I don't believe, things that you didn't use to believe. Do you actually believe them now?"

"Yes, I do. I think."

"We used to have the same faith. Jim, I'm not sure we even believe in the same God anymore."

I didn't answer.

"Look at all this." She gestured at my notebooks and stacks of note cards. "If you did all this in your spare time, I'd say, 'Fine,' but this is all you do now. You're holed up in this room all day, every day."

"What am I supposed to do? Am I just supposed to pretend that Buck never existed?"

Grace raised her eyes to the ceiling. She took a deep breath and then continued. "Jim, I am so scared."

We'd had this conversation before—many times—and I couldn't make her understand. "What am I supposed to do? My son is *gone*. The son I raised for five years. Just gone. Maybe I can't bring him back, but I have to know…have to make sense of what it all means." There was an emptiness inside me that grew by the hour. I couldn't stand it. I didn't know how to combat it. In truth…*in truth*, my memory of Buck was fading, and that upset me as much as losing him in the first place. I remembered less and less about Buck now. There were things that his older brother Thomas did that made me remember, little things, certain gestures or facial expressions. And when I read the journal entries I'd made about Buck, I could feel again what it was like to have him with me. I could remember his grin and the way he would bounce up and down beside me, pulling on my shirt to get my attention, but I couldn't remember much else.

She picked her words carefully. Or maybe they were words that she had been rehearsing over and over again in her head—and so maybe they seemed old and tired words to her. She said, "You have a son. Thomas. What about him? What about me?"

"I know."

"This is an illness."

"No." I shook my head. "You don't understand."

"An illness that you cling to. As if you love your delusions more than you love us."

"That's not how it is." I thought about trying to tell her about the other person whom I'd lost. It was her. I'd seen an alternate reality in which we—Grace and I—were happy. That was lost to me, too.

"Jim, listen to me. We're headed for a train wreck." She looked at me to be sure I understood. She didn't want to explicitly threaten me with divorce, but I understood exactly what she was saying.

When you've been married for a long time, there are things about the idea of divorce that are not frightening at all—in fact, the idea of greater solitude and less daily conflict was appealing. But I would miss Grace. I knew that. And it was a certainty that I would be the loser in any custody dispute—I was mentally ill, right? And the knowledge that as a result, I would lose my other son Thomas too was something I could not bear. I would have nothing left. I said, "What do you want me to do?"

"Well," she said, "I've been talking to Elaine." It was no secret between us that Grace talked to Elaine a lot about my struggles with bi-polar disorder. "Elaine has an idea about something—it was actually something that you and Barry talked about in his office—something about you getting re-baptized. She thinks it might... *might* trigger some kind of new resolve, give you a sense of a fresh start. What do you think?" Elaine couldn't officially see me—or Grace—as a patient, because we're friends, but as a psychologist she often had ideas of things I should try, new drugs, new routines, and so on.

"Wasn't it her idea for me to read <u>Reflections from the Multiverse</u>?"

Grace rolled her eyes. I was just giving Grace a hard time. I knew that in her opinion, loaning me that book wasn't one of Elaine's best ideas. Grace considered the book to be rambling, incoherent non-sense. She'd said that to me more than once, but she didn't under-stand. And I needed her to understand.

I opened one of my desk drawers and pulled Brock's book out. I kept it locked up in my desk when I wasn't there in my study. I'd read it and reread it, line by incredible line, five or six times—maybe ten or twenty times—I don't know—and each time I found new insights, new revelations. I wanted Grace to understand. I said, "Let me read you something. I don't know why it took me so long to...catch what it was really saying."

She stared at the garish cover of <u>Reflections from the Multiverse</u> as I pulled it out of the drawer and then began to laugh. "Jim, it looks like a...porcupine now. I mean you've got a thousand little sticky tags on there. Look at that."

I'd started out by marking important passages so I could refer back to them easily. I used little yellow tags for that. Then I began marking all the passages that related to my ideas on additional spatial dimen-sions—those I marked with lime green stickers. I used pink stickers for good quotes, sentences that said what I thought, but used words better than what I could come up with. I don't remember what the red stickers were for originally. I used so many of them, I ran out. Blue stickers marked parts that explained how time in the Multiverse works.

I laughed too. I didn't see what was so funny, but I was glad for anything that improved the mood. I had an extra chair in the room that Thomas liked to sit in and read comic books—and sometimes listen to me talk about my research. I gestured toward the chair and Grace sat down in it. I rolled my desk chair over beside it. Eve hung onto my shirt to keep from toppling out of my lap. I'd forgotten she was there.

I opened the book and turned it so that Grace could read along with me. She pointed. "Jim, you've...." She let her finger glide down the page. Then she tentatively turned a page with the tip of her fingernail. And then another.

I'd been highlighting passages with different colored highlighting pens. I'd found so many layers of meaning in Brock's writing that most of the words on the pages were highlighted in one color or another. There were a few pages where I'd actually used a black marker to mark out words that were wrong somehow. If the words were just wrong, what else could I do but mark them out so that they couldn't confuse things? And I made notes in the margins. Some pages had lots of my comments, some not so many.

I laughed again, hoping to get her to laugh again too.

She looked into my eyes as if she were struggling to recognize me. I didn't look away. I love Grace. I had nothing to hide.

As I watched, her eyes filled with tears. Her blue eyes became indistinct beneath a film of tears. And then one tear—one—escaped and rolled slowly down the side of her nose and hung there, until I brushed it away with my fingertip. I said, "Grace?"

She shook her head from side to side slowly. She put her hand on my leg for a second and then patted it and said in a quiet voice, "It's okay, Jim. It's okay." Then she stood up, turned and walked out of my study.

I spent the rest of the afternoon in my study, reading and thinking. Around six o'clock I heard Grace and Thomas milling around downstairs, and then I heard the back door closing and the sound of a key locking a stubborn deadbolt. It was a Friday evening. Before I'd lost my job, it would have been typical for us to all be getting into the car at about that time for a trip to our favorite Mexican food restaurant.

From the window of my study, I could see her car backing out of our driveway and then going down the street. Grace was driving and Thomas was in the back seat. Maybe they were going to pick up a pizza. Maybe they were going to dinner without me. Maybe they were driving over to Grace's parents' house to eat—or maybe to spend the night. I didn't know. I didn't know what I would have done if our roles were reversed and somehow Grace couldn't...function.

I stared at the floor. The pill Grace had made me take earlier that afternoon was working its magic, and I felt both sleepy and a bit more focused—or maybe that was my imagination. Or a delusion. Maybe I was delusional about being less delusional.

I stared at the monkey.

Eve had gotten into the habit of loping around my study, as though she was looking for something. Periodically, she would stop and sigh— and sometimes lie down in the middle of the floor.

I knew what she was thinking.

This was Buck's room. I knew that the room had been my study for more than ten years—since before Thomas was born. I *knew* it. I could remember buying the desk and getting Grace's brother to help me carry it up the stairs. He'd hurt his back doing it. I remembered buying a tall bookshelf and then a second one that matched it a few years later, as my collection of books expanded. When Thomas was going through chemotherapy, I put a TV in there, and Thomas and I watched cartoons on the cable cartoon channel at night when he couldn't sleep. But there was a kind of translucence about my memories of the room, as though I could perceive vague images behind them, images of different furniture, different activities. I had a sensation of where Buck's bed had been and that his bedspread was brightly colored. I couldn't remember what color, exactly, but I remembered him rolling up in it, pretending to be a snake. Maybe the sensation of Buck's existence *was*, in all its subtlety, only a delusion. That's what Grace said. That's what my psychiatrist said.

I stared at the monkey.

I had begun to wonder if Eve was the thing that had given me awareness of the nearly unfathomable nature of the Multiverse. Somehow. I didn't know how. I remembered specific moments when reality changed around me, and *she was there*. She was there each time. I didn't remember *any* instances of changes happening when she wasn't there.

And I knew that *she knew*—as much as a monkey can have intellectual cognition of anything. She was just a monkey. But I could see in her eyes that she was aware.

Indulge me as I say something that makes absolutely no sense.

I know it to be true that a monkey—even a monkey whose DNA contains human chromosomes—cannot, alone or in combination with someone like me, transform genuine reality to an alternate reality. I know it, with as much conviction as a man can know anything.

But I *believe* something different.

Chapter 21

I had set myself on fire.

My thoughts were accelerating beyond the speed at which they could be safely contained. And the fire that was burning within me began to consume the things I touched…as bitter proof of what is more real than not.

I couldn't stop thinking about space and time—the dimensions which we so easily perceive and also the additional dimensions which seem beyond our perception.

I was exhausted from my efforts to understand Bock's magnificent epistle–and the books and articles that I'd been accumulating for my own research, but more than that, frustrated at the timidity of scientists who wrote them, at their hesitation to seek answers to the fundamental questions posed by their insights.

I was desperate to find useful information about the eleven dimensions that some physicists believe to exist—the three spatial dimensions that we readily perceive, plus time, plus seven more. *Seven more.* What I'd found in my research consisted of mostly lengthy, incomprehensible mathematical proofs–useless to me. What I needed were words, words that described the nature of those extra seven dimensions, and in particular, I wanted to find something that explained what it would mean for there to be more than one dimension of time. I had some ideas, but who am I?

Brock's book repeatedly explained the Multiverse with references to other dimensions, but it didn't explain how that could be true. Sometimes the characters in his book who were scientists bantered about the difficulty—actually the impossibility—of visualizing extra spatial dimensions and almost taunted the reader with fleeting references to extra dimensions of time. One of the extra dimensions of time is—according to Brock's characters—infinitesimally small and circular—I can't figure out yet how to picture the way in which we would experience it—if, indeed, we would experience it at all. Another of the extra dimensions of time could be crudely described as being perpendicular in its point of departure from the "linear time" that we so easily perceive—those are my words, not Brock's. So, maybe time is more like a flat plane than a straight line. That could explain a lot, or it could explain nothing.

I was trying as hard as I could, but I didn't have any illusions. I wasn't going to be able, through my own efforts, to advance the level of knowledge and understanding in the field of quantum physics. I just wanted to know whatever there was to know. But no matter what I learned or what was revealed to me, I wouldn't be able to change a thing. I knew that. I couldn't build a device or create some kind of vortex of forces that would allow me to change my circumstances—and find Buck—I knew that. I just wanted to understand. And I didn't—not yet.

I noticed that Grace rarely left me alone now with Thomas. I asked her about that, asked if she thought I'd become dangerous somehow. It was an afternoon when she was planning to take him along with her as she ran errands, rather than leaving him home with me. He was sitting in her car as we spoke. We stood in the yard with our backs to him, speaking in low voices, so he wouldn't hear.

She said, "No, Jim. Not dangerous."

"What, then?"

"The things you say are confusing him—the way you're always talking about other dimensions and about having...another son."

"His name is Buck." She wouldn't make eye contact with me, so I said it a little louder. "Buck."

She didn't respond.

I asked, "Did he say that—that I'm confusing him?"

"No. He says it's like being in a comic book—whatever that means."

I said, "Please, Grace. Please don't do this. Don't take Thomas away from me. What am I going to have left?"

She gripped her forehead in the palms of her hands as if she had a raging headache. She glanced at me, but still refused to make eye contact with me. "Okay. Jim, I'm trusting you."

She walked quickly to her car, opened the door and said, "Thomas, why don't you stay here. You've got homework, right? Do that. Okay?"

I could see his mouth moving, but couldn't hear his voice, since he was in the car.

She said, "Tell your dad."

Thomas got out of the car. He said, "Hey, Dad," as he passed me on the sidewalk.

Grace turned to me and called out, "He needs some help with his science project. It's due on Friday." Then she got into her car, started the engine and backed it out of the driveway. I caught up with Thomas at the front door. He was waiting for me, bent over, under a backpack that contained twenty pounds of school books. I flung the door open, and he dropped his load on the floor en route to the kitchen. Eve was waiting for us, inside the front door. She jumped, wanting him to catch and carry her, but he batted her down, as if she were an unruly dog. He said, "Get away from me. Go climb on Dad."

Eve sighed loudly and then shuffled away, into the den. I heard her dump out her basket of toys and books.

Thomas didn't like the monkey very much. He said that she was always bothering him and getting into his stuff when he was gone, and he was tired of it. He said, "I mean…who has a monkey for a pet?"

I understood and tried to reassure him that she wouldn't be living with us forever.

Bonnie had stayed in touch—had actually called several times in the last few months—asking about Eve and reminding me that she was going to help me find a suitable home for her. In her most recent call, Bonnie had said, with excitement, that she had worked things out with St. Anthony's University, a small university in San Marcos, Texas. Bonnie had been accepted into the doctoral program there and gotten a financial aid package that included a paid position in the sociology lab, a lab that housed middle-aged monkeys used in research on aging.

It sounded promising, but I wanted more concrete information than Bonnie could give me. I wanted to know what size cage Eve would have and whether she would ever get to spend any time outside. I asked questions about the level of interaction that she would have with humans and other monkeys—including male monkeys with whom she could mate—and about the medical care that would be available to her, as her Parkinson's progressed. Bonnie got defensive with me and said, "I don't know everything, okay? I haven't even started yet."

It made me anxious to think about letting Eve go, but the opportunity Bonnie was describing sounded like a good one—certainly better than anything I had come up with. But I realized after we finished talking that Bonnie hadn't said whether she'd actually talked to people at the university about Eve—and confirmed that they were willing to take her. I called Bonnie a few times to ask that question, but only got her voicemail.

I watched Thomas as he walked toward the kitchen. He still had a pronounced limp, a lingering side effect from damage done to his body by the chemotherapy. And he was still so thin and fragile looking. The doctors had said he would probably regain his strength and muscle mass as he got older. I called after him, "Hungry?"

"Well, yeah."

While he waited for me to fix him something to eat, he rummaged through the stack of newspapers on the table, looking for the section of the Chronicle that had the comics. When he found it, he opened it and hunched over the page of comics that he wanted to read first.

I brought a plate of cheese and Ritz crackers and a cup of milk to the table and set it near his line of vision. He mumbled, "Thanks," but didn't look up.

"Your mom said you've got a science project due tomorrow."

"Yep." He glanced up at me. "I'm supposed to do an invention."

"Build it?"

"No. Just do a poster."

"So…what's your invention?"

He pushed the newspaper aside. "A time machine."

I waited for a second to see if he was going to say more about it, but he didn't. So I asked, "Doesn't your teacher want it to be something that somebody could actually build?"

One of the round Ritz crackers slid off of his plate. He thumped it with his index finger in short bursts across the tabletop toward me. "I don't know. She didn't say that."

I thumped it back in his direction. A sliver of the cracker broke off. "So what's your idea? How would it work?"

As he thumped the cracker back in my direction, another small piece broke off. It slowed to a stop in the middle of the table. He said, defensively, "I figured you'd have some ideas—it doesn't have to really work, but it can't be something crazy."

"And you're sure your invention doesn't have to actually work."

He shrugged. "I guess."

So I gave him a simple explanation of Einstein's theory about how speed alters time and was describing a device he could draw on his poster that would accelerate a person faster and faster around a large circular track, when he interrupted me to say, "Or maybe it could just be a revolving door that goes really fast." He reached out and picked up the cracker. "Like with a really big motor on top. Now that would be cool."

He smiled. This unanticipated, fun solution to his homework problem had put him in a good mood. He turned his chair around, held the Ritz cracker in the air, and called, "Hey, monkey. Look what I've got."

From the den, Eve looked in our direction and seeing food, bounded into the kitchen, stopping abruptly at the foot of Thomas' chair. Her John the Baptist book was dangling from one hand.

I said, "Be careful she doesn't bite you."

Heeding my warning, he quickly stood up and let the cracker drop from his hand. Before it hit the ground, Eve grabbed it out of the air and ate it. Then she jumped up on the table—with the book still in one hand—and licked up the cracker pieces that were scattered there and on Thomas' plate. This was something Grace refused to tolerate—a monkey on our kitchen table—with good reason, so I yelled, "Hey! Get down!"

Eve slid from the tabletop onto my lap. She dropped her book on the table in front of me and combed her fingers through the hair around her mouth to see if there were any crumbs there to eat.

Thomas took a step back away from the table and stretched. His arms were thin, too thin. He said, "I wish I could draw better. I'd do my poster like a comic strip, with a kid and his crazy dad, where the dad invents a *revolving door of time* and installs it at the front door of their house—because he's...you know."

Crazy. I'm not sure Thomas was even aware of the insulting associations he was making—it had all become such a routine part of his life.

He continued. "And, like, the kid discovers that he can go around in circles in this revolving door—you know how kids like to go around and around in revolving doors? Except this one has a *big frickin'* motor on top that turns it around. And every time he looks out, he sees stuff and then—whoosh—he goes around another circle and when he looks out again stuff is all a little bit different. And, like, this is the thing: the door makes people go back in time. Not, like, to the stone age, but...*back.*" He looked at me to be sure I was paying attention. "That's my invention, right? Like we were talking about."

I could actually imagine a comic book with Thomas' storyline—a dark, but funny story about a father's and son's shared descent into madness. It made me want to cry. It made me think that Grace might be right on target in her fears that my delusions were affecting Thomas—and dangerous.

"The title at the top needs to be in creepy letters." He wiggled his fingers like snakes. "It'll say: <u>Dad's Really Disturbing Revolving Door of Time</u>."

"Isn't it supposed to be your invention?"

He ignored the question. "I wish I could get somebody to draw the pictures for me, because my drawing sucks. What I'm thinking is that it would be funny for all the pictures to be kind of lame, like in kids' books. Like in that one." He pointed at the book Eve had brought over to the table. She'd opened it to her favorite page—where Jesus is being baptized. Thomas walked around the table so that he stood next to me and pointed at the characters on the pages. "See? They all have these oval heads and pug noses and little dot eyes? Very lame here, but it would be cool on my poster. It would be…"

"Ironic?"

"What's that mean?"

"It means…" It took me a few seconds to come up with a definition. "where the words or images you use actually convey an opposite meaning to what—"

"No, that's not it." He put his arm around my shoulder and pointed again at the page in Eve's book. "Is that what you're going to do?"

"Maybe. Who told you?"

"Mom…and Elaine. They said you wanted to get baptized again, because you thought it might…I can't remember what they said you thought it might do."

I thought for a moment before answering. I didn't particularly want to confide in Thomas, but I didn't want him hearing things about me from Grace and Elaine that weren't accurate. I decided to give him the very short version of the answer. "It's a symbol of rebirth."

"Cool." He nodded, probably relieved that I didn't want to say more about it. "Are you going to do it in a river…like Jesus?"

"No." As I said the word no, I suddenly realized that I wanted to do it in a river. I'd never even thought about that before. I wasn't sure if Barry would consider it. He'd agreed to re-baptize me by immersion, but we'd both been thinking about doing it in Grace's church, in its baptistery. So I said, "Well…maybe."

"Cool."

"Yep."

"Yep. Get Barry to do the monkey too. Eve wants to be baptized too, don't you, dog-breath?" He poked Eve with his finger.

"She's a monkey."

"So?"

The phone rang. I could reach it from the table, if I leaned back in my chair a little bit. Eve held onto my shirt to keep from tumbling out of my lap. It was Grace on the phone, calling to check on things. She asked me if Thomas was working on his science project. I said, "Not yet." She said, with apparent annoyance, "What are y'all doing?"

"Well," I said. "I fixed him a snack. And we talked about it."

"Good. I'm glad that you're–"

"He's doing a time machine: 'Dad's Disturbing Revolving Door of Time.'"

It was quiet on her end of the line for a few seconds. Then she said that she'd be home in a little bit and hung up.

I started to tell Thomas that it had been his mother on the phone, but he had slipped out of the kitchen quietly while I was talking to her. So I told Eve about it.

She looked up at me from my lap, made eye contact for a few seconds and then looked away. Animals aren't comfortable making extended eye contact—it's a byproduct of their ingrained animal nature. But as I've mentioned before, sometimes my eye contact with Eve seemed to linger, as it might with another human being. And over time, I saw glimpses of things that made me understand what we at the university had done by injecting her embryo with those mysterious strands of "junk" human DNA, strands whose exact function we do not understand, even in humans. What did we do? We accidentally gave Eve a spiritual nature. We didn't make her fully human. We didn't make her smarter. But we made her into a creature that instinctively and helplessly seeks God. How do I know that? I just do.

And the other thing we did was to somehow create a creature who had the power to set in motion the connections we'd been making with alternate realities. She was always there when they happened. They never happened before I brought her home. If she could have talked, maybe she'd have said the same thing about me—that she never had those disorienting shared déjà vu experiences before I came into her life. Or maybe it was Buck who caused it all to happen—yes, Buck, in whatever alternate dimension he was in right then. Or maybe I'm crazy, and that's a complete explanation.

But I think it was Eve that was causing it all to happen. I think she was setting these disruptions in motion—these miracles…of sorts—because she had an instinctive spiritual longing to do so, but she didn't have the intellectual prowess to question the outcome. She was just a monkey and didn't have the mental capacity for doubt.

I said, "Evie, tell me something—you will be honest with me, won't you? Tell me…am I fucking crazy?"

She nodded, one clipped nod, barely more than a twitch of her head. If she'd had the capacity to understand the limits of normal human behavior—and even rudimentary human speech—her nod might have truly signified agreement. She understood fundamental things about me, just as I did about her. In her own way, she'd even come to love me, as I had come to love her. But she hadn't understood a single word of what I was saying. She was just a monkey. I knew that.

She sighed.

Then I sighed.

She made a loose fist, tapped her chest with it and then touched the page of the book that was open in front of us. What did that mean? It could have meant, "Read to me." Or maybe, "This is *my* book." Or it could have meant something about baptism—she'd pointed at the page where John the Baptist was lifting Jesus from the shining water of the Jordan River, surrounded by yellow beams of sunlight. Thomas had said that Eve wanted to be baptized, and maybe he was right. It wasn't the first time that he—or Buck—had said it. I couldn't remember when, or in what context, but I was pretty sure that Buck had said essentially the same thing. And I knew that they were right. But what would that signify to a monkey? I didn't know—maybe a stripped-down, primal version of what it meant to me, something equally compelling to both of us because of our shared DNA, something instinctual stemming from what it means to be human.

Chapter 22

Psychologists want us to confront our demons. They believe in *interventions* for stubborn souls like me who refuse to do so on their own. Grace and Elaine and Barry appear at the door of my study one morning after Thomas is gone to school. Elaine says, "We're here because we love you, Jim." Barry says, "That's right, Jim." I look at Grace, and she nods and looks away. I wonder, Is this a prelude to asking me to agree to be committed to a mental hospital? And so I ask that very question, and they all say, "No, no, no."

"No."

"No?"

"No."

I see humor in that extended conversation of monosyllables—it was like a badly scripted movie, and I laugh. Barry laughs too. I think he understands why I think it's so funny. I know that Grace doesn't—I can tell from the fear in her eyes. She thinks that me laughing in a serious context such as this is more evidence—if any is needed— that I'm *not right*, not right mentally and certainly no longer right with God. To her way of thinking, that explains a lot too.

They don't know it, but I'm already prepared to make a deal, to do almost anything they ask of me, if it will help me get my old life back. And my family. I want us all to be able to carry on our lives in a normal way again. I want Grace to be in my bed when I wake up in the morning. I don't want to lose Thomas. I don't want to fight losing

161

battles anymore. I understand that my son Buck is gone forever, and that's how it is. He's gone, and that's the way God...well, he's just gone—let's leave it at that.

Barry says, "Do you remember the conversation we had in my office a couple of months ago."

I remember it well. Actually, I remember two—at least two—alternate versions of the meeting in his office. In one of them—no doubt the one Barry would like to talk about—I had asked him if he would be willing to re-baptize me. In another version of the same moment in time, Buck was there—my son who no longer exists. And it was Buck who said that he wanted to be baptized—not me. I decide that I will only talk about the first version today, the version that Barry remembers too, the one that will make everyone relatively happy with me. And so I say, "Yes, indeed," and smile.

He says, "It all seemed very important to you that day, but you haven't called me back to work out the details. Is it something you still want to do?"

I do, but my reasons are confusing—even to me. I think that part of what you get when you're human is a longing that can only be satisfied by religious rituals you don't fully understand. And so I answer Barry's question: "Yes, I do."

Elaine looks at the other two for confirmation that it is her turn to talk. I think they've rehearsed what each of them is supposed to say. "Talk to us about what it—baptism—means...to you."

I tell them. Things and symbols of things inhabit our minds. It shackles them to say that they denote literal truth, and yet, it trivializes them to say that they are simply metaphors. They are, inexplicably, something different—and higher. Ritualized immersion in water is such a thing. It has meaning. It is transforming. I know that to be true, and I say so.

Barry nods. His brow is furrowed. He says, "I couldn't have said it better." He means it, but I'm not sure he really understands. If he had spoken the identical words, they would not have had the same meaning as I have given them. I don't know how to explain that, but it is true.

I have an irrational urge to call the monkey, to let her come in and be part of this gathering. But the monkey is downstairs somewhere, probably whimpering in her crate in the laundry room. Grace is putting her there more frequently now. Grace has started saying that if I don't find a home for Eve soon, she will just take her to the Houston zoo and toss her over the fence. She has told me several times that the monkey is a big part of my problem.

Elaine says, "You were baptized in the Baptist church when you were young, weren't you?"

"I was eight." A couple of years younger than Thomas is now, a few years older than Buck.

"Do you want to talk about it? What you remember from that... experience?" Elaine's tone of voice is that of a professional, not that of an old friend. But I understand. I know she is doing the best she can to be helpful.

"A lot, actually." And I turn to Grace and say, "Do you remember your baptism?"

And she recoils, as if I am attacking her. But I'm not. I just want to know. I believe that Grace and I are more alike than we are different, and sometimes I really just want to know what she thinks and remembers. But she treats my questions as if I'm trying to build a trap for her. I don't understand.

Barry intervenes. He says, "You talked about it a little bit that day when you came by my office. I remember you saying that you felt cut off from your faith—not drawn in. Isn't that what you said?"

"Yes. Something like that."

I remember darkness and soft amber light. I remember snow falling, swirling, lit by the pale lights over the doors of the church. I remember my mother's arm around my shoulder and the faint smell of moth balls in her winter coat.

I am eight and I am a true believer. Belief is an easy, uncomplicated thing for me. I have been a child of God since before I can remember.

My parents, my sister and I rarely go to church on Sunday nights. Instead, we watch The Wonderful World of Walt Disney on television and, after that, read until bedtime. But at our church, baptisms are done on Sunday evenings, and so we are there at the church, instead of enjoying our normal routine at home. But it's fine with me. I want to be baptized.

Under my winter coat I am wearing a white shirt with no tie and black pants. My mother has brought a change of clothes because I am going to get wet from head to toe. I am excited. My feet do a clumsy tap dance in the hallway outside the preacher's office. I am *joining the church.*

My imagination is at work. This night can be the beginning of an adventure for me. In my imagination, boys like me are often moments away from the beginning of adventure. In recent months, I have imagined myself in a variety of them: floating down a river with my best friends on a raft of my own design...inventing and patenting a perpetual motion machine...writing a beautiful hymn that is performed in my grandmother's stately, high-ceilinged, big-city church.

Our preacher invites me into his office. I am one of two people being baptized that evening. The other is a teenage girl with a grown woman's body who doesn't say a word to me. She seems very old. She also seems unhappy about something, but I don't concern myself with that. I had expected a conversation with the preacher about what this all means, but instead, he mostly talks to me about how I should stand and what I should do as he is preparing to dunk me under the water. He shows me how I can raise my hands in a prayerful, reverent manner as I'm being lowered into the water and use one of them to hold my nose. He asks if I'd like to be introduced as "James," "Jim," or "Jimmy." To my recollection I'd never been called James or Jim in my life to that point, and so I say, "Jimmy," and look at my mother and dad for confirmation. They both smile and nod.

I have told my best friends and my second grade teacher that I am joining the church. I am only eight, but I have a clear sense of what that must mean, based on a theology that is partly my own—my own understanding of what happens to a boy like me when he *joins the church.* I will be changed. I will belong. I will understand mysteries.

A deacon escorts me to a small room behind the sanctuary, where I am to wait until they come get me for the baptism. My mother leaves the sack with my extra clothes, because this is also the room in which I will change into dry clothes afterwards. Then my mother and dad leave, so that they can get seats in the sanctuary that are near the front.

The deacon pats my shoulder and says, "I'll be back to get you in a little bit." I hear organ music through the wall. The evening worship service is starting.

I am alone now. I wonder what kind of show I'm missing on The Wonderful World of Walt Disney. It could be a cartoon. It could be an adventure story with Zorro or Daniel Boone. It could be a documentary about birds or possums. That's what I hope. I don't mind missing a show that is nothing more than close-ups of mother birds feeding baby birds or possums doing the normal things that possums do.

I have brought nothing with me to keep me occupied while I wait. I stare at a picture of Jesus across the room. I like Jesus.

I am wearing socks but no shoes. I see that my socks don't quite match.

The organ music stops. I think about pipe organs and pipes. I invented something using a three-foot long pipe that was in our garage. You can talk through it, which is useful sometimes, or you can pucker your lips and play music with it.

The door opens and the deacon is there with a white choir robe, which he helps me put on. He says, "Ready?" The teenage girl is standing in the hallway when we come out of the little room. She's wearing a white robe too. I stand on my tiptoes, but I still don't reach her shoulders.

We walk down a short, dark hallway and stand at the foot of the steps that lead up to the baptistery—the deep pool of water where people are baptized. It's at the front of the sanctuary, behind the choir, high enough so that people in the audience can see what's going on, as long as the choir is sitting down. There's an opening without glass or anything between the sanctuary and the baptistery, so that people can hear the preacher talking when he's back there. A polished wooden cross is on the wall, over the water.

Things begin to move quickly. The preacher comes through a door. He is also wearing a white robe. I see that he is wearing green rubber waders under his robe, the kind of waders that hunters use. He says, "You're first, Jimmy." And he turns and walks down the steps into the baptistery. The deacon gently pushes me, so that I know to follow closely behind him.

The preacher is speaking to the people in the congregation as I am walking into the warm water next to him. He introduces me by name and says familiar words about baptism. The lights have been dimmed in the sanctuary, and I can't see my family. There are light bulbs under the water like they have at swimming pools at Thunderbird Motels.

He turns to face me and says, "Jimmy, I baptize you in the name of the Father, the Son and the Holy Spirit." He takes hold of me and says something about Jesus and then tightens his grip on the back of my neck. He tilts me backwards into the water and I hear these words as I am going under: "Buried with him in baptism," and these words as I come up out of the water: "Raised to walk in newness of life."

And then he turns me and pushes me firmly toward the steps that lead out of the baptistery. The deacon takes my hand to steady me as I come up the steps. I pass the teenage girl, who seems to be staring at my nose.

It was over quickly. I am not yet disappointed, but I am not changed in any way. I am not happier. I am not more enlightened—although at that age I would not know how to articulate such a concept. I am simply wet.

The deacon hands me a towel, and we walk down the hallway to the room where I'd been. I'm cold, and I shiver as we walk. He says, "When you're done changing, I'll take you out there to sit with your parents." When we get back to the room where I had waited earlier, he says, "Got everything you need?" and then he closes the door, saying, "I'll be here when you're done. Just come on out."

I remember the deacon escorting me to the row in the sanctuary where my parents and sister are sitting. My parents and others on that row smile at me and then look away. My baptism is over. Their minds are on other things—possibly the sermon, which the preacher is now giving in his hoarse, old-man voice, or possibly the mundane affairs of life that occupy our thoughts most of our waking hours. I remember almost nothing else about that evening or the weeks after.

I had faith in miraculous possibilities, but I remain unchanged.

Grace interrupts my musings. "Jim?" Her face is unnaturally tense, but otherwise devoid of indications of emotion. "Jim, I just have to say this. You always expect too much. From everything. You look for meaning...in everything, meaning which doesn't exist. You just set yourself up for disappointment."

I let my mind drift. It is a defensive mechanism that I use. It's been pointed out to me by several therapists over the years that I avoid confrontation by retreating inward. I don't deny it. I say, "Maybe I forgot to take my medicine this morning."

Elaine has been sitting in my rolling desk chair. She gets excited, because she wants to make an important point, and so she rolls my chair so close to me that our knees bang together and she says, "Jim, stop it! You're just playing with us. You need to face your demons. You know exactly what I'm talking about. You're choosing—*choosing*—a world of delusions. This..." She points at my cluttered desk and at the patchwork quilt of colored note cards and outlines that are tacked to the wall of my study, and then she completes her sentence. "...bizarre research of yours into parallel dimensions. Jim, a part of you knows that this is all crazy. I can see it in your eyes, like you're playing a big joke on everyone."

I say, "Jesus had to face his demons too, I guess."

They see this as a potentially positive, but cryptic comment on my part. Elaine and Grace look at Barry. It is his turn to talk.

Barry says, "You mean when Christ healed the people who were possessed by demons?"

"No."

Christ had to stand up to delusion. That's the truth of it, but if I say that, it won't be pleasant.

"I'm sorry. I guess I don't follow." Barry is genuinely trying to understand. If it were only the two of us here, talking over a glass of wine, I'd tell him what I really think. But I don't want to get into it with Grace and Elaine listening. It will only make things worse.

I say, "Never mind."

Barry nods. He thinks before he speaks. He says, "Jim, we've been friends for almost twenty years, right? I know you. You know me. We can't bullshit each other. You're one of the smartest guys I know. And it's like you're choosing insanity to deal with your disappointments. You're mourning over something and creating your own myth to come to terms with it. You've created another son…Buck? That's his name, right? Maybe Buck is the child in you, and you're mourning the loss of that ideal. I don't know. That may be bullshit. But if we're going to mourn something, maybe we need to stop talking about baptism, and instead talk about a funeral. Maybe we should help you build a funeral pyre where we symbolically put the things that you need to turn loose of on that pyre and just light it up."

Grace is suddenly restless. I know why—it has to do with things my mother told her after we got married. She gestures to Barry that he should stop, but he is too caught up in what he is saying. It's not at all what I want to do, but it's certainly not a stupid idea.

He nods vigorously as he talks and a smile begins to form on his face. "We can build that funeral pyre, set it aflame and put your disappointments there, your losses, your—"

Grace stands up. "Please. Please, don't say that." Grace's eyes dart back and forth among us. "I'd just rather we not talk about setting anything on fire."

I smile.[3]

---

3 **LAWRENCE, KANSAS – March 21, 1971** Emergency crews responded on Saturday afternoon to reports of a fire at a residence at the 1100 block of Clay Street. Units arriving on the scene were told that the fire was accidentally started by the nine-year-old son of the homeowners, who was conducting experiments with his chemistry set in the kitchen. Douglas County emergency dispatchers advised that the fire was extinguished by the occupants before the units arrived on the scene and that there were no injuries. There have been two prior reports of fires called in from this location within the prior twelve months, including a grass fire in a field adjacent to Clay Street that required additional units from Jefferson County to contain.

Chapter 23

Circa 85 C.E.

In this account, Theophilus, I've described the Master's series of temptations which prepared him for what lay ahead. Take heed, so that you may better understand the mysteries that you have been taught.

After the Master had been baptized in the Jordan River, the Spirit drove him out into a dry and barren wilderness where both angels and serpents existed in close proximity. There was no food for the Master there and he became exceedingly hungry, and to add to his torment, the Devil was always near at hand and frequently appeared at his side to discuss with him matters of consequence.

After forty days of solitude in the wilderness, the Devil found the Master sitting in a dry creek bed in the shade of a low bluff. The Devil bowed low and said, "Rabbi, you are starving."

The Master did not respond.

"Is that how the prophesies are to be fulfilled?" The Devil squatted down near the Master's feet and picked up an oblong stone with a smooth gray surface. He held it out. "Take...eat."

The Master took the stone and scratched at its surface with his fingernail. "What you've given me is only a stone."

"Rabbi, if you wanted that stone to become a warm loaf of bread, well...that would be a simple matter for you, wouldn't it? Come! Turn the stone into bread...and eat—if you are really the son of God. Do it! And live another day."

The Master answered, "It is written, 'Man does not live by bread alone, but by every word that comes from God's mouth.'"

"Ah, so you would prefer to starve—die here and now—rather than face what lies ahead. I see...."

The Master shut his eyes. His long fast had made him weak, and the relentless burning heat of the desert sun affected his perception of things both physical and spiritual. With his eyes closed he had the sensation of spinning and falling. He heard the footsteps of the Devil departing from him and he began to doze, and in his fitful sleep felt a cool breeze against his dry skin, a breeze that grew into a cold, swirling wind. He felt himself soaring. He heard the murmurs of angels. He awoke to the sound of the Devil's gentle voice.

"Rabbi," the Devil said. "I have something to show you."

The Master opened his eyes and struggled to his feet. They stood in the pale, crisp light of dawn on an unfamiliar mountain peak. A stiff, cold wind made the Master's loose robe billow like a sail.

The Devil said, "Look, Rabbi. Look around you."

The Master looked down at the Gentile lands far below: Rome, with its sprawling empire along the northern shore of the great sea and, on the southern shore, Egypt and its bustling provinces that stretched the length of the mighty Nile River, magnificent places that the Master had never been—places where a carpenter's son from Judah, even one descended from the legendary King David, would be scorned.

"The empires hunger for an enlightened leader like you, Master. Have you never dreamed of ascending to a throne? You were born for such a thing. In Rome, they would make you Caesar—with a word from me. In Egypt, why...they would make you a god."

The Master tried to imagine what it would be like to be a powerful man—or even to be a welcomed guest—in one of these ancient capitals of the world.

"And look!" The Devil swiveled sharply and pointed in the direction from which the sun was rising.

The Master turned his eyes away from Rome and looked toward the eastern horizon. He saw the ornate, glittering palaces and temples that lined magnificent boulevards in Persia and neighboring kingdoms. He saw the towers, walls and fortresses of other proud civilizations in the far distance, strange countries separated from the known world by oceans and impassible mountain ranges.

The Devil said, "It's yours to have. I would love for you to have it, Rabbi. Do you understand? Everything that you see could be yours to have, to rule with your gentle wisdom. Look around you one more time and consider carefully. All I ask... all I ask of you in return for *the world* is that you acknowledge me for what I am. And disavow all else."

"No."

"No? I'm offering you the fulfillment of your grandest dreams."

The Master turned his back to the Devil and gazed down from the mountaintop at Jerusalem, at the maze of dusty, narrow streets within its walls. And as he looked down at the holy temple in the heart of the city, he saw the new temple that existed in its place, and as his eyes took in the fading wonders of the city that he knew well and loved so deeply, he saw the new Jerusalem there, superimposed upon the old, and as he looked up at the golden sky, lit by the morning sun, he saw a new heaven, and as he looked down at the brittle works of humankind spread out before him, he saw a new earth—there beneath him—somehow coexisting with the old. New and awakening. And the Master turned and said, "No. For it is written, 'The Lord only is God.' And he alone shall we serve."

Like all men, the Master had dreams, powerful dreams that could, in the first waking moments, be mistaken for reality. But this was no dream. And like many of the prophets of old, the Master had visions, but the Master understood that this was no vision.

As the Master looked around, the rising sun blazed more brightly, filling the sky with white light. Gold and brass objects and ornaments that adorned the wondrous capital cities of the world reflected the sun's light as though they were on fire. The glare from it all was blinding, and the Master shielded his eyes with his hands, and even then, his eyes burned from the light. He felt the heat of the desert returning. He squinted and caught a glimpse of a gray, furry scavenger scurrying behind one of the boulders in the dry creek bed where he had been sitting when the Devil first appeared to him. Then he closed his eyes tightly to block out the painful glare.

The sound of the wind that had blown on the mountain peak transformed into the sound of a thousand urgent voices. In place of the cold wind was a hot, faltering breeze that smelled of dust and livestock.

"Rabbi." The Devil made no attempt to hide his contempt. "I've returned you to your insignificant little fiefdom."

The Master opened his eyes and saw that he was now standing on the roof of the highest spire of the holy temple. A crowd had gathered below and was growing as men streamed out of the temple and women and children left their homes to see the spectacle of a madman who would soon surely fall to his death.

The tiles were not securely fastened on the roof of the spire where they stood. The Master's sandal slid sideways as a tile broke loose and fell. The Devil took the Master's arm to steady him, but rather than pulling the Master away, the Devil pushed him toward the edge of the small, sloping roof. He turned his face to the Master and said, "If you are truly the Son of God—the Messiah—then throw yourself down from here.

Your people will be...entertained. No! They will be moved... changed! They will worship you. Now. In this world."

The Master understood, but didn't answer.

The Devil said, "Why do you hesitate? It is written that your God will command his angels to protect you. The scriptures say, 'They will lift you up in their hands, so that you will not even strike your foot against a stone.'"

The Master looked down. His vision blurred and then came into focus and then separated again into multiple images. The weeks of solitude and hunger had left him with disjointed, feverish thinking, but also greater clarity about things seen and unseen. His mind moved in circles, following the thread of all alternatives and then returning to the Devil's simple, seductive proposition. If he returned to the wilderness from which the Devil had plucked him, he might wind up dying there of starvation, slowly and painfully, and if he didn't, he would die later at the hands of those he had come to save. He knew that much. If he fled to one of the distant lands that the Devil had shown him from the mountaintop...well, there would be no place to hide from the gaze of the Father and from the prophesies that were his to fulfill. And he would die. If he jumped now, angels would catch him, and even if they didn't, he would die a quick, easy death. And live again? Possibly. The Master understood certain things to be true, but much had not been revealed to him yet.

The Master was sorely tempted.

The Devil's eyes glittered as if they were made of purest gold.

Chapter 24

There was no enemy. I mean…really, who was there to fight? There was no one. Everyone was on *my* side. That was the truth of it.

I wanted a normal life again and was willing to do what I had to do to obtain it.

After Elaine and Barry left our house, Grace and I talked for more than an hour about what it would take for us to live together again as man and wife, about what each of us was willing—and not willing—to do, to make things work.

I had to take medicine: lithium, anti-psychotics, antidepressants and whatever else the doctors might prescribe to go along with them. I had to. That was her non-negotiable demand.

Grace had said that, for her part, she would be willing to order new prescriptions for me and pick them up from the pharmacy, but she wasn't willing to nag me daily to take them. That was understandable. I didn't want that either.

And so I began to take the pills regularly, as prescribed and, after two weeks, I was a different person. Different is really the best word for it. Fewer things were funny to me, but I laughed more. I had less on my mind, but I talked more. Honestly, I preferred the person I had been, but that was no longer a choice.

I had said to Grace that, for my part, I would do whatever was necessary to get a job, but that I wanted work that I found meaningful, even if it paid less than other alternatives. She agreed and asked if I wanted her to look for a full time job too. I said, "Let's wait and see."

Once I focused my energies on getting a job, it wasn't all that hard. I got back in touch with the recruiter at Rice University and the interviews that she set up couldn't have gone better. Everyone who interviewed me agreed that I was a perfect match for the job, and they made an offer to hire me within days.

Another of Grace's requirements was that I find a new home for Evie—and that we set a deadline. She said, "I'm sorry."

I agreed to get it done by the first week of April, no matter what. So I called Bonnie, and left her a message to the effect that I had decided to let her have Eve. And I told her about my deadline. But days passed with no return call from Bonnie, and so, in frustration, I called again and left a short message to the effect that, if I didn't hear back from her soon, I was going to have to give Eve to the first zoo that agreed to take her. I got a call back from Bonnie within minutes.

She was angry. She'd said, "What's with you? The last time I offered to help, all you wanted to do was cross-examine me, and now, all of a sudden, it's all about you and your deadlines."

I interrupted her and said, "Things have changed."

"And so now you need my help."

"Are you there yet—at St. Anthony's? Last time we talked you hadn't even started."

It was obvious from her tone of voice that she didn't like questions. "Yeah...."

"And do you still think it would be a good place for Evie to come live?"

She hesitated before answering, but her voice was confident, even a bit strident. "Yeah, it would be a great place for her." She went into some detail as to why that was so. Eve would be one of five old monkeys living in the lab. They spent their days loose in the lab, hanging out with coeds who were earning extra credit in their undergraduate psychology classes. Eve would be given a variety of psychological tests on a regular basis. They would probably try to teach her sign language. It was all pretty laid back—Bonnie thought that the lab's activities were carried out more as a teaching tool for students than as a genuine research effort.

I said, "Okay. Let's do it."

She hesitated again. "I still have to talk to some people, but it won't be a problem. I'll call you back. Tomorrow, okay?"

As it turned out, Bonnie didn't call me back as she had promised, and so I began calling and leaving messages on her cell phone, messages of increasing urgency. I had to get this done. But then, one day when I called, planning to leave a final ultimatum on her voicemail, to my surprise, she answered her phone and said, in a chipper voice, that things were all arranged. She said, "So...can you bring her out here—not this weekend...or next—that wouldn't work either. How about the last week in March?"

When Grace told Elaine about my job offer from Rice University, Elaine insisted that we all get together right away to celebrate. She suggested that we meet for dinner at one of our old favorite restaurants in a hip part of Houston near Rice. We agreed to go, but Grace and I were both hesitant about it at first—each for our own reasons. I think Grace had a lingering sense of shame about things, and as for me...well, I just didn't think it would be much fun—for obvious reasons.

But I was wrong. It was okay. As it turned out, the way that we behaved around each other had not changed all that much. Nothing appeared to have been damaged in our relationships with each other.

We were finishing dessert when Elaine mentioned a vacation they were planning during Spring Break to their weekend house on the Brazos River, near New Braunfels. She asked if we'd like to bring Thomas and join them there for the week. Grace and I had stayed there many times in the years before any of us had children, but hadn't been back since Thomas was born. At first, it had seemed too hard to deal with an infant in such a rustic place, and then, we'd had his cancer to deal with, and then, the years had just slipped by.

Barry nodded enthusiastically. "This is the best time of year to go. The weather is cool at night. The wildflowers are blooming. Our kids can run around outside until dark—Brandy and Katie would love having Thomas there to play with."

Grace and I exchanged glances. We had no legitimate reason not to accept their invitation—other than our fear of awkwardness that might linger from the things that were said—and not said—in my study a couple of weeks earlier. But the dinner that we were finishing—and actually lingering over—had been thoroughly enjoyable. We'd laughed and talked all evening without ever hitting a raw nerve.

That's when the idea popped into my head. I mentioned it as though I were joking, but I wasn't. I said, "Maybe you could baptize me there in the Brazos River."

Barry's face lit up. He said, "I've always wanted to do that."

Everyone thought it was a superb idea, imagining it as a something quaint and entertaining—but entirely serious, too. An old-fashioned baptism, the way our forefathers would have done it. No one could have imagined at the time how such a good idea could go so wrong—but I'm getting ahead of myself.

We parted ways after our dinner, exchanging hugs and allocating responsibility for things to buy and bring for our adventure.

And so Grace and I made plans to spend Spring Break at Barry's and Elaine's house on the Brazos River—and also to drop off the monkey at St. Anthony's University on our way out there. It all went wrong, but it had seemed to make a lot of sense at the time. San Marcos, where the university is located, is less than an hour from Barry's and Elaine's house, so that would save me an extra trip—and it was clear that Grace, despite her mostly unkind words about the monkey, had developed some affection for her and wanted to see her off properly. She began joking frequently about "getting our little girl ready to go off to college."

I cleaned out my study. I threw away all my note cards and the colored scraps of paper that I had been using to capture and organize my thoughts and the conclusions from my research. I also threw away an assortment of half-filled spiral notebooks and journals in which I'd been outlining my theories on time and space, but I also kept a few. Of the ones that I kept, I packed all but one into a box, along with the books that I'd accumulated—including my thoroughly-annotated copy of Brock's life-changing book, <u>Reflections from the Multiverse</u>.

The only journal that I *didn't* pack away was the one in which I'd begun jotting notes and ideas on what it means to be human. The topic still interests me.

The afternoon I was packing things up, Grace stuck her head in my study and asked if I was okay. It was an open-ended question meant to uncover any possible bitterness that I might be feeling. I think she felt guilty about the ultimatums that she'd given me—now that the battle of wills was mostly behind us—and worried that I might harbor anger toward her.

I've mentioned before that my study has a kind of translucence. I sometimes perceive things differently there. It struck me at the instant when Grace asked if I was okay, that I could simultaneously see another version of Grace, almost identical, mouthing similar words, but with a style and delivery filled with love that triggered a similar loving response from me.

I said, "Yes."

The exchange of words was nearly identical, but the feelings behind them for each of us were vastly different—in each of the two realities that I could perceive.

She smiled timidly, maybe uncertain whether she should pursue the topic, and said, "Are you sure?"

I told her, "Yes, babe, I'm fine," and that seemed to satisfy her concern.

It was an honest answer on my part. In return for the things which I had given up, I had received an opportunity.

What I didn't tell Grace—*couldn't* tell her—was that I'd decided to experiment with the dosages of my prescriptions. I'd broken the pills and was taking only half or a quarter of the prescribed amounts.

My psychiatrist had obviously prescribed dosages that were too high. After several weeks of having taken the pills, as prescribed, there were a variety of annoying side effects, but the side effect that had forced me to take action was that under their influence, my mind had grown silent. I could no longer hear my thoughts. What would you have done if it had been you—and your mind had become as still and silent as a graveyard? I couldn't stand it.

Chapter 25

I remember saying goodbye to our family dog when, as a teenager,
I left home for college. He was *my dog*—I had selected him out of a
large litter of Labrador puppies. I'd grown up with him, spent count-
less hours with him, but I couldn't take him with me. He died before
I graduated, in the middle of the fall semester of my sophomore year.
That was hard, but different.

I'm over forty now. I've had a lot of pets in my life, and I've given
a few away, left a few behind, watched a few die—experienced almost
every kind of parting that you can have with a pet. Sometimes it was
easy. Sometimes it was almost as hard as if I were losing a child. But
this was different.

Eve was more than a pet, more than a devoted companion.

As the day approached on which we were to pack up Eve's belongings and take her away, I set aside time more than once to be alone
with her and say goodbye. But I didn't know how to do it. I am setting
myself up as an easy butt for jokes to say this, but…it was like ending
an affair. I loved her—and she loved me. I had been spending more
of my waking hours with her than I did my wife, son, or anyone else.
The two of us had a connection that I'd never had with anyone else. If
it weren't for her, I would have been alone. All alone.

I'll give Grace credit for this: she understood that this was hard
for me. She didn't make light of it in any way. She allowed me to
spend time alone with Eve—without making any comment—during

the last few days before our departure to St. Anthony's University. So Eve and I revisited comfortable places around the house where we'd spent countless hours together over the prior months—the couch in the den, my desk chair and the gazebo in the back yard. And we just sat together, with Eve nestled in the crook of my arm, where she liked to be. I didn't talk to her, didn't say goodbye, because she wouldn't have understood my words. But she understood that a change was coming.

We had a cat once who could tell when Grace and I were getting ready to leave town. It made him crazy. He'd sprint in circles around the house and climb the drapes.

Even animals far less intelligent than a monkey see the signs of change.

I'm certain Eve understood that she was leaving us. She saw us folding and putting her clothes in a small, old duffle bag that I used to take to the gym. Her toys were no longer in their usual place, the wicker basket in the den. We'd put them, along with her books, dishes and other belongings in a small trunk that Grace bought for Eve to take to her new home.

And so Eve was understandably restless the last evening she spent at our house.

Grace made the rounds at ten o'clock, confirming with Thomas and me that we were both completely packed for our weeklong stay with Barry and Elaine—and checking under furniture in the den to be sure that none of Eve's favorite toys were being left behind. Satisfied that everything was done and we were all ready for an early morning departure, Grace announced that she was going upstairs to bed.

Before putting Eve in her crate for the night, I turned the downstairs lights off and stood one more time at the window that looked out at the gazebo in the backyard, holding her against my chest. I knew that it was necessary for my marriage—and not an altogether bad thing for Evie—for her to leave us now, to live with other monkeys at the university. But I felt guilty about it—guilty and disloyal. So as I stroked the fur around her face, I said, "I'm sorry. I'm so sorry." I stopped talking, but continued stroking the fur between her ears and on her forehead. After a while, she looked up abruptly and nipped my fingers lightly with her teeth to make me stop. Then she climbed out of my arms, dropped to the floor, and headed toward the front of the house in her crouched, shuffling gait. She paused to see if I was following her and then continued into the front hallway, where she opened the closet door.

Something had happened there once—there in the hall closet. It was in one of my journals, but I had no clear recollection of it any-more. Buck had been there—that had been the essential point of my journal entry. Buck had discovered a place behind the wine storage vault where Eve liked to go. And in at least one of the alternate reali-ties in the Multiverse, it had been a place that frightened him, maybe a dangerous place...for him. For me—and for the rest of us—it was just a hall closet.

Turning once more to be sure I was still following her, Eve went inside. I stood at the open door for a few moments, searching my memory for any tangible recollections of Buck, but there were none. Instead, to my surprise, fleeting images appeared of me and Grace, of her in a long, formal gown and of me taking some kind of coat or wool wrap from the closet and holding it for her to wear. Of the two of us slow dancing in the hallway. Of her soft hand placed lovingly on my cheek. The images were joyful—but no more real than any I might have conjured up of Buck. Those kinds of romantic, loving times with Grace had never happened, had simply never happened—not in any reality of which I was now a part.

As I looked down, the monkey was at my feet, holding out a small, smudged mirror with a gold rim, probably a makeup mirror that belonged to Grace. When I reached down and took it, Eve turned and scampered back into the space between the wall and the wine refrig-erator. Before disappearing into the dark, she turned and looked at me. She wanted me to follow.

I realized that she probably had a cache of other "treasures" back there. Thomas complained once that he saw her taking one of his movie DVDs back there—which prompted us to joke about her hav-ing set up her own home theater in the warm darkness behind the refrigerator. We already knew it was a place she liked to go, and it was okay with us. It was her private retreat—we didn't bother her when she was back there.

The gap through which she'd gone was maybe two feet wide, narrower than my shoulders. I'd never done it before, but there was just enough room for me to slide in there on my side with my arm outstretched, and then, to bring my arm around to grab whatever might be back behind the refrigerator that needed to be collected and packed with Eve's other belongings.

So I lay on my side and slid into the darkness next to the wine refrigerator. The hall closet was under the stairs, which made the closet much wider at the bottom than at the top, and so there was ample room behind the refrigerator for my head and shoulders—and for my free arm. My head was inches from the refrigerator, and its low-pitched hum filled my ears. The motor inside the refrigerator kicked on and hot air from some unseen vent blew into my face.

The first thing I saw in the dim light was my flashlight. I'd accidentally dropped it back there months earlier when I'd been inspecting for signs of rodent activity. I'd forgotten about it.

I turned on the flashlight and shone it around the area behind the refrigerator. Eve stood a couple of feet away beside a pile of things that glittered in the gleam of my flashlight. She was weaving from side to side, shifting her weight from foot to foot. She was baring her teeth and grimacing at me—a warning that I clearly understood. The clutter behind her—the treasures she had accumulated and piled there in the corner—were hers. Not mine. I understood. But she had wanted me to see it. Small objects and toys and scraps of paper and shards of colored glass and pieces of foil were carefully arranged there—not just piled up.

I understood immediately what it was. It was a holy place of some kind.

I felt it.

And I remembered then that Buck had discovered this very place once and that, like me, he had understood what it was.

I set the flashlight down. Then I extended my arm straight out over my head, letting it go limp on the floor, and lay my head on it. As

I lay there on my side, I stared at what Eve had been inspired—maybe even compelled—to build, letting my eyes go out of focus. I knew what it was.

I sensed a presence there and thought of Buck. I longed to have him back—not just his physical presence, but the joy and the love that we had shared. I remembered that more than I remember him. And the same with Grace: I wanted to have with her the things that I had glimpsed, things that were probably true or that could have been true in another reality. I closed my eyes.

And I emptied myself, hoping that these feelings of love and sensations of *presence* would become stronger. Emptied. It's a word—maybe a bad translation of better word—bandied about in Zen literature and other religious books I've read and forgotten. I think Paul said it about Jesus too: that in becoming what he was, he emptied himself. It's just a word, but it's a good one to describe how I understood things. I was almost there anyway—empty. I was tired to my soul. The medicines that I had been taking—even in lower doses—had caused an unprecedented stillness in my mind. I inhaled deeply and breathed out completely. I emptied myself.

And the humming of the refrigerator became like the voices of angels, the hot air blowing on me like tongues of fire.

I didn't expect what happened next.

For an instant I was thirteen years old again, sitting in the grass in a Baptist summer camp in Falls Creek, Oklahoma. In the presence of God—or of something beyond my ability to comprehend—perceiving things from the inside out. In complete awe.

I finally understood how the multiple dimensions of time work. All alternatives are a single reality. That doesn't explain everything, but it explained enough for me. All alternatives are a single reality.

Chapter 26

We were standing the next day in drizzling rain on the campus of St. Anthony's University, outside of a fairly modern three-story lime-stone building that housed the lab that was supposed to be Evie's new home—the place where Bonnie had said to meet her. I was certain that we were at the right place. But the front doors were locked and there was no one to be seen inside—or outside.

"Great," Grace said. "This is just great."

Bonnie had left me a detailed voicemail message to meet her on Sunday afternoon at 1:00 at Merrick Hall at the entrance that faced the stallion sculpture. I had Bonnie's cell phone number and a map. But every time I called her phone number, I got the same rambling voicemail message: "Hi! This is Bonnie. I...well, I can't answer my phone right now. Sorry."

"I thought the two of you had everything worked out." Grace held her umbrella so that there was also room for Thomas under it, but he seemed indifferent to the light rain and stood a foot away from her. In her other hand she was holding my old gym bag that held Grace's clothes. The little trunk with Eve's other belongings was still in the car.

"I did. I talked to her less than a week ago and got a voicemail message from her day before yesterday. She said that everything was arranged." I pounded on the heavy metal door—more out of anger than from any expectation that someone would finally hear me and open the door. It was dark inside. We'd been standing outside in the rain for almost half an hour.

"Are you sure this is the right building?"

I looked at my damp map one more time. She'd said to meet her at Merrick Hall. That's where we were. There was a bronze sign that said so. I'd already walked around the building and checked all the doors.

Thomas surveyed the empty sidewalks that fanned out in several directions from the building and said, "It's obviously Spring Break here too."

Eve was whimpering in her crate and clawing at its door. I had a trash bag wrapped around her crate to protect her from the rain. I drummed my fingers on the top of it and said, "Sorry, Evie."

She became quiet for a few moments and then started whimpering again, louder than before.

"What are we going to do?" Grace asked, although the answer was obvious.

"We don't have much choice except to bring her with us—unless we want to just go back home. Let's call Elaine and ask if it's okay—it should be. And anyway, when I hear back from Bonnie, I'll put Evie in the car and bring her right back over here."

"Great. All of us crammed together in that old house…with a smelly little monkey. And the kids can't go outside because it's raining."

"The rain's supposed to stop tomorrow."

"I hope so."

To add our misery, a band of dark clouds overhead began to deliver sheets of rain on us as we ran back to the car. We ran faster, but our shoes got soaked as we ran down sidewalks that had become shallow rivers. Grace and Thomas jumped into the car, and I opened the tailgate and shoved Eve's crate in the back among the luggage and sacks of food and wine. I pulled the black trash bag from around the crate, which made Evie stop whimpering—since she could now see me through the slits in the plastic. I said, "It's okay, Evie. Everything's okay now." A part of me was relieved that parting ways with Eve had been put off, but I was still furious at Bonnie for being unreliable, for causing us so much wasted time and trouble.

I climbed into the driver's seat. We dried off with a shared roll of paper towels that I had grabbed from the back.

Thomas broke the silence after I started the engine. "Well, *that* was fun."

I turned around in my seat, prepared to deliver a lecture on the inappropriateness of sarcasm in times of stress. Before I could say anything, he transformed his face into a look of innocence and said, "What? Aren't we allowed to have any fun?"

"You were being sarcastic."

"No, I wasn't."

Grace tapped me on the leg. "Let it go…just let it go." She sighed. "Do you want to call Elaine with the good news, or should I?"

"Why don't you do it." I told Grace what I though she should say to Elaine, raising my voice so that it could be heard over the thunder and the slapping sound of our windshield wipers.

There was a lake of water forming in the parking lot, and on the street, the water was up to the curbs.

Thomas slapped me on the back and said, "Is that—?"

I slammed on the brakes. "Where?"

"Never mind. For a second. I thought I saw a body floating by."

We both turned around in our seats and glared at him.

He smiled. "Just kidding."

"Not funny, Buck. Not funny at all."

Then they both stared at me. He spoke first. "What did you call me? Did you call me Buck?"

"I don't know. Whatever…I meant, 'Thomas.'"

"Well, yeah. That *is* my name."

Thomas looked out the window at the rain, smiling again. For him, my slip of the tongue was a timely diversion of focus away from him. But it changed the dynamics of Grace's emotional state from irritable chattiness to morose silence.

After a few minutes of the silence, I leaned over, attempting to talk in a voice that Thomas couldn't readily hear. I said, "I'm okay, Grace." It was true. I'd been taking my medicine daily for over five weeks now, and I was okay. True, I had been experimenting with the dosages—decreasing them, as I've said—but my delusions, if that's what they were, were no longer a problem for me. I was focused and functioning at a high level. A very high level.

Grace smiled at me bravely and then turned away to face the falling rain outside her window.

The last half mile to Elaine's and Barry's house was on a gravel road that sloped down from the main highway toward the river. There was an old hand-lettered sign at the turn that said, "Private Road—No River Access," with mailboxes fastened to the signpost under it. There were five or six houses along the road, mostly hidden behind low, thick trees and vine-covered fences. Their house was at the end of the road, a two story house with reddish brown cedar siding and wide porches on all sides. Their Volvo was parked on a bare, muddy patch near the front steps, an area that had been cleared for several cars to park—so I pulled our car in next to it. I took a deep breath and let it out slowly. I hate driving in heavy traffic when the weather is bad like that.

Grace said, "You notice that I didn't say a word as you were careening around that last corner."

"I appreciate it."

"And I didn't comment when you missed the turn back in town."

"Thanks."

"I'm being good."

"Yes, you are."

She smiled and I leaned over and kissed her on the forehead.

Elaine and one of their daughters, Brandy, came out of the house and stood on the porch, leaning out as far as they could without getting drenched by the runoff from the roof. Brandy was five, I think. She had a round face and big, expressive eyes that couldn't hide whatever happened to be on her mind at the moment.

The rain was still falling steadily. It was only five o'clock, but the sky was as dark as night from the thick clouds.

As we were getting out of our car, Elaine yelled, "Unpack your car later. Come on in. Hey, Thomas! Look at you. You've grown an inch."

I carried the animal carrier as I ran toward the porch.

Brandy screamed, "The monkey. Katie! They're here."

Barry met me at the door and ignoring my outstretched hand, gave me a bear hug. He said, "Jim," as if I were returning after years in exile. I understood. A lot of things in our relationship had almost been lost. No other friend had cared enough or had enough courage to call bullshit on what I'd been up to. But Barry had.

After we were all in the house and the front door was closed, I said, "Can I let Eve out?"

Brandy came up to me and stood close and said, "Don't let her go down near the river. Snakes are there. Water moccasins."

Barry shook his head. "No, honey."

Brandy's jaw dropped open. "You said."

"All I *said* was that when it floods like this you have to watch out. Snakes get washed up out of the nooks and crannies onto higher land...and sometimes they turn up where you don't expect them."

Grace called Eve's name. "Come on, girlfriend. Let's put you in something nice." Grace was much more upbeat in her interactions with Eve when other people were around. They went into one of the downstairs bedrooms for a few minutes and then came out again with Eve wearing a pink dress with a light blue pony on the skirt. Brandy and her older sister Katie loved it. They held hands and danced around her, calling out, "Eve, Eve, Eve."

Low, rolling thunder filled the room, as if a hulking intruder had thrown open the doors and sauntered in. The lights flickered, but stayed on. Eve scampered across the floor and climbed up my pants leg into my arms. I could tell that Grace had put a diaper on her. It probably wasn't necessary, but it would make Elaine feel better about things. It was fine. Eve didn't care.

Barry said, "This reminds me of that evening at your house when it was raining so hard and we sat out under the gazebo and discussed monkey theology. I love to tell people what you said that night. I've been wanting to work it into one of my sermons, but I haven't found the right context yet." Barry's face became serious and he jutted out his chin as if he were launching into a sermon then and there. "Monkeys come from the tears of God, dear friends—"

Elaine interrupted. "The girls and I made some appetizers. Anybody hungry? It's almost six o'clock."

From a chair in the corner came Thomas' voice—a little too loud and bit strident. "I am."

Elaine said, "Well, of course you are. You're a growing boy. We'll be right back with some tasty snacks." She herded her daughters ahead of her toward the kitchen. Grace followed them. Thomas took a quick look at me and Barry and then got out of his chair and went in the opposite direction from where the women had gone, toward a screen porch on one side of the house. He said, without turning around, "Call me when the food is here."

I sat down on the couch and propped my feet on a sturdy, old table which was there for that purpose. Eve settled back into the crook of my arm, pulled up her skirt and began chewing on the edge of it.

Barry plopped his lanky frame into a chair opposite me, slipped off his shoes and put his feet on the table too. He slowly nodded his head as if contemplating something. "Monkeys coming from the tears of God. Heady stuff."

"Yeah."

"So…are you still writing?"

"Some." The satisfaction of having gotten an essay published in the Houston Chronicle—the one about random outpourings from the mind of God–gave me the motivation to finish another one in the series. I had been jotting down notes and writing some—but mostly thinking about it. I decided to get his reaction. "Her monkey theology, as you call it—well…it's driven by a spiritual quest."

He smiled broadly and his eyes twinkled. "Indeed."

Barry wasn't taking me seriously—he thought I was joking —probably because of the understated way in which I'd said what I thought. But I'd meant it. Eve was on a spiritual quest. In humans, there's *something* in us that draws us to the god we perceive. That's a critical part of what it means to be human. That's what I'd been writing about. It's just there. We don't learn it in church. We're born with it. Well…

Eve had it too. She was a monkey with human DNA, yes, but still just a monkey—with a god she had found that was knowable by a monkey. She had created her own myths and sacred rituals. She pondered archetypal dreams. She had her own understanding of suffering and of prayer. And she'd had—along with me—unexplainable mystical experiences. I was suddenly curious what Barry would think about *that*—sharing mystical experiences with a monkey.

I heard the sound of fabric ripping and looked down. Eve was happily gnawing at the brightly-colored pony that was appliquéd onto her skirt, trying to tear it off with her teeth. I said, "Stop it," yanked the skirt out of her mouth, and pulled it down over her legs again.

I decided to begin by fielding only an abstract question: "So... what's your take on spiritual gifts?" In the early church, believers described having been given a variety of spiritual gifts, in other words, supernatural powers. I'd been wondering whether and to what extent I could explain my sensation of reality having changed around us by attributing it to a spiritual gift of some sort in... one of us. I still resisted the idea that what I'd experienced was all delusion on my part. I knew that I was bi-polar. But that didn't explain everything. In fact, I wondered if being bi-polar—and my greater openness to unreality--made me a more accepting beneficiary of spiritual gifts. And of genuine revelation.

Barry looked confused, not sure where I was going with my question. "Like?"

"In New Testament times, people were given the power to work miracles—heal the sick, raise the dead—"

"Right..."

"Handle snakes."

"Wrong."

"So what's that all about? Is it still going on? Is God still bestowing spiritual gifts on his people? Or is that a thing of the past? Or is it something that might have never actually happened at all?" Barry and I had had candid discussions a number of times in which he acknowledged that he didn't believe that all the stories in the Bible were literally true.

He stared at me and then at Eve and then said, "Hmm," quietly, as if he found the topic mildly amusing. A few seconds went by, and it didn't appear as if he was going to say anything else in answer to my question, but then he began speaking, softly at first, and the volume and intensity in his voice grew as his words poured out, as if he were preaching:

"Probably a thing of the past. But it's because the church—the organized church—has lost touch with love. We're afraid to give love or to experience love. We talk endlessly about the wonder of love, but we insulate ourselves from any genuine experience of it...so what you're talking about—spiritual gifts—I'm afraid it's a thing of the past. Do you remember what the Apostle Paul said?"

He quoted from memory: "'If I speak in the tongues of angels, but have not love, I am only a resounding gong or a clanging cymbal.

"'If I have the gift of prophesy and can fathom all mysteries and all knowledge, and if I have faith that can move mountains, but have not love, I am nothing.

"'If I give all I possess to the poor and surrender my body to the flames, but have not love, I gain nothing.'"

He shook his head sadly. "Nothing."

Brandy came skipping into the room with a cheese ball on a plate. She beamed and said, "I made it. It's got almonds."

Eve sat up straight. I tightened my grip around her waist to be sure she didn't try to jump out of my lap and fight Brandy for the cheese ball.

Barry looked at me. "Sorry. Elaine tells me I'm really tiresome when I get on my soapbox like that."

"It's okay. I asked you a question, and you gave me an honest answer."

"You're very kind."

Grace came into the room next, carrying a tray with several kinds of crackers and some grapes. She looked at me and Eve and said, "Would you...?" Her voice trailed off, but I knew what she was asking.

I stood up and said, "Come on, Evie, let's go." Her crate was still by the front door. I put Eve in it, shut its door, and then I grabbed the handle and carried the crate to the bedroom that Grace and I would share. The room smelled of cedar and Christmas candles. I left the light on and shut the bedroom door.

When I got back, all the seats were taken, except for a spot on the couch between Thomas and the older daughter, Katie. She was sitting politely and quietly, with her knees touching and a plate of food on her lap. There was a glass of wine waiting for me. I put food on a plate and took my glass of wine and sat down.

There was a loud clap of thunder. Within seconds, the lights went out. The only light in the room was faint, indirect light from a candle that was burning in the kitchen. For a few moments no one said anything. We just listened to the rain on the tin roof of the front porch. The sound got louder as the rain intensified.

I was the one who broke the silence. "Do you think I'm going to have to wear a life jacket for my baptism?"

Barry's deep, resonant voice came out of the shadows across the room. "That might not be such a bad idea. Seriously."

Elaine said, "Everyone sit still. I'm going to get out some more candles." She went into the kitchen and then quickly came back with two large candles in glass jars. She set them in the middle of the table and lit them.

I felt Katie fidgeting next to me on the couch. I smiled down at her and said, "Hello there."

"Hi."

"You okay?"

"Yes, I'm fine. But your monkey is crying."

"I don't hear anything."

"I do." Her voice was quiet, but confident.

We all stopped talking and listened for a second. Katie was right. Eve was crying.

Elaine smiled. "Poor thing. I bet she's scared."

"No." Katie's face showed very little emotion. "She's crying like someone who is very, very sad about things in her life."

It was a surprisingly nuanced assessment from a nine-year-old, even the precocious daughter of a psychologist. I feigned skepticism.

"Hmm. Is that your professional opinion, Dr. Katie?" I had the urge to tickle her—or to do something else to prompt a happy, more childlike response from her.

"Yes." She nodded seriously. "Definitely."

"I should do something."

"Yes. You should." Her voice was flat, almost deadpan.

The rain stopped the next day, which was Monday, and the weather forecast was for sunny skies the rest of the week and warmer temperatures. Barry and I took a walk along the shoreline after breakfast. We talked about doing my baptism on Tuesday. The ground was muddy and the water level in the river was at least a foot higher than normal, but that seemed to pose no real problem. Their house was next to a slight bend in the river that had a relatively shallow area with a flat bottom. The river's current was faster there than in deeper and wider stretches of the river—and according to Barry, a little swifter than normal because of the rain—but we saw some fishermen in the water and they weren't having any trouble standing up. There were also a few college students floating by on inner tubes. I yelled to a group of them, "How's the water?" They responded by shooting in our direction with a large water gun made with green plastic pipe and whooping loudly.

I was anxious. It had little to do with the swollen river, but watching the current heightened my anxiety. I could feel turmoil in my mind. This was another one of those times when things around me seemed almost translucent, as though I could perceive faintly beneath everything another layer of reality—and another layer below that. I had a growing, disorienting sensation of crowdedness, as if I were standing near the intersection of a confluence of fluid paths. I trusted my feelings, and I was afraid, afraid that the turbulence at the intersection of paths...alternate realities...fates—whatever you want to call them—would be more than I could handle.

At the same time, the natural beauty—the beauty of God's creation—that surrounded us had a calming effect on me as we went about our day. The winding stretch of the Brazos River on which Elaine and Barry had their weekend home was gorgeous in the springtime. Stocky, wide-limbed live oak trees and towering pecan trees were scattered along the shoreline as far as you could see. Unkempt Bermuda grass that had probably been planted by early homeowners formed a thin carpet in the open spaces, broken up by outcroppings of rock and dotted by clusters of spring wildflowers—bluebonnets and some kind of yellow flowers with brown centers. There was a lush smell in the air when you stood by the water, the smell of algae and fertile river mud.

With the possible exception of Thomas, everyone was looking forward to the novelty of my baptism, but I think the one who was most excited out of all of us was Brandy. She told me at least three different times, "We're going to do it just like in the Bible." She asked me privately, "My daddy doesn't have to preach, does he?" I said no. She said, "Good."

Monday after lunch, Elaine and I sat in lawn chairs near the water, talking a little bit and trying to identify birds that were perched nearby. Neither of us was very good at it. Grace was in the kitchen helping Barry clean up our dishes from lunch.

I thought about confiding in Elaine about my sense of unease, about my premonitions—but I couldn't. She would have asked questions about my medications, and I would have had to admit that I wasn't taking the full dosage of any of them.

Brandy came skipping up to where we were sitting. She made silly, dramatic faces while she waited for us to stop our conversation and let her say something.

Elaine finally turned to her daughter and said, "Yes, Brandy?"

"Granny Gee and Pops want me to come over to play with Emily. Can I go? I told them we should all watch out for snakes—what Daddy said...you know."

There was an elderly couple standing outside the back porch of the house. A little girl with a long blond ponytail was with them: Emily, their granddaughter, I assumed. The man had a cane. The old woman was thin, but stood erect with her shoulders squared and her chin up. She reminded me, even from that distance, of my grandmother.

Elaine said, "Our neighbors. They've owned the place next door for forty years." Then she turned to Brandy. "It's okay with me. Just don't stay too long, okay?"

Brandy looked at me. "Is anyone singing tomorrow? I can sing. I can get my friend Emily to come over too. So is anyone singing?"

I understood that she was asking about my baptism ceremony. I thought about it for a second and decided that I didn't want children singing. I didn't want it to turn into something cute. So I said, "Maybe you can sing after it's all over. Is that okay?"

"Sure." She shrugged her shoulders. "It's your funeral."

Elaine stared at Brandy. "What did you say?"

"Nothing. I mean...that's what my friends always say when—oh, never mind."

"I think you need to apologize to Mr. Jim."

I signaled for Elaine to let it go. I said, "Don't worry about. I've heard far worse. I've got boys."

Elaine looked at me curiously, and I realized what I'd said.

I corrected myself. "Only one, actually...as everyone knows. But he's got a split personality."

Now Elaine looked stunned. She smiled stiffly at Brandy. "Go. Have fun."

Brandy said, "Okay, bye," and skipped away.

Elaine said, "Are you okay?"

I nodded. I had been distracted and wasn't thinking carefully about what I was saying. Then I'd been trying to be funny, making light of my first slip of the tongue—about having more than one boy. But I'd made things worse.

She said, "I hope you don't say things like that in front of Thomas—or Grace."

I checked my cell phone later that afternoon to see if Bonnie had called me back. She had called, leaving a message that said, "I am *so* sorry. At the last minute, the dean sent me an email asking me where the monkey came from, and I thought I was going to have to come up with official papers or something. So I freaked, because...well, you know. But then this morning, I saw him, and he asked why the monkey wasn't in the lab yet, and he was, like, 'I was just curious. No big deal.' So can we do it later this week, like on Friday?"

We couldn't keep the monkey cooped up in her crate all week, and Grace didn't feel good about letting her roam freely in Elaine's and Barry's home. So we took Barry up on a rather novel suggestion that we put Eve on a long tether that was in the backyard, in the wide expanse of lawn between the house and the lake. They used to have a dog. Since there was no fence, they had a cable— maybe fifty yards long—that was fastened securely to a bracket next to the back door. There had been times when we needed to put Eve on a leash, and so we had a harness that we'd bought for her. I think it was made for dachshunds or other skinny dogs. We hooked the cable onto the back of her harness, and it all worked perfectly. There were a couple of trees near the house that she could climb. And there were an abundance of bugs in the grass that she could eat. For the first couple of hours, she just roamed around plucking bugs out of the dirt, eating them on the spot. Later in the day we noticed her sitting in the sun as close as she could get to the river, staring at the water. I knew that the river—and the water in it—had meaning for her.

As it did for me. I think that I had misunderstood up until that moment what draws us to the original ritual of baptism. I'd misunderstood because the church baptizes believers in standing water or with droplets of water. What's missing in those kinds of ceremonies is the *current*. It's the water's current that is the essence of the sacrament— the moving, fluid molecules of water. Jesus and his followers were baptized in a river, in the irresistible currents of flowing water. I was stunned by this sudden revelation, uncertain as to what it might mean, but also exhilarated. I was ready. Ready for whatever might come next in God's marvelous creation.

Around five o'clock we were in the kitchen, which looks out onto the river. Elaine was cutting fruit. At her request, I was unwrapping pieces of cheese and searching for serving dishes and utensils.

Grace was standing by the window. She said, "One of us should get a camera. Look."

We all crowded around Grace at the window to look out. Thomas and Katie were sitting in the grass on either side of the monkey, with their backs to us, nearly motionless, all three of them watching the river. They were lit by the warm light of the setting sun. Ripples in the moss-green water caught the sun and sparkled with amber light.

"I'm glad Thomas and Katie have stopped ignoring each other."

"It's an awkward age."

"True."

"Having Eve there makes it easier for them."

"Would anyone like a glass of wine?" Barry asked.

"I thought you'd never ask. We brought a few bottles of wine too, if you don't want to exhaust your whole collection."

"Shall we sit out side?"

"Let's do. On the patio."

"Do you have a tray we can put this food on?"

"How many knives do you want me to get?"

"We don't need napkins do we?"

"We need to do this more often."

"Jim, you look great."

"Thanks."

"What about me? Don't I look great?

"Of course. You always look great."

"I've got two bottles open. Who wants white and who wants red?"

"White."

"White."

"I'll be different."

"Did you notice Elaine's t-shirt? It's from our trip to Sonora."

"Jim gave *my* t-shirt away."

"No, I didn't."

"Or used it to wax the car."

"Well....So?"

"You're not carrying anything. Would you hold the door for us?"

No one spoke at first as we filed out the back door. In the stillness of that secluded stretch of the river, I could hear a faint ringing in my ears—and then the quiet noise of locusts in the trees around us, cascading from right to left. I turned to face the breeze from the south. It was cool and moist. It carried the bountiful odors of a swollen river and the promises of springtime. It made me smile.

Chapter 27

I am the first to step into the river. The cold rush of water is a shock at first but my body adapts, with barely a shiver. My white robe clings to my legs as I move into deeper water. Barry is also wearing a robe—a black one–along with his emerald-colored clerical stole. I feel his hand on my shoulder. He smiles and says, "Hey, don't forget to give your friend to Thomas." I am carrying Eve. He thinks I have forgotten that I am still holding her, but I haven't.

I say, "No, today is her day too."

He stops. His posture is rigid. He says, "We're not going to make this into a big joke."

I say, "It isn't." I stroke the fur between Eve's wide-spaced ears. Being baptized is something she's wanted since the first time she saw it depicted in our John the Baptist book—without knowing why…almost certainly, as a matter of instinct, without understanding or knowing why.

He can see that I'm not joking, and his anger is then mostly gone, but it's replaced by discomfort and even distrust. He worries about what I might do next. I can see it in his eyes.

We're still only a few feet from the shore. Our families can hear our conversation. I see Grace turn away, ashamed at what is taking place.

I say, "I'll just hold her in my arms—like this." And I demonstrate how I plan to cross my arms across my chest and hold her tight against my shoulder, when he is about to lower me into the water. Eve is very still, almost limp in my arms. She's wearing a new dress that Grace bought her, one with red and white stripes.

Barry shakes his head and says, "Why?"

I don't know how to explain—nothing I can think of would make him feel good enough about what I am asking him to do—and so I just say, "Please, Barry. Just ignore her. She won't cause any harm…or sacrilege. You don't have to acknowledge her in anything you say. Okay?"

He says, "Fine." But there's a remnant of anger in his eyes. He feels tricked.

I remain still for a moment wondering if I should relent and give the monkey to someone on the shore—or maybe forget about the whole thing. Somehow the crisp, spring morning has lost some of its luster. I feel very alone.

He puts his hand on my shoulder and says, "Come on. Let's just do it."

I say, "Are you sure?"

He shrugs and says, "This is for you. We'll do it however you want."

And so I turn and walk further into the river. The current is stiffer than it appears from the shore, but it's okay. I take slow, careful steps.

A canoe full of boy scouts and then a second and a third paddle into view. They see me and Barry standing in the river in our robes, and the scouts slow down and stop on the far shore, out of respect—and curiosity, no doubt.

I hear faint singing. Brandy and her friend Emily are on the shore singing earnestly. I can't hear them well. As we walk further into the river, the noise from the flowing water blocks out more and more of the sounds from the shore. Emily's grandparents are setting up lawn chairs on their dock and sitting down to watch us too. I see broken limbs and river trash trapped under their dock, deposited there by the rain-swollen river.

The water is up to my waist—not quite so high on Barry, since he is taller than I am. I stop to evaluate things. The current is manageable, but the water is too low here for Barry to lower me underwater and easily lift me back up. I think that the water level needs to be part-way up my chest. So we walk further into the river.

A broken Styrofoam cooler floats by, something washed by the rains into the river.

We walk a few more feet and then stop. The river bottom is flat here. The current is gentler in the deeper water. It is easy to stand. We turn and face our families, who are maybe thirty or forty yards away. Grace takes our picture.

I turn to Barry. "Are you going to be too cold?"

"No. I'll be fine." He smiles warmly at me, his earlier irritation with me now gone. "Hey. I'm honored, Jim. To be part of this. You know that, don't you?"

"Thank you."

"Are you ready?"

I say yes, and we begin. My mind jumps around as Barry says a few words about the sacrament of baptism. I hear him, but I also take in everything that's around me. I am hoping for powerful sensations of some kind. I want to experience these moments fully, whatever they may hold.

His voice is loud and resonant, so those on both shores of the river can surely hear him. He departs from the traditional Presbyterian liturgy and talks about our lord Jesus Christ and his baptism in the Jordan River. He talks about the symbolic significance of water. He talks about John the Baptist's proclamation about the one coming after him who would baptize with fire.

The boy scouts look away from us. Some point upriver. I look in the direction they're pointing and see a tangle of thin, broken limbs floating toward us. The wind picks up. There's movement among the branches—something gray. The branches aren't far away, but the wind and the current appear to be sending them just off to the side of us. Barry is facing downriver. He doesn't see them, isn't aware. He says, "And the skies opened and the voice of God proclaimed his pleasure, saying, 'This is my son in whom I am well pleased.'"

Barry pauses. I look into his face, the face of my best friend. Our eyes meet and we share a moment of understanding, I think. He is a deeply religious man and, despite our differences in belief, he empathizes with my struggles of faith—more than anyone else.

Out of the corner of my eye I see the old man on the dock—Emily's grandfather—standing up. He cups his hands around his mouth, as if to yell—at the scouts...or maybe at us. But I hear nothing. The current and the wind in the trees along the shore muffle almost all sound from the shore.

Barry can't see what I see and continues the ceremony with warmth and enthusiasm. He puts one hand behind my neck and with the other grips one of my wrists and says, "Jim, child of God, I baptize you in the name of the Father, the Son and the Holy Spirit."

I look down at the monkey, and we make eye contact briefly. She's aware that something of significance is happening. I can tell. I pull her close to my chest. For the first time, I wonder if she will struggle—even bite me—as I pull her underwater with me. I think not...hope not. She is looking in the direction of the floating tangle of branches too and begins to chatter and point. She's upset. The meandering current is bringing the branches directly toward us now. I can't stop myself from looking again just as Barry is lowering me backwards into the water. They're several feet away.

As I go underwater I notice a writhing, brownish-gray mass floating among the branches. My face is underwater, but I see blunt-nosed heads lifting up and dark eye slits. It is a nest of water moccasins that has been washed into the river by the rains. I can't count them.

I feel Barry suddenly begin to twist and thrash. He lets go of my wrist, but his grip on my neck tightens and he jerks me up out of the water, just as the nest of snakes floats into my chest. The monkey screams and jumps from my arms onto the top of the pile of floating brush. Barry is backing away as quickly as he can, shouting at me to run. He has a thick, broken branch in his hand. Then he comes back towards me, shouting, clubbing the snakes, trying to push them away from me with the stick—but there are too many of them. I don't see Eve, don't know if she's fallen into the river, don't know if she can swim. I feel the snakes' soft, cold flesh—and feel the icy rush of terror, but have no way to escape. The deep water doesn't allow me to run.

I feel the prick of fangs biting into my chest and then again on my neck. I feel one and then another gliding around my chest and past me—but I see the scaly heads and emotionless black eyes of two more in the churning water right in front of me. I swing my arm to knock them away and feel their bite on my wrist and hand. They're cold where their flesh touches mine, but it burns where they bite me. I feel nothing else. I stumble, think maybe if I dive down underwater they can't follow me there. But now they've all moved past me, gliding away in the current. I see the monkey ten feet away, still perched on the branches...safe. She's okay. I feel an instant of relief, but then feel my knees trembling and then buckling. I can't breathe in, physically cannot inhale—the muscles in my chest and gut are still, inert. I try to say something, but can't. My voice has been silenced. My eyes are open as I slip down, into the water. I see the sun through the ripples above me. Water comes into my mouth, but it's not an unpleasant sensation. It's calming and seems to connect me with the sense of movement in the river and in the molecules that form the substance of all things. I sense, rather than see the tumult on the shore, among those watching me—family, friends and strangers alike. I feel Grace's terror, and for a moment I'm sad for her and then that emotion seems foreign to me. I float away in a current of some kind. As I drift, the pressure of water against my body becomes less tangible and the touch of the current in which I'm carried grows warm. And I become warmer—and lighter—until my substance is changed. I am mostly water now too, a thinning mist of water. And air. And I am soaring now, somewhere above the river, high above everything. Sparkling, crackling light is both inside and outside of me. I have an urge to test my voice again, and in that instant, thunder fills the air. My voice is now the sound of thunder. I love it. I speak again—louder now—and all of creation trembles at the explosive sound of my voice. My body extends beyond the limits of my comprehension. I am changing again. I am now developing mass and form and I feel the sensation of falling. I am shattered into a million liquid pieces and I am falling, gaining velocity as I plummet downward, to a place where I am absorbed, come together and harden. I am a catalyst in something I am not able to understand. Slabs of rock and fields of ice around me break apart and mountains that have been buried for eons thrust upward carrying me inside. Magnificent edifices that have been hidden within the rock stand revealed at the foot of a mountain, glittering with crystalline adornments.

And I, without knowing what comes next, rise up out of the mountain peak and stand face to face with a white-haired man who looks vaguely familiar to me. His dark, heavily lidded eyes appear to be staring through me—in fact, I wonder if he can see me at all, sense that he is looking at something beyond me. I turn. I am standing amid jagged rocks on a pinnacle carved by wind and rain. Far below me from every direction, orange light appears on the horizons, a distant line of fiery light encircling me on all sides, as though the world is in flames. A young woman is there behind me and another man too, also young, standing at the edge of the precipice. Their clothes are faintly luminous. They ignore me, as if they're waiting for someone else. I turn again and see a child. The child is not looking at me—he's looking down from the peak on which we're standing at glittering cities stretched out across the plains below us. I approach the child. Without looking up at me, he speaks to me, says, "The angels will catch you. They will catch you in their arms."

The light at the horizon is, indeed, fire. And it is coming closer. I have set the world aflame. My mother would not be surprised.

I am to be baptized in fire.

Fire envelopes the plains below me, spreading rapidly, erupting from crevices. The flames have jagged edges that shoot into the sky and arc across the plain like lightning, touching and illuminating the vain constructs of humankind below.

I have delayed long enough.

I turn and, with my back to the flaming abyss, lean backwards and let that subtle, arching movement of my body be the irreversible force that propels me.

I fall through the fire. I feel a warm hand on mine and another behind my neck, slowing my fall and then lifting me back up, through a curtain of water into sunlight.

The return is jarring. Barry lifts me out of the water into the sunlight. A film of water that clings to my eyes blinds me for a few seconds. I don't understand what is happening to me. Barry holds onto me until he is sure that I am steady on my feet, able to stand in the current of the river without toppling over. I use the wet sleeve of my robe to wipe my eyes and then look around. Barry smiles at me, squeezes my shoulder as he says final words to me about the love of God—and then he turns to Buck. My younger son Buck stands beside me in his white robe holding Eve in his arms. He grins. Buck is going to be next.

I gasp when I see him. He'd been lost to me, but now...I try to make sense of it. I *can't* make sense out of it—out of the jumble of incomprehensible memories of me dying and of the painful, former reality in which I had existed, *but he hadn't.* I glance toward Grace, who's standing at the water's edge, seeking evidence from her...of some kind. Something. Grace smiles at me. Even from the middle of the river, I feel the warmth in her smile, sense her joy.

Barry is talking to Buck now. I face them.

I have trouble trusting the things that are before my eyes. Buck is happily bobbing up and down in the water, waiting for his turn. His blond hair shines in the sun. Eve's red and white striped skirt floats on the surface of the water. Her tail twitches near Buck's ear. She stares at me, as though she knows what I know.

Now Barry is talking in a loud voice about the example that has Christ set—talking to me and Buck and to those on shore. I turn around again and see Grace, standing with her arm around Thomas. Thomas waves at me awkwardly and then drops his arm to his side. Grace blows me a kiss in a quick, flirty way, a loving gesture that's familiar to me—and unfamiliar at the same time. Things are different. Underlying her love for me is a genuine desire.

As I stand in the peaceful flow of the river, as my gaze travels and settles on these people whom I love, I find that my disorientation is lessening, and that I am able to focus on and understand what is happening around me. I am aware of my circumstances as if they are the only ones I have ever encountered. But I know better—in my gut.

I try to shut out other thoughts and listen only to Barry's words. He is speaking to me now—and to my wife. "Grace and Jim, do you bring this child for baptism, in faith, trusting that God desires to receive your child into his family?" I say, "We do." I hear the faint echo of my words from the shore—Grace's voice. I am still distracted, but I am aware of my present surroundings, and I understand what is happening. Buck and I are *both* here to be baptized. I force myself to focus on what is in front of me, but disturbing memories continue to crowd out other thoughts in my mind, making me question my perception of things around me. I can't help it. I remember a vastly different reality—a bleak one in which Grace and I had never known the loving intimacy that seems to exist between us here and now, a sad one in which we'd settled for merely pragmatic love. And one in which Buck did not even exist. But he is here, next to me, smiling. I am afraid and I don't know why. I look around once again…to be absolutely sure of things. Grace and Thomas are still there—Elaine, too, with her daughters. Fishermen are standing in the water near the shore on the other side of the river.

But now something is going wrong in this reality. I know it before they do, but I don't know exactly what will happen. The fishermen begin waving wildly and pointing, signaling for us to get out of the river. They're shouting, but their words are muffled by the murmur of the river's current and the wind.

There is a floating tangle of branches approaching us. Moments earlier it had been stuck amid low hanging limbs from an oak tree a few hundred yards upriver, along with other flotsam. But the current has broken it free, along with other trash—plastic bags, broken pieces of a Styrofoam cooler, a partially inflated inner tube. The sight of it fills me with terror, but I don't know why.

Now Grace comes bounding into the river, but she stops when she's half-way to us. She is screaming the word, "Snakes." Her voice is shrill.

Eve begins to scream too, but it's a scream of rage, not fear. She leans out, away from Buck, thrusting her fist at the floating tangle.

I see them when they are five or six feet away.

The branches have formed a crude cross and snakes are in the crook of it, a twisting, undulating brown mass, with heads that peek out and are then hidden again. The current carries them toward Buck and Eve.

Barry is closer to Buck than I am—he had been seconds away from baptizing Buck. He grabs for Buck's arm, to pull him out of the path of the snakes. They are only a few feet away now. But Eve snaps at his hand, drawing blood. Barry yells in pain and anger and reaches again for Buck.

Eve jumps onto Barry's arm and then launches herself into the middle of the nest of snakes, screeching at them with savage fury.

I yell her name. I yell for her to get away, words she does not understand.

Barry yanks Buck from the water into his arms and turns toward the far shore, but I am momentarily frozen, terror-filled, staring at the thrashing water where Eve is surrounded by snakes.

I see a severed body in her hand where she has bitten off one of their heads, but snakes surround her, biting her face and shoulders. Splotches of blood are on her dress. She howls in anger—and in pain. Our eyes meet one more time. Her motions are a blur, as she bats snakes away and bites at others. I grab a branch and lift it, intending to fight for her, but another snake falls from it, near me. And I hear Grace screaming at me to get away, cursing at me in her desperate attempt to get my attention, to make me listen. She is right behind me now, arms around my chest, pulling me backwards. I slip, but I fall into her arms, and she holds me and drags me away with a strength I didn't know she possessed.

I yell Eve's name, yell that I'm coming to help her.

But the snakes, one by one, are gliding away now, down the river, angling toward the opposite shore.

I tell Grace to let me go, to let me go help Eve.

But it's too late. Eve has stopped fighting now. She rolls over, sideways into the water, facing me and Grace with an impassive stare, and then she turns face down into the water and, motionless, floats downstream. The skirt of her beautiful, striped baptism gown clings to the surface of the river, carrying her motionless body on the face of the water like a summer leaf.

I refuse to acknowledge the reality of what I am seeing, can't believe it. I pull away from Grace, struggling in the deep water to catch up with Eve. But her limp body is moving faster in the water than I can. I shout for someone to help, but no one does. It would be pointless—I know that, even as I am screaming at everyone along the shore to help her—to do something—screaming until my voice breaks.

And then I stop. There's no point. And I watch her body linger in an eddy until the floating crisscrossed branches catch up to her, and then, nestled in a crook, she continues her journey.

Chapter 28

I waited for what might come next, desperately hoping that what had happened to Eve on her baptism day was one bitter alternative out of a series of different alternatives, but not a final, unchangeable set of facts. But nothing happened then or later to change the fact of the monkey's death and burial.

I still wait. Among other things I wait for understanding. I don't know why I have been given a glimpse of things beyond my ability to understand. I truly thought that reality was composed of multiple possible outcomes. I've reread some of my journals, which detail my experiences and seem to provide evidence. But as time passes, my conviction fades that I ever experienced moments in time twice or three times with differing outcomes. Looking back, it feels now like ordinary déjà vu, and maybe that's all it was—and is. Since Eve died, nothing of that kind has happened again. I don't understand.

And I should be happier than I am. I have a wonderful marriage to a woman who loves me more than I deserve. When I wake up in the morning and find Grace's arms around me and her soft skin pressed against me...well, I have moments when it's like I'm in my twenties again, experiencing it all for the first time. I'm blessed—I know that—I am truly blessed.

I mentioned some of what has been on my mind to Elaine, and she said that she thought I was just depressed, that I had been projecting a lot of my unresolved conflicts on Eve—and when she died, my quest for self-discovery died too. I don't know if I believe that. She must have talked to Barry about it afterwards, because he sent me a short hand-written note in which he quoted from Psalms: "Wait for the Lord; be strong and take heart and wait for the Lord."

I continue to wait.

A couple of months later, Buck talked me into going on a father-son camping trip to celebrate the end of the school year. At first, Thomas said he'd come with us too, but after thinking about it, he said he'd rather not go, that he had better things to do. Grace thought it was a great idea, and she began to plan a girls' night out with Elaine for one of the evenings when we'd be gone. She said that Buck and I both needed to get away and do something that was fun and different.

So Buck and I considered all the possibilities and picked Caprock Canyons State Park, a big Texas park that doesn't have any rivers or large bodies of water. It's a long drive from Houston, but that was okay with both of us. Road trips can be fun. Grace let us take her SUV, since it has so much room for big gear like the tent and our folding chairs.

We took a slight detour from the direct route and stopped at the Dr. Pepper Museum in Dublin, Texas. Buck still says that it was the best museum he's ever visited. Original recipe Dr. Pepper is bottled there in small quantities. We took a tour of the room where that's done. Across the front of the museum was a big room full of souvenirs and Dr. Pepper products that were for sale, staffed by wholesome, smiling college kids from Waco. We spent half an hour there too, carefully evaluating the alternatives.

In that part of Texas, storms can roll in pretty quickly. That may be true too everywhere else in the world, but we like to say that about our state, as though it's unique. Maybe it is, maybe it isn't. When we went into the museum, the sky was blue and the sun was out, but by the time we'd finished touring the museum and picking out souvenirs for ourselves and gifts for Grace and Thomas, the sky had darkened and rain was falling in cascading sheets. We could have run to the car, which was parked down the block and across the street. It didn't matter if we got our camping clothes wet, and if we didn't like being wet, we had plenty of dry clothes within easy reach. But we were in no hurry. So we sat on a bench under a wide awning, drank original recipe Dr. Pepper from glass bottles, and watched the rain come down.

After a thunderclap, I turned to Buck and said, "Have I ever told you about the times when I was a kid, when I would just sit on my grandparents' porch and watch the thunderstorms?"

He nodded. "Yeah. I think so."

We were both quiet for a couple of minutes. Then he tapped my knee with the cold bottom of his Dr. Pepper bottle. "But you can talk about it again. I don't care."

I hesitated and then realized that the story I really wanted to tell was the story of the afternoon that Eve and I had first watched a thunderstorm together and shared the wonder of what it signified to each of us. That was a story that I had not told to Buck—I was fairly certain of that—but I didn't think it would have any real meaning to him yet. And it would have involved bringing up Eve's name. We had not spoken of her since the day we buried her in our backyard behind the garage.

At least for me, the burden of keeping my memories of her in abeyance had become greater than any burden I would have suffered from allowing those memories to stay fresh and talking about them. I wasn't sure the same was true for a child of Buck's age, but it made sense to me that he wouldn't be different from me in that regard.

So I said, "You know, Eve liked thunderstorms a lot."

He nodded, but didn't appear to have anything he wanted to say in response. I looked away, staring at the patterns that the falling sheets of rain made on the blacktop road in front of us.

Out of the corner of my eye I could tell that Buck was looking at me, but still keeping his thoughts to himself.

I scooted over on the bench, so that I was closer, and I put my arm loosely around him.

He said, "You know, Eve saved me."

I nodded. "Me too."

"Yep."

"Yep."

About the Author

W. W. Singer is a lawyer with a national firm and the author of many short stories, several of which have been selected for recognition. He has also written two full-length plays, one of which was performed as a staged reading. An excerpt from his first novel was read as part of the Texas Bound series at the Dallas Museum of Art. *When I Set Myself on Fire* is his fourth novel. He lives in Dallas, Texas, with his wife.

Contact the author at www.wwsinger.com.

www.ingramcontent.com/pod-product-compliance
Lightning Source LLC
Chambersburg PA
CBHW061134200626
46817CB00016B/1387